EVERY C..... ....CA FOR
SOUTHERN DISCOMFORT

* * *

"[THE] READER WILL BE WELL REWARDED . . . by shifting into summertime gear and enjoying the feel of Maron's languid, richly tilled earth . . . Knott's powers are persuasive. Her landscapes glow with some of the mysterious fecundity of Thomas Hart Benton's jarring pastoral paintings."   *—Washington Post*

* * *

"A GOOD GUIDE INTO THE SOUL, CHARM AND MALEVOLENCE OF THE RURAL SOUTH."   *—Chicago Tribune*

* * *

"WE'RE GLAD TO BE CAUGHT IN THE GENTLE SPELL OF THIS SOFT PLACE. . . . Narrating the story in a honeyed accent that melts in the mouth, Deborah shrewdly uses the folksy idiom."   *—Marilyn Stasio,*
New York Times Book Review

* * *

"A WELL-WRITTEN STORY, RICH IN LOCAL COLOR AND INTERESTING CHARACTERS. It will leave many readers eager for the next in the Knott Series."

—St. Louis Post-Dispatch

* * *

"SUSPENSE IS SKILLFULLY SUSTAINED BY MEASURED PACING AND SUBTLY PLACED CLUES—all wrapped in the humidity of a sultry Southern summer."   *—Publishers Weekly*

* * *

more...

By Margaret Maron

PAST IMPERFECT
CORPUS CHRISTMAS
BABY DOLL GAMES
THE RIGHT JACK
BLOODY KIN
DEATH IN BLUE FOLDERS
DEATH OF A BUTTERFLY
ONE COFFEE WITH

A Deborah Knott Mystery

BOOTLEGGER'S DAUGHTER*

*Published by
THE MYSTERIOUS PRESS

MARGARET MARON

SOUTHERN DISCOMFORT

THE MYSTERIOUS PRESS

Published by Warner Books

A Time Warner Company

All definitions of building terms used at the beginning of the chapters were taken from the 6th edition of *Rate Training Manual NAVPERS 10648-F*, prepared by the Bureau of Naval Personnel, Department of the Navy.

MYSTERIOUS PRESS EDITION

Copyright © 1993 by Margaret Maron
All rights reserved.

Cover design by Jackie Merri Meyer
Cover illustration by Phil Huling

The Mysterious Press name and logo are registered trademarks of Warner Books, Inc.

 Mysterious Press Books are published by
Warner Books, Inc.
1271 Avenue of the Americas
New York, NY 10020

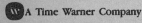 A Time Warner Company

Printed in the United States of America

Originally published in hardcover by The Mysterious Press.

First Printed in Paperback: June, 1994

10 9 8 7 6 5 4 3 2 1

For Vicky Bijur, who knows the line
between agenting and friendship,
yet crosses it anyhow

My thanks to all the officers of courts in Johnston, Wake, Harnett and Lee counties who patiently answered questions, especially District Attorney Thomas Lock, Chief District Court Judge William Christian and Magistrate Jean Massengill; to Dr. Shirley Osterhout, Director of the Duke University Poison Control Center; to Denise Cumbee Long; and, as always, to Special Agent Henry Poole of the SBI.

Prologue
Plans and Specifications

"The construction drawings, plus the specifications to be described later, are the chief sources of information for the supervisors and craftsmen responsible for the actual work of construction."

i

The male mockingbird teeters on the edge of a whitewashed brick wall and flexes his wings in a motion designed to flush unwary insects from the ground below.

Nothing.

He glides down to an open patch of sunlit grass between the wall and a rhododendron bush and again flicks open gray-feathered wings, exposing flashes of white.

A startled cricket hastily dives under a sheltering blade of centipede grass.

Too late.

The mockingbird pounces, tweezers it from the grass with a sharp and deadly accurate bill, then flies up to a crepe myrtle and checks for enemies. At the far end of the long wall, a big yellow cat drowses in the shade provided by tall rhododendrons, extravagant in lavender bloom.

They are old adversaries who long ago established a

modus vivendi of mutual respect. He knows she would eat his babies were they left unguarded, but a warning chirr usually discourages her predatory nature. His nest is well hidden among spindly, difficult to climb twigs; and if she tries, his outraged screams will marshall other birds to hurl raucous threats and help peck her unprotected back.

Only this morning, he and his mate banded with the thrashers and blue jays that inhabit this quiet suburban street to chase a snake from their territory. The sleeping cat is no real threat. The mocker swoops down onto the wall, pauses a moment to pound the cricket into a more easily digested mush, then hops along the bricks to where dogwood twigs brush the top of the wall at this corner.

Here in mid-May, the dogwood has finished blooming. No white flowers gleam among the broad leaves, only swelling green berries that will redden in the fall and provide sustenance when spiders and insects have buried themselves out of sight against winter's coming.

Here in the heart of the tree, the mockingbird and his mate have built a nest safe from prying eyes, and four half-fledged babies open their soft bright yellow beaks the instant they sense his arrival. He stuffs the broken cricket down the most insistent gaping mouth and flies off in search of more food.

All is quiet on this tree-lined street save the drone of a nearby power mower, and nothing disturbs the orderly coming and going of birds at work.

Cars pass, occasional screen doors slam, the lawn mower goes silent, and the mockingbirds shuttle back and forth with their beaks full of grasshoppers and beetles to stuff those insatiable little gullets.

Babies must be fed. The young are always hungry . . .

Into the silence comes the sound of a crooning voice.

The mockingbird buzzes a raspy alarm and watches as a human at the end of the wall stretches out a hand to the cat. She rises, sniffs the strange hand, then allows it to stroke her sleek back.

No threat to his mate or their babies, the mockingbird decides, and goes back to scanning the yard. His eye locks onto a huge grasshopper there at the base of a nearby flowering judas. It's one of those big brown-and-green creatures, enough to fill at least three ravenous beaks. The instant the bird approaches, it springs up; but the bird is quicker and catches it on the wing.

Intent on smashing the struggling grasshopper into manageable bits, the mockingbird pays no attention to what's happening at the far end of the wall; and by the time he flies up to the nest to distribute his grisly morsels, the cat has vanished from his tiny brain as completely and as finally as she has vanished from the wall.

There are babies to feed.

Only the babies matter.

ii

Boxer shorts.

That's how she always thinks of him.

The old-fashioned kind made of striped cotton. With snap fasteners. Except that half the time they'll be unsnapped, with a little circle of damp where he's gotten up to use the bathroom and has been careless about the last drop or two before tucking his thing back inside the striped cotton.

If it's after midnight and her light is still on, he comes into her room without knocking, as if hoping to catch her doing something forbidden.

"Time you were asleep," he growls before lumbering back down the hall.

That's okay. A lot of fathers do stuff like that.

What's not okay are the nights she gets home after they've gone upstairs and he comes to the head of the stairs and stands there looking down at her, his bathrobe hanging open. Or he's waiting in the living room, sitting spraddle-legged in his lounge chair, and he makes her sit down on the couch across from him while he cross-examines her about the evening.

"Why is your skirt so wrinkled? Were you in the backseat of his car? Did you let him put his tongue in your mouth?

That's the first thing men want with a girl—to get their hands inside her blouse, put their hands in her panties. Did you let him? Did you? Is my daughter nothing but a slut? Look at me when I talk to you, young lady!''

But she doesn't know where to look. At his eyes, hot and greedy for something she doesn't understand? At the gaping slit in those boxer shorts where his thing hangs dark and disturbing against those wrinkled hairy lumps?

When he sees her looking there, the striped fabric quivers and rises as the thing beneath engorges and swells. He usually stands then. "I just want your solemn word that you're still a virgin," he says.

Sobbing now, she swears that she is.

And now he knots his robe around him and retires in patriarchal seemliness to the master bedroom.

Her mother often complains of insomnia; yet somehow, she never wakes up when he lectures her at night like this.

iii

The kitchen is even filthier than the rest of the trailer—every surface littered with fast-food cartons, soft drink cans, wilted lettuce leaves, dirty dishes, gummy knives and forks.

"What'd you expect," she bristles. "*House Beautiful*? Supper on the table? When half the time you don't even come home for three days? What's the matter? Couldn't find any fresh meat to poke it into tonight?"

And now she's in there on the couch crying 'cause she got the slapping she was begging for. Well, damn it all to frigging hell, a woman pushes a man like that, what's she expect?

A bunch of roses?

All her fault.

Yeah, and it's her fault, too, if he has to go looking for what he can't find at home anymore.

Including a clean glass.

Every single glass they own is sitting dirty on the narrow counter. Enraged, he sweeps them all to the floor and bangs out of the back door to go where it'll be cool and quiet and clean glasses appear with the snap of a finger.

iv

George Jones's nasal twang fills the flashy little car—two speakers in the rear and one on each door—but the thief's mind isn't on cheating and hurting songs at the moment, and it's certainly not on the lush green trees and fields flashing past the closed car windows. No, it's remembering details from those articles in the *News and Observer* last summer.

They made it sound so easy. Like Velma Barfield, the "Death Row Granny" and last woman executed in North Carolina. Five or six people died before anybody started really noticing. A woman's crime. Middle-aged women. Women like Blanche Taylor Moore, who's sitting up there on death row right this minute. Before her trial actually began, they were saying she might have poisoned as many as nine people.

So who'll notice one more? Anyhow, you really can't count that first time. Because you don't know for sure that's what did it.

There had been only a few syrupy drops left in that little bottle under the sink in the church kitchen. Like liquid saccharine and who's to say it really made much of a difference to that last glass of iced tea? He might've gone on and died anyhow.

But those few drops emptied the bottle and where to get more?

It's just like all the old-timers keep mouthing: nobody ever notices what's slipping away till it's mostly already gone.

Isn't there one single old-fashioned honest-to-God country store left in the whole state of North Carolina? Used to be you could count on a storekeeper *keeping* stuff—old stock pushed to the back of the shelves, new stuff shoved in at the front. Root around a little and you could find 1979 goods still marked at 1979 prices and the owner would never dream of saying, "Hold on a minute, I b'lieve that's gone up a dime or two since I shelved it."

When did hick stores start acting like 7-Eleven quick-stops with computerized inventory controls, wide and brightly lit aisles, even video cameras to record everybody who steps up to the cash register?

After driving up and down every back road in Colleton County this steamy Saturday morning in mid-June, the thief's almost ready to consider other alternatives when suddenly, at a nothing-looking crossroads in the middle of tobacco and sweet potato fields, here it is: a big shabby cinderblock with battered gas pumps and a promising air of neglect. The hard-packed dirt yard is thickly cobbled with forty years' worth of rusty bottle caps and the dirty plate glass windows hold faded announcements of long past gospel sings or benefit fish frys. From the number of pickups and cars parked out front, business is pretty good, which means that whoever runs the store must be too lazy and/or too tight to spend money fixing things up.

Coming in out of the bright noonday sun makes the crowded interior seem even dimmer than normal, but a quick glance around through dark glasses confirms that all the white, black and brown faces belong to strangers. Anyhow, most of them seem to be migrant workers who mill around the cash register to pay for the weekend's wine and beer or to settle up for lunchtime drinks and beans and wedges of hoop cheese bought on the tab all week.

The fat white man behind the counter nods and his sallow-faced wife says, "Let me know if you need any help," but both are too busy making sure their dark-skinned customers aren't stealing to pay much attention to an ordinary white person.

The narrow aisles are crammed head-high with canned goods, farm implements, seed bins and fishing poles; and the smell of fertilizer mingles with sweat and cigarette smoke. Towards the back, mops and brooms are jammed upright between plastic and tin buckets, mothballs and rat traps. Next to these, at eye level, is a shelf full of assorted insecticides. Modern aerosol cans, all with labels claiming to protect Earth's ozone layer, have been dumped in beside pump bottles of evil green liquids that may have been sitting in this very same spot since before what's her name—Rachel Carson?—wrote that book.

With quickening excitement, the thief pushes aside dried-out rolls of flypaper and boxes of shiny tin ant traps that never work worth a flip and spots a stack of orange cardboard boxes: *Terro Ant Killer*. The top ones have a little Roman numeral II after the name and are priced at $2.19. According to the box, each bottle of clear syrup is laced with "sodium tetraborate decahydrate (borax)."

Borax? Isn't that for washing clothes? What good is borax?

A little further digging unearths a battered and faded box marked 98¢. On the back, small black letters read:

Active ingredients:
Sodium Arsenate 2.27%
Total Arsenic (as Metallic)....................0.91%
Arsenic in water soluble
   form (as Metallic)............................0.91%

This is followed by a large orange *WARNING: May be fatal if swallowed*.

There are two small bottles left on the shelf.

Shielded by a support post in the middle of the aisle, the thief slips one in each pocket, crams the empty boxes back where they came from, and looks around for something innocuous to buy.

•   •   •

Back up at the front, the fat owner rings up $6.75 for a rusty mole trap and ninety-nine cents for the mothballs. Plus tax. "That'll be eight twenty," he says.

"Looks like somebody's fixing to get rid of some pests," says his gaunt wife as she bags the two items.

Thinking how much nicer life is soon going to be for a certain person, the thief smiles and hands over a ten-dollar bill. "We sure plan to try."

1

Grading the Plot

"Grade elevations of the surface area around a structure are indicated on the plot plan.... This grading operation involves removing earth from areas which are higher than the prescribed elevation (cut) and filling earth into areas which are below the prescribed elevation (fill)."

My swearing-in ceremony was held on a hot and humid Monday afternoon in Colleton County's oldest courtroom, a big cavernous space paneled in dark oak and weighty with the stone-footed majesty of nineteenth-century law. The high vaulted ceiling is plastered with acanthus leaves; pierced brass lanterns hang down on long black cords above solid oak benches. Now that three bright-colored modern courtrooms have been added on to the top floor of the new jail annex, this part of the courthouse is used so infrequently that the air was cool and musty even though the place was jammed with well-wishers and a bailiff said the air-conditioning wasn't working right.

If and when we ever got around to the actual robing— put a microphone in front of some people and they never hush talking—I knew I'd appreciate the room's coolness. That heavy black garment had started out miles too big, but Aunt

Zell had gathered and stitched and cut and hemmed till it no longer swam on me. Not that I'm the dainty flower of southern womanhood God probably meant for me to be—I came out of my mother's womb a size fourteen and it's been a struggle to get down to a twelve ever since—but Carly Jernigan had been six one; and back when he served two terms on the district bench sometime in the late seventies, he must've weighed two-forty easy.

My sister-in-law Minnie was the closest thing I had to a campaign manager when I ran for judge, and since Carly Jernigan had been Minnie's mother's oldest brother, his widow thought it'd be nice to pass his robe on to me.

"I'm real sorry about the smell," Miss Abby apologized the day she and Minnie brought it over to Aunt Zell and Uncle Ash's house, where I live.

A homemade potpourri of rose petals and heartleaves fills a Chinese bowl that sits atop a Queen Anne chest amid the formality of Aunt Zell's pink and green living room, but its delicate fragrance was blotted up by coarse mothball fumes the minute I opened the long fiberboard coat box.

"I've had that thing hanging on my back porch for a week," said Miss Abby. "Ever since Minnie told me you were going to be appointed. I'm afraid it'll have to get dry-cleaned before you can stand to wear it, though."

After pricing new robes in a catalog of judicial accoutrements that a soon-to-be colleague had loaned me, a dry-cleaning bill was nothing; and I sincerely meant it when I told Miss Abby how much I appreciated her generosity.

Nevertheless, a faint aroma of naphthalene still met my nose whenever Aunt Zell shifted the robe from one arm to the other as we bowed our heads that afternoon for Barry Blackman's invocation. Barry is pastor at Bethel Baptist Church. Sweetwater Missionary Baptist was actually my home church, but the new minister had only been there two months whereas I'd known Barry forever—in fact, he was the first boy I'd ever kissed for real—so it was nice that I could get him to come pray God's blessing on my new career without hurting anybody's feelings. (Politics makes you sensitive to stuff like that.)

We'd already been called to order by Ellis Glover, Colleton County's clerk of court, and we'd been welcomed by Pete Taylor, current president of the county bar association.

Programs rustled up and down the aisle as Barry said Amen and returned to his seat in the old jury box. My brother Haywood's Stevie was videotaping the ceremony and he took advantage of the momentary stir to switch camera angles.

Ellis came back to the microphone set up in front of the high carved bench where the Honorable Frances Tripp reposed in unselfconscious dignity. Forever a politician, Ellis spent the next ten minutes recognizing just about everybody in the audience. He began with the elected: two state representatives, four judges, the sheriff, three mayors, a police chief, six county commissioners, four members of the school board, and the register of deeds.

(If Colleton County ever goes back to electing dog catchers or town criers, our clerk of court will recognize them, too.)

We clapped for two preachers, the head of the Democratic Women, the head of the Democratic Men, the leader of the county's Black Caucus, the president of the local Jaycees, a fire chief, the dean of our local community college, and somebody from the state auditor's office who had innocently wandered over from Raleigh on other business and now had to wait till I was sworn in before courthouse routine would return to normal.

After at least a third of the crowd had stood for polite applause, Ellis asked anxiously, "Now did I miss anybody?" No one leaped up, so he said, "Then how 'bout I ask for all of Miss Knott's family to stand and be recognized?"

There was a slight hesitation, then another third of the audience got up—all my brothers and their wives and children, cousins, aunts and uncles and finally, from his seat beside me, my father, like an Old Testament patriarch, still vigorous and straight-backed even though his hair was silvered by more than eighty years of hard living.

Running for district judge was not Daddy's idea of what his only daughter should be doing with her life. Not ladylike enough. Not by a long shot. But back in his younger days he'd been one of the biggest bootleggers in eastern North Carolina and when an anonymous mudslinger started linking my reputation to his towards the end of my campaign, he changed his attitude. Far as he was concerned, judging the scum of the district might not be a ladylike occupation, but by damn, nobody else but him better try to tell me I couldn't do it. He'd even pulled strings to get me appointed after a disastrous runoff primary last month.

I was still a little sensitive about that.

"Will you just quit it?" scolded the pragmatist that lives in the back of my skull. *"Half the judges on the bench today were first appointed. It's not like your daddy ever killed anybody to put you here."*

"Then how come he knows where so many political bodies are buried?" asked the preacher who shares the same skull space.

A valedictory tone in Ellis's voice brought me back to attention. "—of the North Carolina Court of Appeals will administer the oath of office."

Down from the high bench came Judge Frances Tripp, a majestically tall black woman who moves with such solemn deliberation it always comes as a surprise to realize there's an infectious sense of the ridiculous down below. A narrow ruffle of white lace banded her neck above her dark robe, and she looked like Justice personified.

We met her at the microphone and Daddy held out my mother's Bible. I placed my right hand on the worn black leather, lifted my left, and listened attentively as Judge Tripp said, "Do you, Deborah Stephenson Knott, solemnly and sincerely swear that you will support the Constitution of the United States; that you will be faithful and bear true allegiance to the State of North Carolina, and to the constitutional powers and authorities which are or may be established for the government thereof; and that you will endeavor to support and maintain and defend the Constitution of the said State, not inconsistent with the Constitution of the United States, to the best of your knowledge and ability; so help you God?"

"I do," I said firmly.

"Furthermore, do you solemnly and sincerely swear that you will administer justice without favoritism to anyone or to the State; that you will not knowingly take, directly or indirectly, any fee, gift, gratuity or reward whatsoever, for any matter or thing done by you or to be done by you by virtue of your office, except the salary and allowances by law provided; and that you will faithfully and impartially discharge all the duties of Judge of the District Court Division of the General Court of Justice to the best of your ability and understanding, and consistent with the Constitution and laws of the State, so help you God?"

The words flowed over me like the sanctified anointment of some sweet-smelling oil.

Solemnly and sincerely, I swore again that I did.

Frances smiled for the first time and held out her cool thin hand to shake mine.

"Welcome to the bench, Judge Knott."

Applause almost muffled out the "Awww-*right!*" from one of my enthusiastic nephews.

Aunt Zell came forward with my robe. I was wearing a splashy red-flowered dress that flamed against the somber oak and leather of the courtroom. It was a dress I'd chosen deliberately because I'm theatrical enough to enjoy symbolism. I was a nun taking holy vows. I was Wisdom abjuring Vanity. I was deep water preparing to run still, by damn.

Aunt Zell handed the robe to my father and he held it open for me, settling its weight onto my shoulders. The zipper ends went together smoothly and every inch of red-flowered silk disappeared beneath the heavy black fabric. As Daddy escorted Aunt Zell back to their seats, I turned to the audience and spoke of my gratitude for the trust now placed in me.

My remarks were simple and direct.

And short.

Good politicians know enough to quit talking before people realize they're tired of being talked at. My name was going to be on the November ballot after all; and even though it was only a formality, since I was unopposed for Perry Byrd's seat, I still aimed to rack up a bunch of votes.

• • •

Weddings, funerals, christenings—most solemn ceremonies are followed by food and fellowship, and a swearing-in is no different. Once all the official documents were signed, we followed the crowd downstairs and through a soaring two-level glass atrium that links the new part of the courthouse with the old.

The shiny brass-and-glass design harkens towards the twenty-first century. It's filled with green plants and sunlight, and it's become a popular setting for receptions, which is probably why Julia Lee won't use it if she can help it. She had directed the Martha Circle of the First Methodist Church to set up their tables in the gloomy rotunda of the old courthouse.

Julia—she's John Claude's wife and therefore my cousin by marriage—gets herself elected president of the Historical Society about every other year, and she thought I ought to stand right where a long line of Colleton County judges had stood in bygone years to greet all the colleagues, friends and family who had crowded against these selfsame marble walls to wish them well.

Julia sometimes gets carried away and forgets that those walls aren't all that historical nor all that old either, if truth be told. Yes, court had been held on this site since the late 1700s, but this particular building was erected in 1921, not 1821. Even so, the rotunda was a better choice for this sweltering July day. Modern air-conditioning couldn't keep the sunny atrium as cool as the thick marble that surrounded us; and Carly Jernigan's robe not only smelled like a wool horse blanket, it was starting to feel like one.

• • •

One of the Marthas handed me a cup of slushy lime punch before I took my place in the receiving line. Too sickly sweet, but at least it was cold and wet.

Against his wishes—"I'm not an invalid and I can damn well stand"—they had brought a chair for Daddy and he was holding his own court at the far end of the line. For the last few years, he doesn't leave the farm all that often, so there were lots of folks to crowd around and shake his hand, glad to see him again.

I stood with Judge Frances Tripp on one side and John Claude Lee, Julia's husband, on the other. John Claude's an older cousin and the current Lee of Lee & Stephenson, the law firm where I was no longer a full partner.

Genealogy is still the favorite parlor game in every southern house that still has a parlor; but for those who don't really care who fits in how, here's the Cliffs Notes version: my mother was a Stephenson, her mother was a Lee. Lee & Stephenson, Attorneys-at-Law was begun in the 1920s by John Herman Lee, my first cousin twice removed on Mother's Lee side, and old Brixton Stephenson, her paternal grandfather. My younger cousin Reid, Brixton's grandson, is this generation's Stephenson.

If you're any good at this sort of thing, then you've already worked it out that, while I'm cousin to Reid and John Claude both, they're no blood kin to each other.

But unless you've got some reason to worry about whether or not you could get a fair trial in my courtroom, the relationships are moot at this point and you don't really have to keep it all straight. The firm of Lee, Stephenson & Knott had gone back to being plain old Lee & Stephenson again. I was legally out of it, and all my personal clients had been shifted to John Claude or Reid, who has trouble keeping his pants zipped, but who's a damn fine attorney.

That's a personal opinion, though, and I promise you it's not something I'm going to let bias me. Sooner or later they'd both be pleading cases before me and I planned to be totally objective.

"Long as you don't bend over backwards to be fair," said John Claude when I was cleaning out my office in the 1867 house his great-grandfather (my great-*great*-grandfather) had built half a block from the courthouse. John Claude's mother was once his second-grade school teacher. His hair is silver now and she's almost ninety, yet he's never forgotten the way she always took the other child's side in any dispute.

"Don't you worry, not one little minute," I soothed. "When it's your turn to take out the kickball, I won't give it to anybody else."

•   •   •

The receiving line from hell continued to snake past.

My fellow attorneys were amiable and friendly, but their joshing remarks lacked the usual barbs.

When Judge Perry Byrd had his stroke, I was in the middle of a runoff campaign for a different judge's seat. Then, instead of getting better, as his doctors had originally thought, Byrd had another stroke and died just as my own campaign crashed to a halt at the runoff primary. In North Carolina, when a judge dies or resigns in the middle of his term, the local bar associations get together and present the governor with a slate of candidates from the judge's same party. Because I'd polled enough votes to force a runoff in the first place, I was put on the slate as a courtesy, but it was generally thought that Chester Nance, a white male ADA from Black Creek, would get it.

To everyone's surprise—everyone who didn't know about the keg of Republican dynamite my daddy was sitting on—our Republican governor appointed me.

I'd been kicked up a notch in the pecking order and as they passed through the line, I could feel my colleagues already beginning to distance themselves from me. No more sharpening our spurs on one another before the bar. Now I would be above the fights, judging their words and deeds, and nobody knew for sure what sort of things I might let ruffle my feathers. They'd be walking on eggs till they got a feel for my way of doing justice.

I just wished certain elderly cousins and aunts would exhibit a similar reticence. In the same breath, they could offer congratulations—loving and completely *sincere* congratulations—and still make it crystal clear that the next time they hugged me in a receiving line, they sure hoped I'd finally be wearing white satin and orange blossoms.

"Oh, it'll have to get a lot colder than this," I said sweetly when Aunt Sister asked if becoming a judge meant I was about ready to settle down.

She gave me a blank smile and passed on, but Frances Tripp put her lips close to my ear and murmured, "Like when hell freezes over?"

"Give or take a few degrees," I muttered back.

All around the rotunda, my brothers and their wives and children were clumped in animated conversation with friends and relatives. Among the teenage girls helping the older women of First Methodist serve were Seth and Minnie's Jessica and Herman and Nadine's Annie Sue. I was glad to see that Annie Sue and Herman seemed to be speaking to each other today. A lot of days, they didn't.

From infancy, Annie Sue had tested the limits of paternal authority; but she'd turned sixteen this spring and now that she had her driver's license, she wanted more freedom and less accountability than ever. According to Minnie, they'd had a monumental clash last weekend. I didn't get all the details; but I gather it involved a broken curfew and confiscation of car keys. Nothing new there except that both my brother and my niece had lost their tempers and Herman had warned Annie Sue—and in front of her friends, which made it twice as humiliating—that she wasn't too big to get a switching if she didn't apologize at once.

"In the same breath as she apologized, she swore she'd never speak to Herman again as long as she lived," Minnie had reported with a shake of her head. "Herman's way too strict, but that child's sure got a talent for pouring kerosene on a hot fire."

I watched her pour Herman a cup of punch with every appearance of daughterly affection and hoped their reconciliation would last a while this time.

A moment later, my spirits were buoyed by the sight of Lu Bingham beaming at me from across the rotunda. The Marthas had set out silver trays of miniature ham biscuits, cucumber sandwiches, and pecan puffs to go with their lime punch and butter mints, and Lu was loading her paper napkin to the spilling point. She has a way with young people and seemed to be bantering with my nieces. Even across the rotunda, I could hear her booming laughter.

We'd gone all through grade school and high school together, but I was still fighting to stay a size twelve while Lu had long since surrendered to an eighteen. On her, though, it was okay. She looked solid and comforting and infinitely capable of shouldering the responsibilities of the world. Not a bad thing since she was the guiding spirit and most of the muscle behind WomenAid.

WomenAid. Women helping women to cope with life's sour lemons—from Cambodian refugees to a battered wife in one of Dobbs's oldest families. My internal preacher nodded approval, but the pragmatist was slowly shaking his head.

Now why was the thought of that nonprofit organization suddenly making me uneasy?

Even as I continued to smile and accept congratulations and good wishes, I kept a wary eye on Lu. She was working her way through the crowd, probably hitting on everyone she spoke to for a donation. She was an ace at writing grant proposals and getting corporate funding, but much of her support came from the grassroots level and working every crowd seemed to have become an automatic reflex.

A member of the Black Caucus momentarily halted the line in front of Frances, and Lu, who would seize an opportunity with the best of them, slid into the gap. Crumbs of pecan puffs showered down the front of my robe as she gave me an enthusiastic hug. "We're so proud of you! And it's going to be such great publicity having a judge out there swinging a pick."

For a moment, I thought she'd said "picket" even though she, of all people, would surely know that judges can't walk a picket line.

She grinned at my bewilderment. "When you spoke to the volunteers of WomenAid in May. Remember? You said you sure wished you could take time off from campaigning and pitch in. Here's your chance. Saturday morning, seven o'clock. While it's still cool. Don't forget to bring your own tools."

(Stevie chose that moment to turn his camera back on my face just as it was beginning to sink in that I was going to have to put my muscles where my mouth was. My brothers think it's a real funny four-second sequence.)

• • •

By five-fifteen, the reception was finally winding down and Frances and I ran upstairs to pick up our briefcases and get out of our robes.

Hers was a cool summer-weight—winning two elections must give a judge the confidence to buy a second robe. As she unzipped, she said, "Didn't anybody tell you judges aren't supposed to make campaign promises?"

Promises made in the spring have a way of coming due in the fall. I knew that. But this was only summer.

"It wasn't really a promise. Besides," I sighed, "I thought they'd be finished building before I finished campaigning. If Perry Byrd hadn't up and died—"

"—you could've got credit for singing with the angels? Without having to show up for choir practice?" She shook her head and laughed. "Child, you really are a politician!"

Back downstairs, the Marthas were packing their leftovers in Tupperware boxes, and after I thanked Frances again and said good-bye, I went over to the table and yielded to the temptation of a single pecan puff. It tasted like fluffy buttered air.

"You didn't eat a bite," said one of the Marthas at my elbow. "Let me fix you a plate."

"Fat cells are just as fluffy as pecan puffs," warned my internal preacher, who also keeps a running total of calories consumed and energy expended.

"Better not," I said regretfully, fishing for her name.

Gladys. Gladys McGee. A sweet face, nondescript body, appropriately Martha-like in a beige-and-rose two-piece dress. The wife—no, the widow of one of Dobbs's independent businessmen. Insurance? Real estate?

Accountant. That was it. Ralph McGee, CPA. A small office next door to my bank, two blocks down Main Street from the courthouse. He'd kept the books for my brother Herman's electrical contracting business. A bit of a domestic bully, I seemed to recall. Gladys had been an attractive blonde once. She couldn't be much past forty, but her hair was now that indeterminate color between light brown and gray. Despite low-keyed makeup, she looked older than forty, and there were deep lines beside her mouth and around her eyes. Continuing grief? Maybe Ralph hadn't left her very well off? And wasn't there a daughter?

The teenage girls who'd helped earlier were gone now like a chattering flock of bright-feathered birds, but among them had been Herman's Annie Sue and a pretty honey blonde.

"That wasn't your Cindy I saw before, was it?"

The worry lines smoothed and Gladys was pretty again when she smiled with maternal pride. "Don't they grow up fast?"

"She's gorgeous!" I said, with only a little exaggeration. I recalled now that Annie Sue had grumbled about how strict her friend Cindy's dad was. Even stricter than Herman, who half the time acted like it was the 1890s if Annie Sue could be believed.

Still smiling, Gladys went back to packing up the pecan puffs. "She's a little headstrong, but a good child, too. It's so easy not to be these days, am I wrong? I'm sure you see plenty of that in court. It's been hard on both of us, losing Ginger and Ralph in the same month—"

Ralph I knew about, but who the hell was Ginger? Then I remembered that Cindy had an older sister.

"—much too young, of course, but she and Tom had been sweethearts since eighth grade and we promised that if she'd at least finish high school, we'd give them a nice wedding right after graduation. And then, only two days after they got back from their honeymoon—"

I knew what was expected of me. "It's been such a shock to everybody. Ralph was still young, wasn't he?"

"Only forty-six," Gladys agreed. "But then they always say that the younger you are, the more serious a heart attack is."

I tried to sound concerned and interested. "And he'd never had any heart trouble before?"

"Not a bit." She snapped the lid shut on the pecan puffs and one of her friends took the box and added it to a growing pile of plastic containers at the end of the table. "He'd had some summer flu—least that's what Dr. Bhagat called it. *I* thought it was too much tension over Ginger's wedding myself. Sometimes you have to wonder about these foreign doctors. Am I wrong? But Ralph swore by him. Anyhow, when he went to him with the flu, if that's what it was, Dr. Bhagat said his liver was a little enlarged and his blood pressure was high, but his heart was just fine. Maybe if he'd gone to an *American* doctor . . ."

She shrugged and shook her head sadly.

As a lawyer, I should be inured to how people can go on and on with the most intimate details of a loved one's final days. Nevertheless, I was relieved when Julia Lee came over to wind it all up. She really is wasted as John Claude's wife. She should have been running a corporation somewhere. No detail was too small to escape her notice.

"Don't you want to take some of those cucumber sandwiches?" she asked. "You've paid for them."

I looked around for Aunt Zell. It's her refrigerator.

Julia correctly interpreted. "Zell already left and she said for you not to bring home anything you weren't going to eat yourself. She's put Ash on another diet. He ate too many chimichangas when he was in Mexico and she doesn't want him tempted."

She gave my hips a critical glance. "The Martha Circle usually gives Lu Bingham whatever's left over, if the client doesn't object. She can give you a receipt for the IRS."

Put like that, there was no way I could gracefully claim some of those yummy little cucumber sandwiches. Already Lu was piling them into a capacious cardboard box.

"The kids at our day care love it when I scrounge party food," she said.

She popped a cucumber sandwich into her mouth and happily licked the mayonnaise from her fingers.

Sheer willpower—okay, sheer willpower and Julia's basilisk eyes—kept me from wrestling her to the ground for one.

2

Layouts and Elevations

"The elevation of any object is its vertical distance above or below an established height on the earth's surface."

District court is the workhorse of North Carolina's three-tiered system of justice. On top, the Appellate Division has our supreme court with seven justices and a court of appeals where twelve judges, sitting in panels of three, act as intermediate appellate courts to take some of the load off the justices.

Next comes the Superior Court Division. Except for a few special categories of cases, superior courts handle all felonies, any criminal *de novo* trials bucked up from below, and any civil disputes involving amounts over $10,000.

At the bottom are the magistrates and judges of the District Court Division.

Sooner or later, every judge has to run for office, but magistrates are appointed for two-years terms and they screen out a lot of the really petty stuff, since they're the first to hear someone who's just been booked. Like the old justices of the peace, they can accept certain misdemeanor guilty pleas and admissions of infractions, settle small claims, and issue warrants. (A magistrate is also, to my private disappointment, the only civil official who can perform marriages. I'd love to be able to marry my nieces and nephews.)

District court judges get all the rest of the non-jury trials. In addition to juvenile court, we conduct preliminary hearings to determine probable cause in felony cases, we have original jurisdiction over misdemeanors, and we adjudicate civil cases involving less than $10,000. Last year 130,000 cases were filed in superior court; 2.3 *million* were filed in district court. Superior court has 77 judges; district court 165—you figure it out.

Considering our caseload, you'd think that judges out here on the barricades of justice would have a few perks, right? If not a personal secretary, at least access to a pool of clerical staff?

Uh-uh. We don't even get a paralegal to look up statutes or precedents.

No personal offices either. When I arrived at the courthouse on Tuesday morning, I robed myself in one of the small bare chambers not being used that day by Ned O'Donnell, a superior court judge sitting in Courtroom 2, or F. Roger Longmire, who would be hearing probable causes in 1. The eight-by-eight cubicle held an empty bookcase, an oak veneer desk, four metal tube chairs, and nothing else. Not even a pencil holder on the desk top.

There were two doors on the left wall. One led to a three-hanger closet, the other to an equally small lavatory. There was another door on the other side of the toilet. Presumably, it led to the room F. Roger Longmire was using today.

I hoped I wouldn't forget to knock before barging on through the door because I certainly didn't know Longmire that well. Ned O'Donnell probably wouldn't give a damn, but I had to grin when I pictured the reaction of a judge like stuffy old Harrison Hobart if I walked in on him sitting there with his pants down. Probably give him a stroke quicker than the one that felled his pal Perry Byrd.

Just the thought of Hobart and Byrd made my temples throb and I opened the medicine cabinet over the sink, hoping to find something for my headache. I shouldn't have drunk that last bourbon-and-Pepsi.

Not that I was hung over exactly. I never drink too much. Well . . . almost never.

Last night, though, some of my rowdier kinfolks had insisted on toasting my appointment a few times more than I should have let them, and another aspirin would certainly have been welcome. Unfortunately, this cupboard was bare, so I wet a paper towel with cold water and pressed it to my forehead a few minutes. That seemed to help.

Back in my chamber, I hung my green-and-white seersucker jacket in the closet and had no sooner zipped up my robe than Phyllis Raynor tapped on the door and handed in a piece of paper.

"Add-ons, Your Honor."

"I hope this means you're clerking for me this morning," I said as I adjusted the heavy folds of my flowing sleeves.

She smiled. "Mr. Glover always assigns me to a new judge's first day."

Very politic of him.

As clerk of the court, Ellis Glover could have sent up anybody he damn well pleased, but he knows that Phyllis is everybody's favorite. An attractive midforties, Phyllis Raynor is efficient, professional, and totally unflappable. She knows as much about courtroom protocol and procedure as any judge or attorney in the courthouse, but she's savvy enough not to flaunt it. She seldom gets backed up, not even when the judge is zapping out decisions, defendants are trying to sort out their judgment papers, and attorneys are clamoring for case numbers. The rare times I *have* seen her get behind, she never snaps or gets all huffy and put-upon.

God knows Ellis had plenty of those he could have sent up if he'd wanted to.

"Anything special on today?" I asked.

Phyllis shook her head reassuringly. "Just the usual."

She continued on down the hall to Courtroom 3, and I scanned the top sheet of the day's calendar—seven pages of traffic violations, assaults on females, worthless checks, and misuse of alcohol. Despite my own misuse of alcohol the night before, the heading gave me a sudden ripple of chill bumps:

IN THE GENERAL COURT OF JUSTICE
DISTRICT COURT DIVISION—COUNTY OF COLLETON
DOBBS DISTRICT COURT
JUDGE PRESIDING: HONORABLE DEBORAH KNOTT

Phyllis had left the door ajar and as I savored the words, Reid Stephenson, my tall, good-looking cousin and ex-partner stuck his curly head in through the opening. Old Spice aftershave wafted in, too, and the familiar smell was comforting.

"Nervous?"

"Nope," I lied and continued reading through the names. "Any of these belong to you?"

"Just a couple of lead-foots who'll probably throw themselves on your mercy."

We walked down the short hallway together. "Mercy?" I said. "What makes you think I have any mercy in me?"

" 'Sweet mercy is nobility's true badge,' " he reminded me, stealing one of John Claude's favorite quotes.

" 'Nothing emboldens sin so much as mercy,' " I retorted from my own stock of Shakespeare.

At the end of the hall, several attorneys were clustered around the coffee maker that was kept plugged in year-round no matter how hot and muggy outside.

"Here come de judge," someone murmured sotto voce.

"Good morning, Your Honor," the others chorused.

"Gentlemen," I said gravely. "Ladies."

Reid held open the courtroom door and grinned. "Go get 'em, tiger!"

• • •

"All rise," said the bailiff.

And they did.

Attorneys, assistant district attorneys, state troopers and town police officers, accused and accuser, character witnesses and anxious parents. Monday and Tuesday sessions of district court are always crowded first thing in the morning, so every row was full of standing (if not upstanding or outstanding) citizens.

I stepped onto the low platform, where Phyllis Raynor stood beside a computer screen that glowed with lists of names and case numbers, then up another shallow riser to the high-backed black leather chair that awaited me.

I was barely a foot above the rest, but as I looked out on all the attentive faces, those twelve inches empowered me as nothing else had ever done.

"Welcome to the bench!" crowed the pragmatist who had schemed and campaigned and compromised an ideal or two for this position and who now delighted in seeing every eye upon me. *"Will you just look at all those people who—"*

My inner preacher hauled me up by the hinges.

"They aren't standing for Deborah Knott," came that stern voice. *"They're showing respect for what you symbolize—the justice to which they're entitled. You're like a priestess now, entrusted with the holy sacraments of Law."*

Suddenly, my pridefulness was gone, and I was filled by a wholly unexpected sense of deep humility.

What am I, Lord, that thou art mindful of me?

O God be merciful to me, a sinner.

To my horror, I felt my eyes begin to puddle—that's Stephenson blood for you. Stephensons will cry just watching one of those sappy greeting card commercials—but somehow I managed to rein in my emotions as I stood and waited with everyone else while the bailiff intoned, "Oyez, oyez, oyez. This honorable court for the County of Colleton is now open and sitting for the dispatch of its business. God save the state and this honorable court, the Honorable Judge Deborah Knott presiding. Be seated."

We sat.

I've been a trial lawyer long enough that I should've had the routine down pat, but there was no denying it: my perspective was suddenly different. I was part and parcel now of an institution as old as the wigs on English judges, or as the Hear ye, Hear ye! in the bailiff's corrupted pronunciation of the old French *Oyez!* A sobering moment. Even so, I think I appeared both competent and confident as I said good morning and began to explain courtroom procedure to those who might be facing it here for the first time.

"Everybody has a right to counsel. It says so in the Constitution of the United States. If you are unable to pay for an attorney, the court will appoint one for you. You do have to meet the standard for financial need, though," I cautioned. "You can't just poor-mouth because you don't like what attorneys charge these days."

A couple of my former colleagues seated on the side bench inside the bar snorted and some of the audience smiled.

"If you think you want an attorney appointed," I continued, "now is the time to say so."

Eight people came forward and a bailiff showed them where to go to fill out the forms.

"Those of you who choose not to use an attorney will be asked to sign a release when you come up to plead your case."

That brought whispers and uneasy stirring and I raised my voice one level. "There will be no talking in the audience during court or you'll be asked to leave."

I uncapped my pen, carefully straightened the papers in front of me, and met the dark brown eyes of the young ADA seated at the table down below.

"Call your calendar, Ms. DeGraffenried."

She inclined her head in formal acknowledgement. "Thank you, Your Honor. And may I say it's a distinct privilege to be here your first day on the bench."

I'll bet.

Cyl DeGraffenried was still an enigma to me. Very pretty, very bright. We heard that she'd graduated in the upper five percent of her law class at Duke, which made some of us wonder why she had immediately chosen to come do donkey work for Douglas Woodall, our current district attorney. She should have been clerking for one of the justices if she wanted a political career, or joined some eyes-on-the-prize law firm in Raleigh or Charlotte if she wanted to stay in

North Carolina and make a million dollars before she was forty.

She was clearly ambitious; I just couldn't define what that ambition was.

It certainly wasn't for the title of Miss Congeniality. In her few months with the DA's office, she'd proven an implacable prosecutor with very little give in what's usually a give-and-take situation. Her rigid adherence to the letter of the law and the way she called for maximum penalties not only had a lot of us defense attorneys grumbling, some of the judges had even spoken a few private words with Douglas Woodall, too. You honestly don't need to make an example out of every shoplifter or Saturday night rowdy. Freshmen ADAs often err on the side of harshness when they first begin, but Cyl DeGraffenried just wouldn't let up.

A loner, too, even though she appeared at all the expedient meetings, both the political gatherings and the professional. When some of us invited her to join us for drinks afterwards, she would come and smile and talk with every semblance of cordiality. Sometimes I wondered if I was the only one who noticed that she managed never to divulge any personal information and that she always left to drive back to her apartment on the other side of Raleigh alone even though she was, as I indicated before, absolutely gorgeous: long fingernails painted a soft pink, a cloud of dark brown hair, a perfectly oval face with cheekbones to kill for, a size six figure draped in softly feminine dresses or suits of tailored silk, a collection of high heels that would turn Imelda pea green.

"I'll bet you a dollar she's a closet Republican," Minnie, my sister-in-law and a yellow-dog Democrat, said darkly when I discussed Cyl with her once. "I'll bet that's why she lives out of the district—so nobody'll know how she's registered."

Minnie's usually a political realist, but she has a hard time understanding why any black person would, of her own volition, deliberately choose to join the same party as Jesse Helms, Strom Thurmond or David Duke. For Minnie, a black Republican was hot ice and wondrous strange snow indeed.

My guess was that if Cyl DeGraffenried were actually registered anywhere, it would be as an Independent.

•   •   •

She read through the calendar briskly. Many of the cases had already been disposed of because Doug Woodall always dismisses a few after the calendar's printed. Before I even entered the courtroom, a dozen or more minor traffic violators had decided to plead guilty and were lined up to pay their automatic fines and leave. Others would be held over because of personal conflicts with work or child-care schedules or because their lawyers had previous commitments in other courts. Seven pages of names could dwindle to three or four in no time.

But now all the preliminaries were done and Cyl half turned in her chair to call, "Jaime Ramiro Chavez?"

A Mexican migrant came forward and took the place Cyl indicated behind the opposite table. His hair was neatly combed and he wore faded but basically clean jeans and T-shirt. He was charged with driving without a valid driver's license and failure to wear a seat belt. There to stand with him and speak in his behalf was a local farmer who said that Chavez possessed a Florida license but it'd been lost and he was, in fact, on his way to take the North Carolina exam when Trooper Ollie Harrold pulled him over.

Cyl asked for a hundred-dollar fine and costs, but I was feeling sentimental.

Jaime Ramiro Chavez.

My very first judgment.

I wanted to reach out and pat his wiry brown arm and assure him that he had not fallen into the hands of an unjust system. Instead I had to make do with memorizing his features. For some reason it felt crucial to me that I not let this moment and this man pass out of my memory, and I wound up concentrating so hard on the swoop of his brows and the cut of his chin that his deepset eyes shifted uneasily from me to the farmer who employed him.

Both waited stolidly.

I said to the farmer, "Are you prepared to see to it that he does go take the driving test?"

The older man nodded. "I can take him over Thursday evening."

"Very well," I said. "I'm going to suspend judgment. All charges against Mr. Chavez will be dismissed if he can bring me a valid driver's license before Friday at noon."

Relief crept over the defendant's face. Evidently he could understand more English than he wanted to admit.

"*Gracias*," he said with simple dignity.

"Call your next case," I told Cyl DeGraffenried.

She always takes a patrolman's schedule into consideration and the next ten or twelve were more traffic cases from Trooper Harrold: speeding, driving while impaired, improper passing, driving while the license was revoked. Depending on circumstances, I fined, accepted prayers for judgment, sent to drivers' refresher courses, or gave suspended jail terms.

One of the young black males was an army lieutenant who had been driving a government vehicle. "I just got back from Germany, Your Honor," he explained.

"You thought Highway Forty-Eight was an autobahn?" I asked, quirking an eyebrow.

He smiled sheepishly.

"Pay the court costs and try to stay inside this state's posted limits," I said, smiling back.

Reid's client pleaded guilty to failure to yield to an emergency vehicle and to speeding fifty-two in a thirty-five zone, something I take a lot more seriously than doing eighty on an open interstate. Despite his attempt at boyish charm, I gave him a hundred-dollar fine and a thirty-day suspended sentence.

A cynical young man who was on probation for four counts of obtaining property by writing worthless checks asked me to activate his two-year sentence.

All morning Phyllis had been guiding me through the routine judgment forms. Now she handed up form AOC-CR-315—Judgment and Commitment upon Revocation of

Probation—and I checked the appropriate boxes and signed on the back under "Order of Commitment."

It went against my grain, but there was nothing I could do about it. He thought it'd be easier to do a month of real time than to have a probation officer looking over his shoulder for three years. He was probably right.

By eleven, we'd disposed of thirty-one cases and I called a fifteen-minute recess.

Phyllis leaned back from her computer screen and flexed her shoulders. "You're doing good," she said.

I thought so, too, but I knew there were heavier things to come.

A quick trip to the lavatory (making sure both doors were locked), fresh lipstick, a fresh cup of coffee, and I was ready to go again at 11:17.

So was Cyl DeGraffenried. "Number sixteen on the add-on calendar, Your Honor. Lydia Marie Duncan, three counts of issuing worthless checks."

Lydia Marie Duncan. White female, approximately nineteen or twenty, and not exactly what a lot of people around here would call a credit to her race. Her lanky blonde hair was three days past needing a shampoo, the neck inside her BORN TO BE BAD T-shirt looked dirty, and her grungy bare feet were thrust into rundown flip-flops.

There to bear witness that she had indeed willfully written checks against a closed account were managers from the Dobbs IGA, the Cotton Grove Winn-Dixie, and the Dik-a-Doo Motel and Lounge out on the bypass.

Cyl finished reading the charges.

"How do you plead?" I asked.

"I need me a lawyer."

"Didn't you hear me tell everyone who wanted an attorney to come forward?" I asked sternly.

She tugged at the T-shirt that skimmed the waistline of her dirty yellow shorts. "Yes, ma'am, but all them won't here then." She gestured with her head toward the three stern-faced complainants. "I figure now I might maybe need somebody speaking for me 'fore they put me under the jail."

"Do you have a job?"

She shook her head. "I did work out at the towel factory, but I got laid off last year and now they've shut down and I ain't found nothing yet,"

That factory closed completely two months ago and more people than she were out of work these days.

"Very well."

Phyllis held out the form and pointed her toward the bailiff standing by the door to my right. I told the complainants, "Sorry, folks."

They knew as well as I did that Lydia Marie Duncan would probably qualify, which meant that the case would have to be rescheduled, which meant losing another day of work and in the end, even if they got the judgments they sought, they'd probably be back in court a time or two to have those judgments enforced.

The mills of justice ground on.

Over Cyl DeGraffenried's objections, I dismissed various charges of possessing drug paraphernalia, making threats, assault with a deadly weapon, and failure to stop for a stop sign. On the other hand, I did find a twenty-nine-year-old black male guilty of trespassing. He got a six-month sentence, suspended for a year on condition that he stay off the premises of the Winn-Dixie, make twenty-four dollars restitution to the store, pay a hundred-dollar fine and costs, pay a hundred twenty-five dollars for his court-appointed counsel, and break no law for one year. This was the second time he'd stolen steaks from the same grocery store—"I get tired of chicken all the time"—and I could sympathize with the manager wanting him to stay out of his store.

Before reading the next charge, Cyl motioned to a shy-faced young woman in the audience. The witness came with head-down reluctance and sat in the chair beside Cyl with a timorous half-smile.

I knew exactly what was coming.

"Line ninety-eight. Jerry Dexter Trogden. Assault on a female."

The young man who'd been seated beside the witness swaggered forward. He had light brown hair that hung almost to his shoulders, a Fu Manchu mustache, and tattooed on his right forearm was a bright green-and-purple dragon. He signed the waiver of counsel with a flourish.

And how did he plead?

"Not guilty."

"Your Honor," said Cyl, "the prosecuting witness refuses to testify and wishes to take up the charges."

She was still a teenager and there was a stand-by-my-man look in her eye. I wondered how many more times he'd knock her around before she'd quit believing he could change.

"Are you sure this is what you really want to do?"

"Yes, ma'am."

"Then I have no choice but to rule the prosecution frivolous and order you to pay court costs."

She followed that egg-sucking hound over to Phyllis's stand to pick up the papers and then out to the cashier in the hall to pay their fifty-one dollars.

It was 12:20.

"Court will be in recess till one forty-five," I said.

• • •

When court's sitting, a table is always reserved for judges at the Bright Leaf Restaurant, a half-block away on Second Street. As Ned O'Donnell and I came down the courthouse steps and headed there, the hot and muggy July day wrapped itself around us like a damp bath towel someone else had used first.

"Rough morning?" I knew that he was hearing a messy statutory rape case.

He shrugged. "I've seen worse. What about you? How do you like the view from the bench?"

I tried to look decorous. "I've seen worse."

Like me, Ned O'Donnell had grown up on a working farm and he gave me a conspiratorial grin. "Beats housing tobacco, don't it?"

• • •

"All rise," said the bailiff. "This honorable court for the County of Colleton has now resumed its sitting for the dispatch of business. God save the state and this court."

It was precisely 1:45.

The ranks had thinned considerably. Now the courtroom held less than a third of what it had this morning.

A perky black teenage girl bounced forward when Cyl called her name. First speeding violation and it was only for sixty-seven in a fifty-five zone.

"What's this contempt of court about?" I asked when she pleaded guilty. "How come you didn't go ahead and just pay the magistrate last night?"

"I might've mouthed off a little last night," she admitted sheepishly. "Might've said a bad word or two."

Mischief danced in her brown eyes and she was so engaging I couldn't help smiling back.

Gwen Utley had been last night's magistrate. She could be very nice, even sympathetic, as long as people were polite to her, but she wouldn't take rudeness from God nor curses from the devil.

"Don't pay to use cuss words in front of some magistrates," I said. "Twenty dollars for two bad words, plus court costs."

She laughed and scampered over to Phyllis.

Cyl DeGraffenried was not amused. "Lines a hundred seven, eight, and nine," she said stoically. "Franklin Ottis Webb. Speeding seventy-five in a fifty-five zone, driving while impaired, driving while his license was revoked, resisting and obstructing a public officer, giving fictitious information to that officer."

Zack Young got up from the lawyers' bench and ambled over to the defense table. "Your Honor, I represent Mr. Webb," he said. "He's suffering from Hodgkin's disease and is under a doctor's care. I'd like to ask that his case be continued."

"Your Honor," Cyl said coldly, "this is the third time Mr. Webb's case has been calendared. The state would like to move on this."

Zack pulled a piece of paper from the stack of dog-eared

manila folders he had piled on the table. "I have here a doctor's certificate—"

"If he's well enough to drive and drink and then strong enough to get out and take a swing at Trooper Harrold—" Cyl began.

"Alleged, Your Honor," said Zack.

I read over the papers both were waving at me. Perry Byrd had given the last continuance, but a Raleigh doctor had scribbled a statement that he was indeed treating Webb for Hodgkin's.

"What's the state asking, Ms. DeGraffenried? Do you want me to issue a warrant for his arrest?"

She didn't like having to back down. "No, Your Honor. We just want a firm deadline."

"You've got it," I said. "I'll hold this over two weeks, Mr. Young, till—" I glanced at Phyllis.

Without missing a beat, she murmured, "Till July seventeenth."

"—till July seventeenth," I echoed. "If he's not here on that date, you'd better bring me his death certificate or sure as the sun comes up that morning, I *will* issue a warrant."

"Thank you, Your Honor," Zack said. He gathered up his messy stack of folders and ambled on out.

Zack's only a few years older than me, but he plays the good ol' country lawyer like Andy Griffith playing Matlock.

We got through some possessions of marijuana with intent to sell and some possession of drug paraphernalia, sent a klepto over to Mental Health for evaluation, and listened to a light-skinned seventeen-year-old boy explain that he really hadn't *stolen* that car, he'd just borrowed it for a few hours and he meant to fill it back up with gas and he would've, too, if that patrolman hadn't picked him up when he did.

When his aunt came forward to pay his fine, I said, "You know, ma'am, you can keep on bailing him out and paying his fines, but he's just going to keep on getting in trouble till you make him face up to things himself."

The old woman looked at her nephew, then she looked me straight in the eye and said, "You prob'ly right, Judge honey, but I love this child and I believe in him, and me and the Lord'll keep praying over him till we'll get him walking straight in the end. You'll see.''

What could I say? Don't call me ''Judge honey''?

It was 4:15. I ruled on a couple of motions and then recessed till the next morning.

And the evening and the morning were the first day.

3

Materials and Scaffolding

"As the working level on a structure rises above the reach of men standing on the ground, temporary elevated platforms called scaffolds *are erected to support the craftsmen, their tools and materials."*

Wednesday was a holiday—Fourth of July picnic at the Jaycee Park, fireworks over the river. Thursday was a duplicate of Tuesday, and I figured that if all the odds and ends left over from the week's calendar could be heard by noon on Friday, it would give me at least half a day to fritter before I had to start toting barrels and lifting bales for Lu Bingham on Saturday.

Which is how I wound up at my brother Herman's on Thursday evening.

• • •

Make an X.
Nip off one of the stabilizing legs and what's left?
You got it, sugar: a lopsided Y, perpetually off-balance.
Every once in a while when my friends and I are skirmishing through yet another battle of the sexes, we speculate about what's actually on that little part of the X

chromosome that we still have and men don't—besides the antidote for testosterone poison, I mean.

Toni Bledsoe, who got married again last year and really wants to make it work this time, swears it holds the gene that'll let a woman ask directions.

"When it's perfectly obvious Pete hasn't got a clue where we are, I tell him I've got to pee. RIGHT THIS MINUTE! Honey, if there's ever been a man willing to argue with a woman's bladder, I never met him. And don't want to. So he heads in at the nearest service station and while I'm inside asking for the ladies' room key, I'm also asking the clerk, 'What's the fastest way to highway whatever from here?' Then back in the car I say, 'Pete-Sweet, I bet we could make up some of the time I just lost us if we took a left at that light up yonder . . . ' *et voilà!* He thinks I've got a great sense of direction and I don't have to watch him pout for the next hour 'cause he feels emasculated."

My sister-in-law Amy, Will's wife, mutters about being the only one in their house with the physical dexterity to put a fresh roll of toilet paper on the hanger; and K.C. Massengill, who used to work undercover for the State Bureau of Investigation, keeps wondering if that's why there's so much hurling and flatulence on *Saturday Night Live* when, presumably, all the eight-year-olds are asleep.

I myself think that extra segment gives us a more rational attitude toward tools.

Ever notice?

It's almost as if their try squares and saws and electric drills are some sort of ceremonial totems that will be profaned by secular (i.e., feminine) use unless ringed by ritual promises and protected by sacred vows. Probably goes back to the Stone Age and the first fire-hardened pointed sticks or roughly flaked rocks: *"You woman. No touch my axe."*

Some men'll let a new puppy mess all over a hundred-year-old Persian rug, use a hand-embroidered guest towel to wipe it up, then get bent out of shape if you pry open a can with one of their screwdrivers or dirty up their hammers cracking black walnuts.

Uncle Ash is a sweetie about most things but he's never real happy if Aunt Zell or I take anything other than simple gardening tools from his well-stocked shed back of the house.

All the same, if I was going to labor in the vineyards of the Lord, I needed to show up with more than empty hands and a willing heart. Fortunately, my brother Herman has four truckloads of tools and he lives right here on the edge of Dobbs. He growls worse than our daddy ever did, but he's not Daddy and I don't pay him too much mind.

* * *

He was growling at Annie Sue when I drove into their backyard after supper that Thursday evening. Annie Sue was huffed up and sir-ing him in that snippy-polite way teenagers do when they want to make sure you know that the respect is only on their lips, not in their hearts.

"I told Lu Bingham I'd wire our WomenAid house and now he says I can't," she told me hotly, her Knott-blue eyes flashing in the late afternoon sunlight. "He never lets me do anything!"

"She never did a circuit box by herself and she don't have a license," said Herman. From the tone of his voice, I gathered he'd already said that more than once before I drove up.

"Reese hasn't got a license and you let him wire everything by himself."

"No, I don't and even if I did—"

"Because I heard you tell Granddaddy and Uncle Seth I know more about how electricity works than he does."

"Miss Big Ears is liable to hear something she don't want to hear, she keeps talking back to me," Herman said darkly.

He still had his work clothes on, as if he'd just come in himself. Hot, tired, dirty and probably hungry, too. There was a pinched look on his face, and I had a feeling this might not be the best time to ask him to lend me a hammer. Or for Annie Sue to goad him into saying things it might be hard to back down from. She always makes a big dramatic deal out of things and since she turned sixteen, she and Herman always seem to be bumping heads.

"Come on, honey," I said. "I bet your daddy could use a big glass of tea about now. I know I sure could."

Annie Sue wanted to stay and urge, but I was already steering Herman to the lawn chairs clustered under their big pecan tree, so she headed for the back door, impatience with adults in every step.

"And bring me that pack of Tums over the sink," he called after her.

The chairs were in deep shade and it was a pleasure to sit for a while though I knew that mosquitoes would chase us once the sun was fully down. I shooed their big lazy tom from my chair, and as soon as I sat down, he jumped back in my lap like a furry rug. A hot furry rug. But I'm always a sucker for a purring cat, and I missed having one around since Aunt Zell's cat disappeared a month or so earlier.

An occasional car passed on the side street and from beyond the thick shrubbery, I heard the muffled laughter of young children splashing in their backyard pool. Nadine's gardenia bushes had almost finished blooming, yet a few creamy white blossoms hung on to perfume the air.

Cindy McGee and another teenage girl pulled up in the drive behind my car, hopped out, and called, "Hey, Mr. Herman!" before heading for the back door with the familiarity of best friends who run in and out of one another's houses a dozen times a week. They were inside only a few minutes till they were out again, carrying two summery dresses on padded hangers. Their high light voices called, "'Bye, Mr. Herman!"

Herman shook his head. "Girls! How they keep up with which dress is whose is beyond me."

"You still working over at Tinker's Landing?" I asked as car doors slammed and they drove away.

He slouched down wearily in one of the wood-slatted chairs he'd built himself. "Yeah, finished up one house all except we were short two switch plates. I thought they were two-gangs, but turned out they were three and Reese didn't stock the trucks like he was supposed to."

He gave a heavy sigh. "Guess I'll have to get Annie Sue to start doing it again."

All his kids had worked there in the summers, but Annie Sue was the only one who actually liked it, a fact that seemed to be lost on my brother.

"I swear," he said, "Reese should've been the girl and her the boy."

Like me, Annie Sue was an accident of nature after Herman and Nadine thought they'd finished their family. They'd begun with twins, Reese and Denise. No surprise since twins ran in both families. Herman was one of two sets our daddy sired—he and Haywood, the "big twins," are seven and eight brothers up from me—and Nadine's grandmother was a twin, too. Edward came along two years later and that seemed to be all she wrote till he was in the second grade and Nadine got pregnant with Annie Sue.

"I thought I was having the change early," Nadine always said.

By that time, Herman had his electrician's license and his own business. Nadine had started doing the paperwork and answering the phone, so she just set up a playpen beside her desk and let Annie Sue teethe on new rubber insulators. The child was barely toddling before Herman stuck her in his truck and started taking her along to be his gofer on local jobs. Soon she was handing him a pair of wire strippers or a line tester before he even asked for it. "Best little helper I ever had," he said. "Even if she *is* a girl."

At the age of twelve Annie Sue rewired her bedroom with outlets every three feet and installed stereo speakers under her bed. Once when she was mad at her parents, she fixed it so that every time Nadine adjusted a stove burner, the front doorbell would ring. Nadine's not the brightest woman God ever made, so it took her two days to realize there was a connection between turning off the peas and running to answer the door when no one was there. Herman thought it was sort of funny till he went to plug in his razor and the bathroom lights went off and on in rhythmical sequence.

He switched her legs good for it, but I heard him

bragging about how much aptitude those monkey tricks took and how he wished Reese or Edward showed half as much.

Reese could pull wire, but he's not really interested in the finer points. Being an electrician is just a paycheck, something that puts beer and barbecue in his belly, new radials on his Corvette, and his half the rent in his trashy girlfriend's hand—none of which meet Herman's approval.

Edward, on the other hand, had no intention of wallowing around under houses, rewiring old fuse boxes. He studied electrical engineering at State and now works with a big outfit headquartered in Charlotte where he designs lighting systems on a grand industrial scale.

Denise worked in the business every summer, too, but she never got out of the office. She still acts like she's not real sure which end of an extension cord plugs into a wall. Not that she'll ever need to know, long as there's a man around to do it for her. And not that Herman ever expected her to. She's a girl, isn't she? True to form—and confirming his second worst fear—right out of high school she married an insurance salesman a bare eight months before the baby came. (Poor Herman's worst fear is that a daughter of his would have a child and no wedding. In Dobbs, "nice" girls still don't.)

Denise now lives in Greensboro, a hundred miles away from her parents' judgmental eyes; but her near brush with scandal has made Herman twice as strict with his younger daughter and she's never been allowed off on anything less than a double date.

Annie Sue gripes loudly to anybody who'll listen that Herman doesn't trust her. She's right. He doesn't. We can tell him he's wrong till our tongues get blisters, he just can't believe she won't make dumb decisions about her life.

·   ·   ·

Annie Sue returned with a tray that held four glasses of ice and a big plastic pitcher of tea. Nadine followed.

"Hey there, Deborah. I didn't know you were out here till Annie Sue told me." She handed Herman the antacid tablets and smiled at the big cat in my lap. "Goldie ever come back?"

I returned her smile. Nadine's all right. We're not terribly close. She's seventeen years older, practically a whole generation ahead of me. Too, she's one of those Blalocks from Black Creek and more straitlaced than most of the Knotts, but that seems to suit Herman. They don't go in for public shows of affection, but their marriage has never caused much gossip in the family. Although Herman's tighter with a dollar than most of the boys, nobody ever hears Nadine complain that she doesn't have everything she needs or wants.

"No," I answered, stroking Mo-Cat (because he purrs like an electric motor all the time). Goldie, short for Goldenrod, was Aunt Zell's big yellow cat that disappeared back in May. "Aunt Zell thinks she must've been hit by a car or something. Miss Sallie's talked her into taking a puppy. Her mama dog strayed off last week, and Miss Sallie was stuck trying to hand-feed four beagle pups around the clock."

We watched Herman take two tablets and wash them down with a big swig of tea.

"Stomach still bothering you, hon?"

"You're not feeling well?" I asked him.

"I'm fine. Just a little stomach virus I can't seem to shake. It comes and goes."

My eyes met Nadine's. "It comes more than it goes," she said. "Awful cramps. He had a real bad spell Monday night after your swearing-in, but will he see a doctor? *I* think it's a bleeding ulcer, but he won't let me look at his stool and—"

"Oh, hey now, woman!" Herman had an old-fashioned delicacy about some things and he fumed in embarrassment. "Deb'rah sure didn't come over here to listen to us talk about something like that."

Unspoken was the sudden question of why I *had* come.

"Actually, I guess I'm here for the same thing you and Annie Sue were fussing about before," I told Herman. "I was hoping you'd let me borrow some of your tools Saturday morning. Uncle Ash is so picky and I'm supposed to work on that WomenAid house, too. What about you, Nadine?''

"Oh, I'm not doing any building, but I did say I'd help some of the other ladies with the picnic lunch."

"What sort of tools?" asked Herman cautiously.

"Just a hammer," I assured him. "Maybe a nail apron if you've got an extra."

"I reckon I could do that right now. Annie Sue, you want to look in that side bin for your aunt?"

"Or I could just drive the truck over Saturday and Deborah could help me string wire."

"Annie Sue—"

Anger was tightening his jaws, but she couldn't let it alone.

"I just don't see why's it such a big deal that I don't have a license. Don't I work for you, too?"

Normally I don't get between my brothers and their children, but I thought Annie Sue was being reasonable.

Each company has to have at least one licensed electrician on staff, and the others are empowered to work under that. Sometimes though, the person who holds the license never does a lick of field work. In fact there's a company at the other end of the county that occasionally swaps work with Herman. Their holder of record is the owner's wife. He can put electricity anywhere you want it, but he couldn't pass the written examination. She could. And did.

"So are y'all furnishing any of the materials?" I asked, hoping to find some ground for compromise.

"They're buying the fixtures and outlets, but we had some extra coils of wire left over from another job," Herman grunted. "I told Lu I'd just donate it. Along with *my* services," he added heavily.

"But don't you see, Dad?" Annie Sue broke in. She sat with her heels resting on the edge of her chair, her hands clasped around suntanned legs drawn up in front. "It's supposed to be only women that's building the house. To make a statement."

"And just what kind of statement, daughter? That women don't need men for anything?"

"Oh, now, hon," said Nadine as I stirred uncomfortably in my chair. "She didn't mean that."

"Yes, ma'am, she did. Just look at her."

Annie Sue had showered since work and was dressed in a cool blue sundress because she had a date later. White sandals on her feet, pale pink polish on her nails, her shining chestnut hair clipped up off her neck. A stranger might have seen only a sturdy young woman who hadn't yet lost all her baby fat, sitting in respectful silence; but there was nothing respectful about the set of her lips or those hot blue eyes.

I waded in with flags flying. "And just what's wrong with women proving they can be self-sufficient?"

His big hand tightened around his glass of half-melted ice. "Now don't you start on me, Deb'rah."

The exact tone of defensive exasperation, even his choice of words, made me smile. "You sound just like Daddy when he gets cranky."

The anger went out of Herman's jaw. He loves our father. So does Annie Sue. She put fresh ice cubes in Herman's glass and filled it up again with tea.

"Look," I said. "What I'm hearing is that you're afraid it'll endanger your license if Annie Sue screws up the wiring, right?"

"No, it's because I don't want another Mary Dupree on my conscience." As soon as he'd blurted it out, I could tell he wished he'd kept that thought to himself.

"Why, Herman Knott!" exclaimed Nadine, clearly surprised. "You still worrying about that after all these years when you know good and well that wasn't your fault?"

"Who's Mary Dupree?" Annie Sue and I asked.

"Tink Dupree that owns the Coffee Pot's mother."

The Coffee Pot is next door to Herman and Nadine's office. It's only open for breakfast and lunch, but half the town walks in and out between six and two. Herman stops off there for a cup of coffee every morning and I think Nadine takes her midmorning break there. It's a family business—Tink and his wife, Retha, and their daughter, Ava—but I didn't remember seeing his mother.

"Happened about ten years ago. During that time you lived off," said Herman. (All my brothers walk gingerly around that patch of wild oats I'd sown back then.) "Tink and Retha were working at the Coffee Pot, but they didn't own it then."

"Didn't have two nickels to rub together," Nadine said, stirring more sugar into her tea.

"His daddy used to work on the base at Fort Bragg and one night they were driving back down to Fayetteville and got in a bad wreck. It was raining and he run off the road and got killed. His mama got banged up so bad she had to come up to stay with Tink and Retha while her leg healed, Tink being their only child and all."

Annie Sue was waiting impatiently to hear what Tink Dupree's mother had to do with wiring the WomenAid house, but Mo-Cat rearranged his bulk on my lap so I could stroke his other side for a while.

"Won't enough room in that old house to cuss a cat without getting hair in your mouth," said Herman, "so they give Ava's room to Miss Mary and they made a little attic room for Ava. It was around Thanksgiving, so that worked out okay as far as it being warm enough up there. Heat rises. She'd've burned up if it'd been summer. But they figured either Miss Mary'd be back in her own house by then or that they'd just build 'em on another room if they needed to. Ava won't happy about having to move, of course, and she pitched a fit to have her hair dryer and her stereo and all the other stuff girls think they've got to have."

Annie Sue rolled her eyes again. I knew what Ava Dupree looked like now, and now I remembered hearing how she got that way; but Herman was so deep into his tale that, like the Ancient Mariner, he was constrained to finish.

"Tink got me to come in and show him how to add another circuit for the attic. That fuse box of his was so old and rusty, I told him right off I didn't feel good about adding anything else to it. But he kept on and on at me, swore it had to be done or Ava wouldn't give him no peace, promised they'd be careful about overloads, and then said he was going to do it whether I helped him or not. The long and short of it was that I told him how it could be done and I give him a good price on the stuff to do it with, but I said not to come blaming me if his house burned down—never for a minute thinking it would.''

"And he didn't," Nadine said loyally, " 'cause it *wasn't* your fault.''

"So you say and so says Tink." Herman set his empty glass back on the tray. "But every time I look at the scars on Ava's face and arms—every time I think of Miss Mary dead in that fire— Well, I know and Tink knows, too, who bears half the blame.''

"If I recall," I said, "it was her insurance policy that gave Tink the money to buy the Coffee Pot?''

"That and selling her mobile home down in Fayetteville," said Nadine. "The insurance wasn't supposed to be all that much but it paid double because of the way she did die. The Lord moves in mysterious ways, doesn't he? Miss Mary used to fret about Tink and Retha living hand to mouth and then she was the cause of them getting the Coffee Pot. I thought they did a real good job fixing Ava's face, don't you? You can't hardly tell she was ever in a fire at all.''

"Mother!" Annie Sue was appalled. "You look at her arms and her hands!''

"Well that's her own choosing. Retha says they've tried to get her to let the plastic surgeon fix those, but she won't and I can't say as I blame her. Long as her face looks all right. Didn't keep her from getting a husband, did it?''

Bass Langley wasn't much of a husband, far as I could tell. Amiable enough, but a full two slices short of a loaf. Did the heavy lifting and cleaning at the Coffee Pot.

"Might've got him, but couldn't keep him," said Herman gloomily. "He's gone.''

"Who's gone?" asked Nadine. "Bass? When? Where?''

"Don't know where. He took off last week sometime. Just packed all his things and left without a word to anybody. Tink was sort of telling me about it around the edges when Ava wasn't nearby.''

"So that's why she was so short with me yesterday," Nadine mused. "How come you didn't tell me?"

Herman shrugged. "Only reason Tink told me was because I was sitting there when somebody came in and said he'd come about a help wanted ad in the paper."

Nadine clearly wanted to cross-question Herman about the details, but the sun was almost down, mosquitoes were starting to rise, and Annie Sue was still champing at the bit.

"Listen," I said to her, "it's all very well to want all the work done by women, honey, but in this county, all the building inspectors are men. Long as one man's going to be inspecting it, what's the harm in a second?"

I turned back to Herman. "What if you just come over and look at what she's done after we knock off Saturday night? Would that ease your mind?"

"I reckon," he said grudgingly.

Not the most gracious acquiescence, but enough to erase Annie Sue's scowl.

I myself was right pleased. I'd come to borrow a hammer and had wound up with the use of a whole truckful of tools.

Maybe I'd have to rethink that chromosome chart.

4

Hard Hat Zones

"When men...are directly below other men working above, the men below must be sheltered against possible falling objects by a protective covering. The men below MUST wear protective headgear."

Superior court had a jury still deliberating Friday morning, but I should have realized that didn't account for so many attorneys cluttering up the hall when I came through robed and ready. Yet even when I saw Doug Woodall himself waiting there to prosecute, no alarm bells went off.

Doug's in his second term and he runs as a "hands on" district attorney, so if I gave his presence a second thought, it was merely that he was a considerate boss who'd let Cyl DeGraffenried and the other ADAs get an early start on their weekend.

On the other hand, Ally Mycroft was clerking, not Phyllis Raynor. Ally's a two-faced priss pot who simpers and coos over male attorneys and gives short shrift to females.

An anticipatory air hung over the crowded front benches. John Claude wasn't there, but Reid was. I beetled my eyebrows at him and he gave a don't-blame-*me* shrug.

"Whatever's up can't be too bad if your own cousin didn't warn you," the preacher comforted.

"Don't bet on it," the pragmatist said sourly. *"He's left you holding the sack at the end of more dirt roads than one."*

"Fair's fair," said the preacher. *"Just remember how many snipe hunts you've taken him on."*

Suppressing a grin at the memory of sticking Reid with the Castleberry sisters—grandmothers now but still at each other's throats under an unbreakable trust that would yoke them till they died—I waited for the bailiff to finish his Oyez, oyez routine and took my chair.

Only five or six people were scattered around the courtroom beyond the rail, yet the attorney's bench was jammed. And there crammed in amongst all the seersucker and linen suits was Dwight Bryant in his summer uniform as detective chief of Colleton County's sheriff's department. He appeared a little embarrassed and wouldn't meet my eyes even though I've known him all my life from when he was a gangly teenager shooting baskets down at the barn with my older brothers.

What the hell—? I looked at my calendar. Nowhere was Dwight listed as a prosecuting witness.

I turned to Ally Mycroft. "Did you forget to give me some add-ons?" I asked coldly.

"Oh, I'm *so* sorry, Your Honor," said that whited sepulcher as she handed up the proper sheet.

I barely had time to scan the amended form when Doug Woodall said, "Line three of the add-ons, Your Honor. State versus Elizabeth Hamilton Englert."

Immediately, Ambrose Daughtridge, the county's most courtly silver-haired attorney, entered through the double doors at the rear of the courtroom, his hand on Mrs. Englert's elbow, as if she might trip on her way down the aisle to the bar of justice. Ambrose couldn't have been more lofty and dignified than if he were escorting her to a concert, but I thought I detected a slightly self-conscious expression on Mrs. Englert's patrician face, the sort of look she might wear if she'd arrived at the concert after the conductor had begun the first movement, so that she now had to inconvenience those already seated and wrapped in music. Ambrose shepherded her to a chair at the defense table as Doug began reading the charge.

I kept my face serene and interested, but inside I was seething. Those bastards. Reid and Dwight. *Wait'll I get my hands on you*, I promised them silently.

The other attorneys might think it funny that Kezzie Knott's daughter was going to have to pass judgment on one of Dobbs's most prominent women for possession of untaxed liquor; but of those present, only Reid and Dwight knew that Mrs. Englert had personally squashed the matrimonial designs her son had on me a few years back. A bootlegger's daughter had been deemed an unsuitable vessel by which to convey Hamilton-Englert genes into the twenty-first century.

Not that I would have had Randolph Englert as a present on a Christmas tree, but it should have been *my* decision, not his mother's. Unfortunately, Reid and Dwight were both there in the lounge of the Holiday Inn the night Randolph suggested that we cool it for a while till his mother came around. I told him our relationship was already cold enough to keep his reptilian relatives in hibernation till the next glacier hit town; then, just in case he still had any hots for me, I dumped an ice bucket in his lap and walked out.

Next day Reid left a package of Frosty Morn frozen sausages on my desk. Said it was Dwight's idea.

Sophomoric enough to be something Dwight'd think up—especially when you look at how teeny those sausages are.

Doug finished reading the charge: unlawful possession of untaxed liquor.

"How does the defendant plead?" I asked.

Ambrose came majestically to his feet. "Not guilty, Your Honor."

"Call Major Dwight Bryant to the stand," said Doug.

Theoretically, I could have disqualified myself since I'd already heard Dwight describe the circumstances under which he'd found two half-gallon Mason jars of white whiskey in Elizabeth Hamilton Englert's basement. On the other hand, Ambrose would be hard put to find a judge in the district who *hadn't* heard. Any time the mighty get humbled, the story goes around faster than blue mold through a tobacco field, particularly when circumstances were this ridiculous.

From time out of mind, Hamiltons had led the fight for an alcohol-free county. Every generation threw up at least one preacher or congressman or state senator who'd ride that hobbyhorse far as he could to the exclusion of all others.

Englerts tended to be less vocal but generally more adamant about the evils of drunkenness. Every Englert generation threw up at least one backslider.

Elizabeth Hamilton had unwittingly married her generation's backslider.

Not that Lawrence Englert was intemperate by normal standards; just that by Hamilton-Englert principles, anybody who looked upon the wine when it was red (or whiskey when it was white, for that matter) was a potential degenerate perched atop the slippery slopes of hell.

So Mr. Englert in his day, like his son Randolph in this generation, had done his drinking on the sly. He had cultivated a connoisseur's taste for smooth apple brandy. I don't *know* that my daddy supplied him—Daddy tells me he hasn't touched a brass worm in years—but they had been known to go hunting together a time or two, and Mr. Englert always tipped his hat to him when Daddy came to town.

Anyhow, Mr. Englert died a couple of years ago and Mrs. Englert's rattled around in that big house all by herself ever since.

On the night in question, she thought she heard someone downstairs and she'd called the sheriff's department rather than the town police, whom she considered incompetent.

Dwight happened to be around and at loose ends that night, so he went along for the ride. "Never hurts to have an Englert appreciate special services the law can provide" is what he told me back when it happened. Not what he was testifying now, of course, when Doug asked him to describe what he'd found upon arriving at the Englert home.

"Mrs. Englert called to us from the upstairs window and then came down and let us in."

"Us?" asked Doug.

"Myself and Deputy Raeford McLamb, who was on duty that night."

"What did you do then?"

"First we searched the ground floor thoroughly and examined all the doors and windows for signs of forced entry."

"And did you find any?"

"No, sir."

"What did you do next?"

"Mrs. Englert stated that she thought the noises she heard might have come from the basement, so we went downstairs and again conducted a thorough search."

"What did you find?"

"No indication of an intruder, but shortly after we entered the basement, the central air conditioner switched on and we heard a rustling noise in one of the ducts. We later ascertained that a piece of trash had fallen into the vent and was causing the noise that Mrs. Englert mistook for an intruder."

"What else did you find around that air conditioner unit, Major Bryant?"

"Objection," said Ambrose. "The prosecution is leading the witness."

"Sustained," I agreed.

"I'll rephrase," said Doug. "Did you find anything else that night?"

"Yes, sir. Deputy McLamb drew my attention to two half-gallon jars of clear liquid behind the air-conditioning unit."

"Permission to approach the witness, Your Honor?" Doug asked.

"Permission granted," I said.

Doug lifted a half-gallon Mason jar from the brown grocery bag beside his chair and carried it up to Dwight. "Major Bryant, I show you this jar and ask if you can identify it as being one of the jars you found in Mrs. Englert's basement on the night of June twenty-eighth."

"It is. That's my mark on the lid."

"I ask that this be entered as state's Exhibit A," said

Doug. I nodded assent and he continued, "Did you open this jar?"

"Yes, sir."

"What does it contain?"

"Objection," said Ambrose, standing with ponderous dignity. "Calls for an informed conclusion this officer is not qualified to make."

There were snickers from the side benches that any Colleton County law officer couldn't recognize moonshine when he saw it.

Doug, too, had a grin on his face. "Your Honor, Major Bryant is a veteran law officer with many years experience. I should call him eminently qualified."

"So should I," I said, "but Mr. Daughtridge is technically correct. Major Bryant is not a chemist. Objection sustained."

"I'm prepared to introduce into evidence a detailed analysis of the contents by an Alcohol Law Enforcement agent," said Doug. "I thought in the interest of saving time and—"

Mrs. Englert had tugged at Ambrose's jacket and as he bent down to listen, the whole courtroom heard her exasperated whisper. "Why do you quibble so, Mr. Daughtridge? Everyone *knows* what it is. Get on with it."

"Your Honor," said Ambrose, "the defense will stipulate as to Major Bryant's expertise in this matter."

"Thank you," said Doug.

As Dwight confirmed that the jars had held untaxed liquor that was probably at least eighty proof, I thought about the things we weren't going to hear from the witness stand today. Things like how a silly combination of circumstances could cause a waste of taxpayer money. Ordinarily, Dwight would have emptied those jars down the nearest sink drain, and that would have been the end of it. But young Raeford McLamb was pushing to go by the book and Dwight knew if he overrode McLamb, he'd lay himself open to charges of kowtowing to the rich and well connected.

Now McLamb might have let someone else's liquor go down the drain; but three days earlier, Mrs. Englert had entered a complaint against his sister because his sister's cat occasionally used Mrs. Englert's herb garden as a litter box. McLambs are pretty clannish. Cut one and you've cut them all. If Mrs. Englert couldn't overlook a little cat urine, no way was Deputy McLamb going to overlook two jars of white lightning.

Nor could Doug overlook them once McLamb brought the ALE in on it. Not that there was any love lost between him and Elizabeth Englert either. As a Republican, she'd supported his opponents in both races.

"No further questions," said Doug.

I looked over at Ambrose. "Cross-examine?"

"No questions," he replied.

"The prosecution rests," said Doug.

"Mr. Daughtridge?"

Ambrose stood, straightened the front of his beautifully cut navy linen jacket, and smoothed his silver hair. "Your Honor, the defense does not dispute that two jars of untaxed liquor were found when and where Major Bryant has so testified. What I do dispute is the implication that these jars were attained by my client or that they were ever in her possession. The district attorney has not proved possession and I would therefore move that this charge be dismissed."

Doug was already on his feet. "Your Honor, is my worthy opponent suggesting that Mrs. Englert does not own the house? If so, I think we can have a copy of the deed up here in ten minutes."

"Motion denied, Mr. Daughtridge," I said. "Present your case."

"I would call Mrs. Elizabeth Englert to the stand."

Mrs. Englert crossed firmly to the stand. The bailiff handed her a Bible and when Ally Mycroft asked if she swore to tell the truth, her frosty reply suggested she felt insulted at being required to swear to veracity. Surely the whole world *knew* a Hamilton never lied?

As expected, she denied any knowledge of how those jars came to be in her basement. When Doug invited her to speculate on cross-examination, she declined. Yes, it was her house. Yes, under the terms of her late husband's will, she now owned its entire contents; but she had not brought every item into the house nor could she possibly know what else might lie hidden within its spacious confines.

Ambrose asked that his client be declared not guilty, while Doug argued that possession is possession is possession.

When they had finished, I sat back in my chair and regarded the participants. Mrs. Englert's eyes met mine and half-narrowed as it finally sank in that I and I alone had the power to prolong this public embarrassment. I suspect she was remembering her past petty snubs.

I hoped she was.

I leaned forward. "Mrs. Englert, the court sincerely regrets any personal emotional pain this incident may have caused you. In this court's opinion, you have been a victim of overzealousness, both on the part of the sheriff's department and the district attorney's office. Possession of untaxed liquor is a serious matter, as I'm sure you know; but you were clearly an unwitting possessor, therefore I find you not guilty of all charges."

I smiled sweetly. Never had revenge tasted so good.

"Thank you, Your Honor," said Ambrose; but Elizabeth Hamilton Englert suddenly looked like a person biting into an unpeeled persimmon. In three sentences, I had patronized her, implied that she was slightly stupid, and then put her in my debt for all time.

Top that, sugar!

Over on the side bench, Reid was grinning broadly and Dwight was trying not to.

As Ambrose escorted Mrs. Englert from the courtroom, most of the attorneys left, too.

No blood drawn from the new kid today.

· · ·

When we resumed after a fifteen-minute recess, Cyl DeGraffenried was back behind the prosecutor's table.

First up was a DWI revoked license and I gave him ninety days of active jail time. Even though it was my toughest sentence yet, I didn't give it a second thought. His daddy owns the largest building supply business between Raleigh and Wilmington, and I guess it was daddy's money paying for the services of Zack Young to defend him.

Zack's probably the best attorney in Colleton County, but I'd seen his client in this particular courtroom a lot of mornings over the last three years since he got his driver's license and I knew he'd had the benefit of doubt extended to him more times than one.

Zack gave notice of appeal and asked for bail.

I looked to Cyl, who stood and said, "Your Honor, he's only nineteen; he can't even buy beer legally, yet this is his fourth DWI. If you'll look at his record, you'll see that not only does he drink, he just will *not* stay off the road when he's drinking. So far, he hasn't killed anyone, but by the law of averages, he's overdue. The state recommends that bail be denied on the grounds that he does pose a danger both to himself and to the community."

For once I thoroughly agreed with her. "But we can't deny bail," I said before Zack could protest. "So how about we make this a half-million cash bond?"

Zack bolted upright. "*Cash* bond? Your Honor, my client's father may own Tri-County Supply, but even he can't raise that kind of cash money at the snap of his fingers."

"Good," I said. "Bailiff, take the defendant into custody."

Three rows back, a fortyish woman in a designer black-and-white polished cotton and white jade necklace rose with a devastated face as Zack came down the aisle to her. They went out together with Zack patting her shoulder.

Mrs. Tri-County Supply. But under the expensive dress and jewelry, a mother too, it would seem.

* * *

We briskly disposed of the rest of the calendar before lunch and I was about to adjourn for the day when a Mexican hurried up to Doug from the back of the room, waving a shiny plastic card. His English was so poor that Doug couldn't understand what he was saying, nor why he kept waving the card toward me.

It was the bailiff who finally recognized him. "Tuesday,"

he reminded me. "Driving without a valid license. You gave him till today to bring you a North Carolina license."

"*Jaime Ramiro Chavez,*" said the preacher. "*The man you were never going to forget.*"

"*Welcome to the bench, Judge Knott,*" said the pragmatist.

5

Load-Bearing Members

"Load-bearing structural members support and transfer the loads on the structure while remaining in equilibrium with each other."

In my teens, Friday nights were TGIF, necking at the only drive-in left in Colleton County, hotdogs with slaw and chili at the Tastee-Freez afterwards, and cruising Cotton Grove in an endless looping traffic jam of open convertibles and loaded pickup trucks, every radio blasting—R&R going head-to-head with the Okie from Muskogee.

All through my twenties, except for the times I lived off, winter Friday nights were dinner dates and dancing at one of the Raleigh clubs; in summer, they were often the beginning of lazy weekends spent shagging at the beach, before everybody drifted off and got married or settled into "meaningful relationships."

Now that I'm in my thirties, a lot of the people I used to party with are back single again, only this time we all have so many strings attached, partying is almost more effort than its worth.

Terry Wilson had called me earlier in the week. His fifteen-year-old son, Stanton, was in a summertime baseball league and they were scheduled to take on the Dobbs team Friday night. Did I want to watch?

"Sure," I said. Terry and I go back a ways and I've known Stanton since he was six and Terry used to get him for the weekends. Terry's been married and divorced again since then. As an SBI agent, he was working narcotics undercover at the time. Hell on marriages. On Friday I played phone tag and finally left a message at SBI headquarters that I'd meet them at the field because I had to drop by a funeral home first.

Just because I had that fall's election wired didn't mean I could let up. The mother of one of the county commissioners had died. I never met the woman, but her son is one who'd remember if I didn't go and offer my condolences. Besides, once you gain elective office, you find yourself treating almost every gathering as another golden opportunity to press the flesh.

I was in and out in under forty minutes, but then I had to go home and change from funeral home decorum to jeans and sneakers.

• • •

The game was tied 1–1 when I got there in the bottom of the second and it stayed that way through the next six innings. Two of my nephews were playing for Dobbs, so I sat on a bleacher between home and third with Terry and my brothers and their wives, and I hollered for both sides indiscriminately. In the top of the ninth, Stanton batted in the go-ahead run for his team; in the bottom, as shortstop, he caught a hard-hit line drive down the middle and stepped on second before my nephew could get back from third. Unassisted doubleplay. A high pop-up to center ended the game.

Terry yelled himself hoarse, hugged me hard, and wanted to take everybody out for pizza, including my two nephews and their parents.

"Can't do it," I said. "We carpenters have to get a full night's sleep."

All through the game, my brothers had teased me about being so out of shape I probably wasn't fit to swing anything heavier than a gavel—I swear, I can't spit in Dobbs without having a brother in California call up the next day and tell me spitting's not very ladylike. They'd heard I was borrowing tools from Herman and thought they'd get my goat singing choruses of "If I Were a Carpenter and You Were a Lady"—words changed to suit my situation, of course.

"Better do a good job," said Will as we climbed down from the bleachers, "or ol' Rufus here'll make you do it all over again."

My eyes met those of a trim, fiftyish man with thinning gray hair and an easy smile who had been seated a few rows down from us and whom we had overtaken on our way out. I'd seen that face around the courthouse occasionally, but couldn't remember that we'd ever been introduced. Will knows everybody by their first names, of course.

"Say what, young man?"

"You know my sister, don't you?" Will said. "Deborah, this is Rufus Dayley. He's the county's chief building inspector."

"Everybody knows who Judge Knott is," he said gallantly. "Pleased to meet you, ma'am. Did I hear Will say you're building something?"

"Only helping," I said.

Will couldn't let it go. "She's gonna be pounding nails tomorrow over at that house those women are building by themselves."

"Oh, yes." Dayley nodded. "I've had to pay one of my men overtime, so we can fit the inspections in around you weekend workers." He seemed to hear the less-than-gracious tone in his voice and backpedaled for my benefit. "Of course, if we're going to have a lady judge on the job, I'll have to tell him to go easy on y'all."

"Oh, *please* don't do that, Mr. Dayley." Girlish sweetness sugared my words till it's a miracle I didn't choke. "Why, I'd just *hate* for him to think you've got a different set of standards for people you know."

He had to use his fingers to work it out, and then he didn't know whether or not to take it as a joke. His laughter sounded forced as he wished us a good evening.

Amy shook her head. "I'm no feminist, but—" she began.

"I'm a feminist, *and*," I grinned.

"Can't take you anywhere," Terry grumbled.

• • •

Out in the clay-and-gravel parking lot, the night air was hot and still. White moths fluttered in the headlights as the cars pulled out in swirls of heavy red dust that fell straight back to the ground. No moon and too hazy to see many stars. Terry's hunted and fished with all my brothers, and we stood and talked lazily about dogs and bass till the boys were released by their coaches.

They were laughing as they came up, loping dark shapes silhouetted by the field lights behind them. It'd been a satisfying, hard-fought game, nothing sloppy on either side and none of the three had been charged with errors, so they felt good about their performances. I hugged all three of them, loving their gangly height, their awkward social graces, their clean sweaty smell like young horses that had galloped through long grassy pastures. Aunts and former-almost-stepmothers can get away with stuff like that.

"Aren't you coming with us?" they chorused as car keys jingled and our group scattered across the nearly empty parking lot. "Aw, come on, Aunt Deb'rah."

"Next time," I promised. I got a brotherly kiss and a "Seeya, gal" from Terry, then he was gone, too.

For a small town Friday night, the main streets back through Dobbs were busy with cars and trucks full of couples sitting close to each other, wrapped in their own bliss. As I drove through the white brick gate and pulled up to the side entrance of the house, WQDR was playing the Judds's "Grandpa, Tell Me 'Bout the Good Old Days."

"And the good old nights," sighed the pragmatist, even as the preacher was patting me on the head in approval. *"'Bout time you quit burning your candle at both ends."*

Lights were still burning down in Aunt Zell and Uncle

Ash's sitting room, but I went on up to my bedroom, brushed my teeth, popped a cassette of *Donovan's Reef* in my VCR and was sound asleep before the drunken Aussies had sung a single chorus of "Waltzing Matilda."

•   •   •

Next morning, Annie Sue came for me well before seven in one of the company's four trucks. She pulled right up to the front veranda and leaned on the horn till Aunt Zell went out and flapped a dishtowel at her to make her hush.

"Some folks in this neighborhood like to sleep on Saturdays," she scolded as Annie Sue followed her back down the wide hall to the kitchen where I was finishing off a plate of sausage and eggs.

"Sorry, Miss Zell," said Annie Sue. She snagged a biscuit and didn't look one bit repentant to me. No, ma'am, she didn't want a glass of milk or a cup of coffee; and no, she didn't want to sit either. Eagerness to get going kept her lithe young body in perpetual motion until she suddenly spotted the cardboard box in the corner of the kitchen.

"Oh, is that the puppy you were telling us about?" She touched the fat little rump and the puppy immediately began to cry and snuffle about. "Oh, he's darling! May I pick him up?"

"And feed him," said Aunt Zell, handing her the pup's nursing bottle as Uncle Ash came into the big sunlit kitchen.

"Here, now, what's all this hoo-hawing this early in the morning?" He cocked his head at my niece and said, "Well, it's plain as those blue eyes in your head that you're a Knott. Haywood's or Herman's?"

She smiled back at him as the wiggly little puppy in her lap suckled noisily. "Herman's, Mr. Ash. I'm sorry if I woke you up."

"Not you, child. It was the smell of Miss Zell's coffee." His face was smooth and rosy from its morning shave. "She's a sneaky lady. Leaves the door open on purpose just to roust me out."

Aunt Zell rosied up herself. Married forty years this May

and they were still like that. I could never decide if it was natural, if they worked at it, or if it was because Uncle Ash was on the road so much as a buyer for one of the big tobacco companies. He'd been saving his frequent flyer miles and in less than two weeks, they were flying off to Paris for a second honeymoon, something Uncle Ash had been wanting to do ever since RDU became an international airport with direct flights to Paris.

From the day he brought home the tickets, there'd been an air of "Let the Games Begin!" Nice to be around.

He gave Aunt Zell a squeeze, then poured himself a cup of coffee and topped my cup, too. The puppy held our attention. It was about two and a half weeks old and required round-the-clock feeding every four hours, which was why there were dark circles under Aunt Zell's eyes.

Still didn't have a name, though. Aunt Zell was of the school that believed an animal would reveal its real name if you waited long enough. Of course, Aunt Zell once owned a dog that was called Dog from the day Uncle Ash brought it home till the day it got hit by a truck three years later.

Today she was trying out the names of gods: Thor, Zeus, Apollo. "What do y'all think of Jupiter?"

"How about Greedyguts?" Uncle Ash teased.

"Poor little orphan," Annie Sue cooed. "What do you reckon happened to its mother?"

Aunt Zell shrugged. "Sallie had her a box fixed out in the garage where she could come and go. She thinks the mama dog must have been moving them somewhere else and either got hit by a car or just stolen because she took one of the puppies and never came back for the other four and that's certainly not natural."

Annie Sue set the pup on the floor and it took a few wobbly steps toward Aunt Zell, who scooped it up and matter-of-factly began to sponge its bottom with a warm damp washcloth. The short lapping strokes she used were supposed to feel like its mama's tongue because that's the way nursing bitches stimulate their babies to urinate and defecate.

Puppies or nieces, Aunt Zell has always been a nurturer

and, as I drained my cup and picked up my gloves and cap, she cautioned, "Now don't you overdo out there today."

"I bet you're gonna have bad sore muscles tonight," said Uncle Ash. "Maybe Miss Zell and me'll let you have the Jacuzzi first tonight."

Annie Sue was thoughtful as we climbed into the truck. "You mean they still get in a Jacuzzi together? At their age? They're older than Mom and Dad."

Not really, I thought. Through closed doors I had heard them splashing and cavorting like teenagers more than once. No way could I imagine Herman and Nadine in a tub together. Both naked *and* with the lights on?

I didn't think Annie Sue could either.

6

Concrete Foundations

"Concrete *is a synthetic construction material made
by mixing* cement, fine aggregate *(usually sand),*
coarse aggregate *(usually gravel or crushed stone)
and water together in proper proportions. The
product is not concrete unless all four of these
ingredients are present. A mixture of cement,
sand, and water, without coarse aggregate, is not
concrete but* mortar *or* grout. *Never fall into
the common error of calling a* concrete *wall or floor
a* cement *wall or floor. There is no such thing
as a cement wall or floor."*

As in a lot of small southern towns that accreted around a
market center in more spacious times, blacks and whites
don't live as rigidly segregated in Dobbs as they seem to do
in more urban areas. We do have an all-white wealthy
section near the river and there is an all-black section over
to the east—shabby old Darkside, in our case—where a
few black professionals have chosen out of sentiment or
pride to build on ground that had been in their families for
several generations.

For everything in between these two extremes, you might
have patches of fine houses facing each other, with backyards

that touch the backyards of quite modest dwellings on the next street over, then a string of trashy shanties the next street after that. One of the white bank presidents lives near the center of town in his grandmother's fifteen-room Victorian "cottage," flanked by two-bedroom bungalows on either side. A white mailman lives in one, a black florist in the other.

• • •

As we drove through town, Annie Sue chattered enthusiastically about how she got roped into WomenAid. "I thought it was just a shelter for battered women. Then around Easter, Lu Bingham came by the office to see if we could give her a rough idea of what an electrician would charge to wire a small house because this is the first one they've ever tried. Cindy and I were there with Mom, and she really got us charged up about making a difference. Doing something tangible and permanent for a homeless woman and her children. It sounded like a lot of fun."

That was Lu, all right. She could make having a root canal sound like fun if it would benefit one of her needy women.

Sometimes it's quid pro quo—as when she helped one of the new Cambodian refugee families set up a lawn service and then convinced me it'd make a great present for Aunt Zell and Uncle Ash's fortieth anniversary this spring. Actually, it did. I no longer have to dragoon a nephew or niece to cut the grass when Uncle Ash is gone; and Aunt Zell thinks they really do a super job with her yard and gardens, so I get Brownie points every time they come. But I didn't think *this* project was going to get me anything but blisters and heat stroke.

"So who's this house for?" I asked.

"Her name's BeeBee Powell. She's a black single mom. I think the little boy's nine, and just the darlingest little six-year-old girl. She works full-time out at the hospital in the billing department and takes part-time courses at Colleton Tech to be a nurse."

"Sounds like an overachiever."

"Well, this isn't just charity, you know. Lu won't help anybody unless she's willing to help herself. We may be giving our time and labor and maybe even some stuff like that leftover wire Dad said I could use, but most of the building supplies have to be bought for cash money and— oops!" Tools shifted loudly in the back of the truck and my body strained against the seat belt as she braked abruptly for a stop sign she almost didn't see till the last minute. "Sorry about that!"

"That's okay," I grinned. "But for future reference, you do *not* want to run a stop sign with a judge sitting beside you."

"Oh gosh, that's right. I keep forgetting. You still just seem like you. Not serious and—" She searched for the word as the intersection cleared and she could drive on. "Not big-headed."

"It's only been a week," I said dryly. "Come back in a year."

"Not you," she said firmly. "Dad said—"

She broke off, embarrassed, and I pretended not to notice. I didn't have to push her to get the drift of what Herman probably said. I'd already heard my brothers speculating about how long it'd be before I forgot about where I was and mouthed off at the wrong time.

"Anyhow," she continued as we crossed under a railroad bridge, "BeeBee got picked by WomenAid's board of directors. Everybody that wanted to could put their name in, but they had to fill out a long questionnaire—education, job history, finances, number of dependents—everything. I guess half the questions were about how bad they needed a house—like, can anybody really believe she and her two sisters and their five kids are all living in a four-room house 'cause they love each other so much? Let's get real here."

Her young voice was hot with newborn awareness of social inequities.

"What was the other half?" I asked.

"Whether or not they could carry the mortgage."

"If it's just for the building materials, that can't be much."

"It's going to take BeeBee about twelve years to pay it off," my niece said indignantly. "Can you believe it? They must be paying her *nothing* at the hospital!"

Reality time.

She turned down a narrow street of shabby houses badly in need of fresh paint and fresh screens on doors and windows, took the right·fork at the next intersection and wound up on Redbud Lane, a tree-lined street at the edge of Darkside where the neighborhood was racially and economically blended. Some of the houses on this street could use paint as well, but they seemed in good repair. Too, the yards were neatly tended and most were bright with red and white petunias and those stiff little blue flowers that I can never remember the name of.

The site was easily identified by a temporary dumpster, two blue portable toilets and stacks of fresh lumber. Directly across the street was an undeveloped wooded lot, which neighborhood children seemed to use as a play place.

Thanks to Annie Sue's enthusiasm, we were twenty-five minutes early, but Lu Bingham was already there, along with several other women. While we waited for the rest to assemble, Lu gave me the fifty-cent tour. When finished, the house would be a no-frills frame: hardboard siding on solid slab, three bedrooms, one-and-a-half baths. This morning it was merely an eleven-hundred-square-foot rectangle of concrete with plastic pipes sticking up here and there where water and sewage lines had been roughed in.

"Took us four weekends to get it to this point," Lu said. "First we had to clear out all the underbrush and rubble. Filled three dumpsters."

Situated two doors up from a neighborhood quick-stop and half again as deep as it was wide, the lot looked to be a little over a quarter acre. There was a tall pine beside the front sidewalk and two sturdy oaks at the rear. Someone had hung two old tractor tires from ropes, and a knot of youngsters, black and white, were already swooping back and forth.

"Saturday before last, we dug the footing by hand and it was poured on Monday. And we finally got the utility companies to come out and give us electricity and water."

Last Saturday, the wife of a brick mason had demonstrated how her portable mixer worked, and what proportions of mortar mix, water and sand to use. Then, while the neophytes kept them supplied with a steady stream of wet concrete blocks and fresh mortar, she and two others had laid a low block wall atop the perimeter footing that would enclose the concrete slab. They were finished by noon. After lunch, the women spread sheets of plastic over the entire dirt floor to act as a vapor barrier, lapped them up a few inches on the side, then laid down steep reinforcing mesh on top of the plastic.

"Everything was picture perfect for concrete to be poured and then the inspector came out and made us pull up the plastic all around so he could inspect every inch of the footing."

"Nitpicking little bastard," said the brick mason's wife, who had joined us. A chunky fortyish, she'd stopped at that nearby convenience store and was drinking a Pepsi from the can. "I help my husband all the time when he gets behind with his jobs and has to work a Saturday. They never make *him* pull back no plastic."

"I'd act surprised," I said, "except that I met his boss last night."

Lu made a face. "Rufus Dayley. Did he tell you how he was having to pay an inspector overtime? You'd think it was money out of his own pocket."

Nitpicking or not though, the inspector had finally passed the footing and the plumbing rough-ins as well. They had poured the slab on schedule last Monday.

"Feel how smooth," said Lu, running her gloved hand across the dark gray surface. In truth, the finish was like marble.

The mason's wife tried to look modest and launched into a monologue about mechanical screeds, rough smoothings, and troweling machines. "Then, 'fore we left, we sprayed the surface with a curing compound so it wouldn't dry out too fast and check on us."

I didn't understand half what she said except to realize this was an artisan who took pride in her abilities. And with good cause, according to Lu.

"Once the carpet goes down, you'll think this is a hardwood floor," she told me. "Smooth, no bumps or dips, and a hundred percent termite proof."

I should hope so. My mother used to drive tobacco sticks into the ground for flower stakes and a month later, the sticks would be riddled with tunnels. Termites do love Colleton County's sandy soil.

"Bet they didn't find any faults with this slab," I said.

The women exchanged glances and Lu Bingham shrugged her ample shoulders. "Some men would fault God if they thought she was a woman."

"Who's this inspector, anyhow?" I asked. "Anybody I know?"

"Bannister?" hazarded the mason's wife. "My husband keeps up with them, but I forgot to ask him."

We walked over to the fluorescent orange building permit that was nailed to the utility post. Five categories were listed under the bold heading INSPECTIONS REQUIRED: Building, Energy, Electrical, Plumbing, and Mechanical. On the *footings* and *foundation/slab* lines, the same signature appeared: C. Bannerman.

For some reason that name touched a chord with me, but I couldn't think in what context. "He from Cotton Grove?"

Neither knew and we quit wondering about him the minute our crew leader arrived.

Betty Ann Edgerton had been three years ahead of me at West Colleton High. She was the oldest daughter of a sharecropper on one of my daddy's farms; and after one frustrating semester spent struggling with office machines and typing, she had single-handedly changed Industrial Arts into a coed department.

"I ain't going to college," she argued before the local school board (of which my mother was a member), "and I shore don't want to spend my life cooped up in no office typing all day, so how come I can't learn how to build a house? Women buy houses, too, don't they?"

She eventually married a classmate who aced Business Skills and these days they own a flourishing little contracting business, work three or four crews, and are building houses all over the county.

"This here's like a holiday," she told me, happily revving up her Skilsaw. "I stay so busy these days estimating bids and then checking in behind our crews, I don't hardly ever get to use a saw no more."

Hers wasn't the only saw that got a workout that day. Annie Sue hooked up some outlets to the utility box so that bright orange extension cords could power the tools; and by eight o'clock, the quiet Saturday morning was shattered by the high-pitched whine of power saws and the pounding of hammers as we anchored a heavy wooden floor plate to the slab. Using a carpenter's rule and some arcane formulae, Betty Ann and another woman who spoke the language quickly marked off where all the outer doors and windows were to go.

We divided into teams and were soon laying out two-by-sixes on each side of the house. Each exterior wall was nailed together flat on the ground, then hoisted into place, up on the plate, with door and window openings already roughed in.

Betty Anne was everywhere, explaining and directing.

Annie Sue couldn't begin wiring until the walls and ceiling rafters were in place, so she fell in with a crew on the other side of the house where her friend Cindy McGee was hammering away.

• • •

The work was grueling, yet at the same time, enormously gratifying. By midmorning though, I was glad I'd been sensible the night before and started the day rested. It'd been years since I'd lifted and hauled under a broiling July sun, but at least I knew enough to wear a loose long-sleeved cotton shirt over my tank top and a baseball cap that shaded my face. Some of the town-bred women came in shorts, tube tops and sweatbands, and by ten o'clock they were turning pink on their shoulders and noses. One worker was the manager of a chain drugstore and she'd thought to bring along a case of sunscreen. Every time any of us took a breather, we'd go slather ourselves. The smell made me feel

I should be pounding through surf at the beach instead of pounding a hammer.

There were over thirty of us; yet even so, I was surprised at how fast the work was going. Despite our self-deprecating chatter, we gradually shaped ourselves into a raggedly efficient work force. In fact, we were setting the exterior wall framing in place when photographers from the Raleigh *News and Observer* and the *Dobbs Ledger* showed up. Without being obvious about it, I made sure I was in several of the pictures and that they got my name spelled right. (Modesty has its place, but nobody ever said you have to hide your altruism under a peach basket; and let's face it: name recognition's half the game in the voting booth.)

By lunchtime, all the exterior and most of the interior walls were set in place.

"At this rate, we'll have the rafters up by quitting time," Betty Ann encouraged us when we broke for lunch.

For the last fifteen minutes, women from two of the local churches had been spreading food on a table constructed of sawbenches and planks. Every whiff of fried chicken and hot cornbread made my mouth water.

A clerk from the quick-stop down the street came up to invite us to use their facilities if the two portable toilets weren't enough, but most of us just lined up at the hose pipe to wash off the morning's grime and sweat, then headed for the food.

Lu stood at the head of the table. Beside her were BeeBee Powell and her two children, who'd been working hard all morning, too. On the other side was a sweaty white girl in green cotton running shorts, a pink T-shirt, and an even pinker nose. She didn't look a day older than Annie Sue and her friends.

"For those who haven't met her yet," said Lu, "I'd like to introduce the Reverend Veronica Norton. Ronnie?"

The young woman wiped her hands on the seat of her shorts, then opened a Bible, and with an impish grin, read the last three verses of the book of Proverbs. It's from the passage that begins "Who can find a virtuous woman?" —the one most preachers will read at an elderly matron's

SOUTHERN DISCOMFORT • 73

funeral when he doesn't really know the least little thing about her except that she'd been somebody's wife and mother. This was the first time I'd heard it read with a spin.

"Many daughters have done virtuously, but thou excellest them all. Favor is deceitful, and beauty is vain, but a woman who feareth the Lord, she shall be praised." In the Reverend Norton's voice, the final words sounded downright subversive: *"Give her of the fruit of her hands, and let her own works praise her in the gates."*

I wasn't the only woman who turned and looked proudfully at the house rising behind us, strong and clean, soon to shelter the young mother who stood among us with her two children.

Lu next called on an elderly black deaconess who gave thanks for the food, both spiritually and temporally, and we fell to. My paper plate was soon loaded with chicken, butterbeans, two thick meaty slices of vine-ripened tomatoes, and a dollop of zucchini casserole, and I carried it over to a stack of plywood shaded from the midday sun by a huge elm tree that was actually growing in the next yard over. Somebody's black-and-white hound was lying in the cool dirt beside the lumber. He looked up at me with a hopeful air and I gave him a bit of crisp chicken skin. Annie Sue, Cindy and a third girl soon joined us, sitting cross-legged on the broad sheets of plywood like day campers on a boat pier.

"Y'all know my Aunt Deb'rah, don't you?" Annie Sue asked.

Cindy McGee I had already recognized. The other, a strawberry blonde who'd been with her Thursday night, looked familiar but I couldn't put a name to her and said so.

"That's because you couldn't come to our spring concert," said Annie Sue. "She and Cindy and me made up a trio, but you had a fund-raiser or something that night."

"I'm Paige Byrd," the girl said shyly. "I think we probably met at my father's funeral."

"Oh. Right," I said, feeling like a clod. "Sorry."

I vaguely knew that Annie Sue and Cindy had begun

running around with Judge Byrd's daughter when they made the senior high school chorus last fall. And I must have seen her at his wake—even though I disliked Perry Byrd personally, I'd still gone to pay my respects to the family—but she had never fully registered.

"That's because she was a total *mess*," Annie Sue told me later. "Fat and frumpy. She's lost at least ten pounds since the funeral and Cindy and me, we made her cut her hair and get a rinse and start wearing bright colors. Can you believe it? Everything in her closet practically was beige. She just flat-out disappeared into the woodwork before."

Now that I knew who she was, I could see the likeness to her father. Perry Byrd had been a redhead with broad flat cheekbones and wide brow, and his daughter had inherited both his bone structure and his coloring. She seemed to have escaped his prejudices though, if helping to build a house for a needy single black woman meant anything.

She wiped her fingers on her napkins and held out her hand like a well-mannered old lady. "I'm pleased to meet you again, Judge Knott," she said awkwardly. "I've been wanting to ever since Annie Sue told me you were going to be appointed."

"Why, thank you, Paige. I guess it must be hard for you and your family to see someone else in his place, but—"

"No," she said firmly, as if this were something she and Annie Sue had already discussed. "I was really glad when I heard it was you going to get his seat. I think there ought to be more women on the bench."

"Hear, Hear!" said Cindy, tapping her hammer on plywood to underline her enthusiasm.

Paige turned beet red and there was a moment of self-conscious silence before Cindy, who was the prettiest of the three and who seemed to be the leader, leaned over and bossily took a buttered biscuit out of Paige's hand.

"You want to put back every pound?" she said sternly, handing the biscuit to the hound, who didn't really need it either, but was willing to oblige. "If you're going to get in that new bathing suit—"

"Doesn't matter whether I can or can't," said Paige. "My mother doesn't want me to go with y'all."

"What?"

Annie Sue stirred uneasily. "My dad won't let me either."

Cindy sat back, looking scornful. "And y'all are just gonna let them tell you what you can do every minute?"

"Easy for you," said Annie Sue. "Now that your dad's gone, you can talk your mother into anything."

That seemed like a callous remark to me, what with Ralph McGee not in his grave a month and Perry Byrd barely a week earlier, but only Paige seemed to notice.

"I could probably talk her into it later," she said quietly. "Just not now. She thinks it wouldn't look right this soon after."

"Where are y'all wanting to go?" I asked.

"My cousin and her new husband have a condo down at Emerald Isle," said Cindy, "and he's got to go to Chicago on business so she's invited us to come stay with her next week. Just four females. It's not like Jet's going to have men over or anything and her new-married."

"Jet Johnson's your cousin?" I asked.

"Jet Ingram now," Cindy said. "Actually, second cousin. Our grandmothers are sisters. Anyhow, she's settled down a lot these last two years and I don't know why Mr. Herman won't trust her to chaperon."

Annie Sue just shrugged, but I could have told Cindy why my straitlaced brother objected. And for once I agreed with him. Jet Johnson's more my age than Cindy's. She grew up in our part of the woods over in Cotton Grove and she didn't get her nickname at the tender age of thirteen just because she had dark eyes and coal black hair. She broke the Colleton County sound barrier, and drugs and sex were only the tip of her wildness. There'd been rumors of dealing and known acts of violence.

True, I'd heard nothing in the last year or so. And maybe I was turning into an old fogy right before my own eyes. All the same, I didn't like hearing that one of Annie Sue's best friends was that closely related, and I was glad old stick-in-the-mud Herman had put his foot down on any beach trip Jet Johnson might be a part of.

"I think he's just being mean," Cindy persisted. "Why don't—"

Paige abruptly nudged her foot and smiled over my shoulder. "Hey, Miss Nadine."

I turned and there was my sister-in-law bearing a box of homemade cookies.

"Ah, here you all are!" said Nadine. "Who wants a fudge delight?"

7

Roughing In

*"Rough carpentry includes the layout, cutting, and
erection of formwork members and of such
wooden structural members as plates, joists, studs,
girders, bridging, bracing, and rafters...sheathing
and subflooring members are also included under
rough carpentry."*

The trusses to support the peaked roof were built of
two-by-fours and looked like big wooden triangles with
W-shaped stiff knees between rafter and joist. They spanned
the full width of the house from one exterior wall to the
other and they looked heavier than they were. Or maybe that
was because many hands really do make light work. I was
afraid we'd need sky hooks to hoist those cumbersome
things up to the women perched like acrobats on those
flimsy-looking skeletal walls. Up they went, though, and
once they were nailed in place, the whole structure suddenly
became rigid and sturdy. A steady stream of half-inch
plywood sheets followed; and as soon as the bottom courses
were secured, several of us swarmed onto the roof to tack
down black tar paper.

"Now let it rain!" we told one another.

As we knocked off in the late afternoon, BeeBee Powell

stood under the waterproof roof with a blissed-out smile on her face.

"Starting to look like a real house, isn't it?" I said.

"Starting to look like home," she answered softly.

Her children were darting in and out between the open studs. "Which is my room, Mama?" they called. "Which is mine?"

Annie Sue approached with the wiring diagram in one hand and a carpenter's pencil in the other. "We don't have to put everything exactly where it is on this, BeeBee. Did you think about where you'd like counter sockets in the kitchen? And what'd you decide about that ceiling light in Kaneesha's room?"

As they went off together to mark off on wall studs and ceiling joists where each socket and light fixture should go, I grabbed a basket and started picking up scraps to carry out to the dumpster.

Most of the women had gone, scattered for the week with promises to come back or send friends in their places next weekend. Still there were Annie Sue's friends who were straightening lumber in the back and Lu Bingham and Betty Ann Edgerton, who sat on the edge of the small front porch and conferred about delivery schedules for next Saturday's supplies. They were hoping to set the doors and windows and get the exterior sheathing on so that the whole house would be dried in, ready for insulation and Sheetrock.

I had emptied two basketfuls of trash when Betty Ann called, "Come and sit a minute."

"I'm afraid my muscles will seize up if I stop moving," I said; but I didn't need to be asked twice.

Out in the side yard, Cindy McGee and Paige Byrd had stepped into a water fight with the Powell kids. Squeals of laughter erupted every time the hose changed hands.

"Where do they get the energy?" Betty Ann groaned as she pulled a crumpled pack of cigarettes from her nail apron and lit up.

"Probably comes with being sixteen," I said.

"Were we ever sixteen?" Lu took out her own cigarettes and offered me one.

I shook my head.

"We *were* sixteen," Lu said. "Because that's when you and I both started smoking. I remember sneaking out of study hall with you to the girls' bathroom. When did you quit?"

"When I was eighteen," I reminded her. "When my mother was dying with cancer."

It was part of yet another secret bargain I had tried to strike with God that summer: *Just let her live and I swear I'll never put another cigarette to my lips.*

God wasn't bargaining that day either.

"Oh, Lordy, that's right," said Betty Ann as Lu's hand hesitated on her lighter. "Will it bother you if we smoke?"

"No," I said honestly.

In truth, I had always loved the smell of mellow tobacco and still missed cigarettes after all these years. Yet even if it did bother me, it would be hypocritical to say so, since part of my income is from the tobacco allotment I inherited from Mother. Besides, some of my sweetest memories had the smell of her cigarettes and Daddy's twining through them.

The sun headed down the western sky behind the tall pines but there was plenty of daylight left. I rested my tired back against a wall stud and waited for Annie Sue to finish up and carry me home. She and her two friends had talked about meeting some guys at a dance over at the Armory, but Aunt Zell and Uncle Ashe's Jacuzzi was the only entertainment I wanted tonight.

Marking on the studs as she talked, Annie Sue and BeeBee came down the newly defined hall into what would be the living room. "—and then over by the front door, we'll have a switch plate for the porch light and that lamp outlet, okay?"

BeeBee nodded. "Sounds fine to me." She grinned at the three of us flaked out on her new porch. "Y'all look plumb worn out."

Before we could retort, her son came around the corner of the house lugging the hose with such mischievous intent that she drew herself up sternly. "Boy, you better think again 'fore you point that thing at me."

Gurgling with laughter, he didn't hesitate and before we could dive for cover, all five of us were swept with a spray of cold water.

"Anthony Carl Powell, I'm gonna wear your bottom out!" his mother threatened as she leaped from the porch.

The child dropped the hose and fled, confident that she wasn't really angry, that the chase would end in a tumbled heap on the long grass under the trees.

Lu and Betty Ann looked at their soggy cigarettes ruefully.

"Time I was getting home anyhow," said Betty Ann and went off to her truck.

"Me, too," said Lu as she headed toward her own car. "You'll be back next Saturday, Deborah?"

"Sure," said Annie Sue. "She's going to help me pull wire, right?"

I sighed. "Right."

"Maybe we could even get started one evening next week?"

"Maybe," I said noncommittally.

Lu laughed and called good-bye to BeeBee, who was toweling her children off with her son's wet T-shirt so they wouldn't get mud on the seat of her car.

"Y'all aren't leaving now?" BeeBee asked.

"My dad's coming by to check that I've got everything marked out right," Annie Sue told her. "I thought he'd be here by now."

"Probably making sure everybody's gone first," I said.

"See you next week then," said BeeBee as she finished buckling little Kaneesha into the backseat. Anthony Carl was buckled up, ready to roll, and both children waved to Paige and Cindy till the car pulled out of sight.

The two girls were drenched to the skin. Their hair hung in wet strands and their thin cotton shirts were plastered to their young bodies, outlining breasts and nipples.

At that moment, a bright red Jeep without its rag top screeched to a halt and a virile young white man pulled himself up by the roll bar. Sunlight glinted off his mirror shades.

"Well, well, well!" A salacious leer spread itself across

his handsome face. "Did someone forget to tell me about the wet T-shirt contest?"

He stepped down from the Jeep, hitched up his low-slung jeans and strolled across the grass. "Hell-*lo*, little ladies! I'm your friendly neighborhood building inspector and I'd be happy to inspect your framing any old time you say."

The girls laughed at his burlesque of crude seducer. I just sat where I was and watched. Motionless on the floor behind the others, my baseball cap perched on one drawn-up knee, I could have been another teenager for all he noticed. He still hadn't pulled his eyes off those wet shirts; but I knew his face and now I remembered his name: C-for-Carver Bannerman, my cousin Reid's lead-foot, the man I'd fined a hundred dollars for grossly speeding in a residential zone and for failure to yield to an ambulance.

"Don't tell me you gals know how to hammer a stud into place?"

He marched right on up to them in that space-invading tactic men like him use, knowing most women will step back. Annie Sue and Paige did. Cindy stood her ground, dimples flashing, her green eyes daring him to further flights of outrageousness. Her back was against a porch support and he reached past her to brace himself, his chest less than six inches from hers. With his free hand, he pulled off his sunglasses and stared straight down into her pretty face.

It seemed a good time to pull the plug on this nonsense. I stuck my cap back on my head and leaned forward. "Good evening, Mr. Bannerman."

"Just wait your turn, dollface," he drawled. "I'll get to—" He hesitated, seeing me now, almost remembering my voice, but unable to think how he knew me.

Paige and Annie Sue were smiling as broadly as Cindy, who slipped out from under his arm and said, "This is Ms. Deborah Knott. *Judge* Deborah Knott."

"Oh, shit!" He downshifted from the cliché of walking penis to the cliché of boyish penitence, which he'd tried to use on me in court Tuesday. "Stepped into it again, didn't I?"

"You do seem prone to it," I agreed.

The smile stayed on his lips, but the eyes went hard before he slipped those concealing glasses on again. A young man who liked to jab, not be jabbed. He kept his cool though. Continued to tease the girls, albeit with considerably less lechery than he'd used initially. They seemed not to notice and laughed when he asked what part I'd worked on "so I can judge the Judge."

They followed him through the house, chattering and giggling. I stayed where I was. Lu had led me to expect a lot of sarcasm and nitpicking, and I didn't want to hear it; but when they returned, Bannerman's only criticism was that two-by-two ledger strips ought to be nailed on the ceiling joists, a valid oversight and something easily corrected.

He dated and signed his okay on the building permit's framing line and hopped back in his red Jeep.

"How old would you say he is?" I heard Cindy ask as Carver Bannerman roared away.

"At least twenty-one," said Paige.

"Twenty-two easy," Annie Sue guessed.

"Well I don't care," said Cindy. "If he's there tonight, I'm dancing with him."

They stirred restlessly.

"I guess Cindy and I'll go on," said Paige. "Want us to come by for you, Annie Sue?"

"Okay." She looked at her watch for the third time in ten minutes. After six and still no Herman. "Give me a call when you're ready to come, in case something comes up."

No sooner had they, too, driven away than a teenage black girl walked into the yard. She was the young clerk who'd come up earlier from the convenience store. From the way the two girls greeted each other, I realized they must be classmates at Dobbs Senior High. "Your mother just called, Annie Sue. Said for me to tell you your daddy's not feeling good and he's not coming."

"Thanks, Patsy," Annie Sue said. "Give you a lift back to the store?"

"No, thanks. I'm through for the day. And it's Saturday night, girl!"

As I feared, I was stiffer than a two-by-two as I rousted myself up off the porch and climbed into the truck.

Annie Sue was almost as lively as she'd been at seven that morning. "He *was* kind of cute, wasn't he, Deb'rah?"

I shrugged.

"You didn't take all that stuff he said serious, did you? He was just playing."

"Half-joke, no fooling," the preacher said starchily.

"Forgotten what it's like to be sixteen?" asked the pragmatist.

Trouble was, I remembered only too well. Still . . . "Yeah, he *was* cute," I said. "Too bad he's too old for you guys."

"He asked for our phone numbers."

"Oh?"

She looked so poised and mature, her hands relaxed and in control of the truck's steering wheel. "Cindy gave them to him."

"You wouldn't go out with him, would you?"

"He probably won't ask me." She sighed wistfully and suddenly looked fourteen. "Anyhow, Dad would kill me!"

8

Framing Squares

"The framing square consists of a wide and long member called the blade *and a narrower and shorter member called the* tongue, *which forms a right angle with the blade....The problems that can be solved with the square are so many and varied that...only a few of the more common uses of the square can be presented here."*

New Deliverance was borderline charismatic and not the sort of church I felt comfortable attending; but at lunch the day before, Nadine had caught me off guard—a fudge delight cookie has the power to cloud minds—and laid on the guilt. "Isabel says you went to her and Haywood's church last Sunday and to Seth and Minnie's Sunday before last, but you haven't been to ours in almost two years."

With Jacob's pottage rich and chocolaty on my tongue, I had no quick words with which to resist.

"Besides," said Nadine. "I know Zell and Ash are driving down to Southern Pines to visit Brix Junior tomorrow, so you can come have Sunday dinner with us afterwards."

Which is how I wound up sitting in the unadorned plainness of New Deliverance on Sunday morning listening to a man who'd dropped out of high school in the tenth grade preaching from I Timothy 2:9–15, my least-favorite passage in the Bible.

"—because Adam was not deceived, my friends. He was doing what God told him to do. It was the *woman* who listened to the serpent, it was the *woman* who picked the apple, and it was the *woman* who talked Adam into eating it. Woe unto mankind the day poor weak Adam listened to the *wo-man*."

I was accustomed to how women my age and older could sit quietly and listen to sanctimonious fossils expound on how woman brought the first sin into the world by tempting man, and how women continue to tempt men by "adorning themselves in contrariness to God's holy ordinance." But when I looked at the Young Folks Choir seated directly behind him, I saw no rebellion or repressed resentment on any of the female faces, teenage faces that were certainly adorned with lipstick, eye shadow, earrings, and necklaces.

On the other hand, most of them didn't seem to be listening very hard. From the half-frown on her lips and the faraway glaze in her eyes, Annie Sue for sure had something else on her mind besides a sermon underpinned by St. Paul's view of woman's place.

There was no way this paternalistic pair of jockey shorts could have known I'd be there this morning, so I didn't have to take his choice of text personally. In this part of the world, antifeminism is but another club with which to bash the hydra-headed beast of secular humanism. As long as a woman knows her place—on a pedestal or on her back— men of the preacher's generation will give her protection and a thousand courtly courtesies. But let her try to climb down or stand up—aagghh!

As soon as he started in on "suffer not a woman to teach, nor to usurp authority over the man, but to be in silence," I knew I either had to tune out or walk out. On the pew beside me, Herman's sigh almost masked mine.

There was a gray drawn look about his face today that made me uneasy. It was so unlike him not to check in behind Annie Sue last night. Even though she hadn't drilled a single hole or put a piece of wire on anything except the utility box, if he'd been able to drag one foot in front of the other, he'd have been there to look over her plans.

It'd be different this week if she followed through on her plan to try to finish the rough-in before Saturday. Last night there'd been an invitation on my answering machine from K.C. Massengill, inviting me up to her place on the lake next weekend. If I helped Annie Sue during the week, surely that would excuse me from stuffing fiberglass insulation in the walls next Saturday? And then—

To my relief, I suddenly realized that the preacher had called for the closing hymn. The pianist swung into a toe-tapping rendition of "Leaning on the Everlasting Arms," and we reached for our hymnals. Herman's slipped from his fingers and fell to the floor. Nadine fished it out and I saw her anxious look as we all stood to sing.

"You okay?" I murmured to him.

He nodded and began to, well, it wasn't what a purist could call singing exactly—in a music-loving family, Herman was the one who could never stay on pitch—but it was certainly a conscientious effort toward making a joyful noise unto the Lord.

A benediction followed, then the preacher placed himself in the doorway and shook everyone's hand as we left. When it was my turn, his craggy face broke into a genuine smile.

"Judge Deborah!" he exclaimed. "We're all just so proud of you!"

Go figure, as Lev Schuster used to tell me.

* * *

"Mom's going to try and make Dad see Dr. Worley tomorrow," said Annie Sue as she rode home with me from New Deliverance. She was so quiet in the car that I remembered her withdrawn look earlier.

"Something bothering you?" I asked.

"Oh, no," she answered hastily. "I'm just a little tired, I guess."

"So how was the dance last night?"

"Okay."

There was a cherry red zit on her chin. It'd started the morning covered with makeup, but she'd touched it so much during preaching that it blazed now. As her hand strayed toward her chin again, I reached over, pushed it down, and asked with a smile, "Did what's his name—Bannerman? —show up?"

There was a stricken silence.

"Honey?"

She twisted in her seat to look me in the face. "Can I tell you something and you won't tell Mom and Dad?"

"Depends." I took my foot off the gas and slowed down a little. "If you're in trouble—"

"Not me. A friend."

"Cindy or Paige?"

"Cindy," she admitted. "Carver Bannerman did drop by the dance last night, and he was coming on strong to all three of us, but Cindy liked him best and she let him take her home."

"And?"

"He didn't take her home. I called over there this morning and Miss Gladys said Cindy was spending the night with Paige. So I called Paige, but she didn't."

"I see," I said slowly. "You think she went home with Bannerman?"

She didn't answer.

"He's lucky. Sixteen used to be statutory rape if a parent found out and wanted to bring charges."

Annie Sue groaned. "I swear I just don't know what's got into Cindy. Ever since her daddy died, it's like she's been on speed or something. I mean, she was always crying about how mean and strict Mr. Ralph was, when I don't think he was half as mean as Judge Byrd and I *know* he wasn't as strict as Dad. But this past month, it's like she's been let out of prison for the first time in her life. If Paige and I didn't pull her in—"

"You can't hold yourself responsible for her bad decisions," I said.

"She swears this is going to be the summer she loses her virginity. That's so stupid."

"And these days pretty dangerous."

"We know." Annie Sue leaned over and patted my hand on the steering wheel. "Honest. We do get AIDS lectures."

"Yeah, but does Cindy listen?"

She shrugged. "The thing is, what if it's not *that*? What if they had a wreck or something?"

"Maybe she's called Paige by now," I suggested. "If you don't hear from her in the next couple of hours though, I think you're going to have to tell her mother."

•   •   •

Annie Sue'd had to put away her choir robe and I'd been stopped by a dozen people who had seen the story on the WomenAid house in the morning paper (I was in the foreground of the picture and, yes, they'd spelled my name right) and either wanted to know if I'd ever met Rosalynn Carter ("She and Jimmy are doing such *fine* work with Habitat") or wanted to know how I liked being a judge. As a result, we were a good fifteen minutes later than Nadine and Herman in getting away from church.

By the time we arrived, the kitchen smelled of biscuits in the oven and a fresh ham roast sat on a platter waiting to be carved. Nadine wore a butcher's apron over her Sunday dress and her plump face was flushed.

"Oh, good," she said when we stepped through the back door. "Annie Sue, Cindy's called twice since we got home. Would you please go call her and tell her not to call back till after dinner?"

"Yes, ma'am," Annie Sue said and darted down the hall to her bedroom.

I took an apron from the pantry and moved to the sink to finish grating the carrots for Nadine's vegetable salad. "Where's Herman?"

"In the den. He *said* to watch the news, but I think he just wanted to stretch out a minute." She quit stirring the gravy and looked at me with anxious eyes. "I'm starting to get real worried about him, Deb'rah. He's never been sick hardly a day in his life and he just won't admit he is now and I never could make him do something he didn't want to.''

So what else was new about most of these Knott men? Nadine could fuss and nag like the rest of my sisters-in-law, but so far as I know, Mother was the only female who could ever turn them all west when they had their minds set to head east.

Dinner was strained. Herman filled his plate with sliced meat and vegetables and pretended that his appetite was normal so Nadine wouldn't fuss, even though it was clear he was merely pushing the food around his plate. Nadine pretended she wasn't noticing, and she and Annie Sue both pretended they were interested in the conversation I was pretending—well, you get the idea.

As soon as I'd helped clear the table and the dishwasher was loaded, I pleaded things to do, told Annie Sue I'd give her a call after court the next day, and escaped.

It was just as well that I went home early. The phone in my sitting room is on a separate line from Aunt Zell and Uncle Ash's and there was a message on my machine from Ned O'Donnell.

''Had calls from Zack Young and Graham Ogburn yesterday,'' he said when I returned his call.

''Oh?'' Graham Ogburn was the influential owner of Tri-County Building Supply and father of Layton, Zack's young DWI to whom I'd given that ninety-day jail sentence.

''Zack's petitioned me for a writ of habeas corpus. You mind telling me how come you set such a high bail?''

As a superior court judge, O'Donnell had the power to overrule me and we both knew it. As objectively as possible, I detailed Layton Ogburn's DWI priors. ''I figured a half-million cash bond might keep him off the road a while.''

There was a long silence at the other end of the wire. Finally I heard O'Donnell sigh. ''Well, if that's what you're aiming for, I reckon it will.''

''Well, well, well!'' said the pragmatist.

''See?'' said the preacher. ''Not everybody goes by what's politically expedient. Go thou and do likewise.''

•   •   •

Monday's court was last Tuesday all over again: same song, different singers. During one of the breaks, I collared Reid and cross-questioned him about Carver Bannerman.

"Bannerman? What about him?"

"For starters, how old is he? What's his background?"

My cousin wrinkled his handsome brow and tried to remember details. "Twenty-five or -six. Comes from Goldsboro originally. Took civil engineering at State. I think he has a double-wide over in Magnolia Park off Seventy. That's where his wife lives, anyhow."

"Wife?"

"Yeah. He's sort of married."

"How can you be sort of married? As if I didn't know."

"Well then, hell, Deborah. Why you asking me?"

"I just love listening to how you rationalize things like that."

"Don't go laying Bannerman's morals on me," Reid said righteously. "Why do you want to know about him anyhow? From the way you came down on him about those traffic violations, I thought maybe he rubbed you the wrong way. What'd he do? Wait around to carry your briefcase after court?"

"*If* I came down on him, it was nothing more than he deserved," I said. "Flying through a residential zone where some child could have been playing? Failure to pull over for an ambulance? Shows a real selfish lack of concern for anybody besides himself, don't you think?"

Reid tapped his watch. "Didn't you tell them you'd resume court at ten-thirty?"

He hates lectures. And smart as he is, he's never caught on to that's how John Claude and I avoided answering some of his questions.

So Carver Bannerman was "sort of married," was he? I wondered if Cindy McGee knew?

•   •   •

"Married?" Annie Sue was stunned when we met at the WomenAid house that evening. "But he wasn't wearing a ring. We looked."

She handed me the long stud drill from a bin inside the van and got out carrying a looped extension cord on one shoulder and a coil of heavy duty wire on the other. Hand tools dangled from the leather utility belt around her sturdy waist.

"Cindy's going to just *die!* She said he was so sweet once they were alone. And gentle. None of that macho raunchy stuff. Oh, golly, Deb'rah! She gave it to a married man? She'll flip. She'll absolutely flip."

Distressed, she followed me across the grass. We had a couple of hours of daylight left, but the interior of the skeletal house was darker than I'd expected because someone had worked there that day and nailed on rigid sheets of silver-backed foam insulation.

Mistake.

As we stepped onto the porch, we heard running footsteps inside. Believing that only the wicked flee when no man pursueth, I instinctively raced through the house in time to see three kids disappearing into the underbrush at the rear of the lot. They couldn't have been more than eight or ten years old, but whether black or suntanned white, male or female was impossible to tell because they had dark hair and wore the summer uniform of preadolescence: shorts, T-shirts and sneakers.

From behind me, Annie Sue was fuming. "Look what they did!"

All along the back wall, big holes had been punched in the insulation. Yes, the sheets were rigid; yes, they had a high R-rating. Nevertheless, they were as fragile as a piece of paper and were supposed to be protected by siding soon after installation. Even a baby could put a fist through them, and the kids I chased had been long enough past infancy to know right from wrong.

No one answered my knock at the house diagonally across the street or next door, so I walked on down to the convenience store, where I borrowed their phone to call

Lonnie Revell's office. I don't have as much confidence in Dobbs's sheriff as I do in Bo Poole, our county sheriff, but these things have to go through channels.

"Say you want somebody to do what?" asked their moronic dispatcher.

Patiently I again described the minor vandalism and how it would be nice if this street were added to the nightly patrol route. My words wouldn't penetrate his lead-shielded brain. Exasperated, I called Lu Bingham over at the WomenAid shelter, explained what had happened, and sicced her on Lonnie's dispatcher. She'd get some action.

"Bet it was those Norris young'uns," said the store clerk when I thanked her for the use of her phone. If people didn't want other people to hear, they'd use the pay phone outside, right? That was Patsy Reddick's sensible attitude. She was the same teenager who'd relayed Nadine's message to Annie Sue Saturday evening and she didn't pretend she hadn't listened to every word I said. "Were they white?"

"They might have been," I answered. "Who are the Norrises?"

Patsy glanced around. Even though the store was empty, she lowered her voice. "You won't tell anybody it was me that said it, will you?"

I promised.

"There's three of 'em. Their mother's Kimberly Norris. I heard that when Miz Bingham and them were studying who was going to get the first house, it was almost a tie between her and BeeBee Powell, only BeeBee won. Kimmer's helping work on this one so she can get the next one, but her kids were meanmouthing here in the store Saturday that the only reason BeeBee got picked first was 'cause she's black and Kimmer's white."

The same old same old.

•   •   •

When I walked back to the WomenAid site, Annie Sue had already drilled a bunch of holes as big as my thumb through the studs and ceiling plates. I told her what I'd done, then fetched a fifty-foot tape from the truck and helped measure off lengths of the flat white electrical cable that would run from the main breaker panel to all the outlets and fixtures.

It wasn't very long before Lu Bingham came by to survey the damage, followed shortly thereafter by one of Lonnie Revell's men. I repeated my vague description of the children but didn't mention the name Norris till after he'd left.

"Do you think the Norris kids are capable of this?" I asked Lu.

"Capable? Of *course* they're capable," she promptly replied. "That's why they were my personal choice for this first house."

Vintage Lu. Put little vandals in a nice house?

"Sure. Give 'em something to be proud of. They'd take care of it," she said and explained that the Norris woman and her children live over in what's called Seaboard City, a handful of dilapidated, cold-water trailers strung along the railroad track less than a quarter mile from where we stood.

"They're at such risk," said Lu. "Another year may be too late for them. The Powell children are living all squashed in with their aunts and cousins and BeeBee certainly deserves better as hard as she works, but at least they're in a caring environment with relatives who love them. The Norris kids have nobody but their mother and she's working just as hard as BeeBee to make a better life for them."

Despite her impassioned pleas, the WomenAid board had decided that a black woman and her better-behaved children would be a more persuasive advertisement for further houses.

"Bunch of amateurs," Lu sighed. "And mostly white. White do-gooders seem to have a harder time with the concept of white poverty. Weird, isn't it? If Kimmer and her kids were down on their luck because of a calamity—if they'd had a major illness or accident, if her house had burned down—that'd get their sympathy. But because she's made 'poor life choices'—? Kaneesha's father was white. Did you notice?"

Actually I hadn't. "And the Norris children?"

She nodded. "The father of Kimmer's first child was

black. It's okay for a white man to sleep with a black woman—that's been going on here for two hundred years—but a white woman with a black man . . .''

Her voice took on the saccharine earnestness we'd heard from otherwise do-good ladies our whole growing-up lives, '' 'Now, honey, we don't want to look like we're *rewarding* miscegenation, do we?' Oh, well, at least they promised that Kimmer will be next. *If* we can get money for a next.''

For a moment, her normal optimism seemed to dim and her shoulders slumped tiredly. ''They always say money's not the problem, but darned if it wouldn't be fun to have enough just once in my life. I do believe I could take care of some of the worst blights. Save a few children anyhow.''

Her eyes narrowed speculatively. ''Which brings us to my next point.''

''Yes?''

''Walk me out to my car?'' She smiled up at Annie Sue, who was perched atop a step ladder to install a ceiling box over our heads, and said, ''Looking good, kid.''

No breeze outside either and the hazy, late afternoon sun kept the humid air heavy, although I thought I heard far-off rumbles of thunder in the western sky. Hopeful images of a cooling rain flickered through my mind as I waited warily to hear what Lu wanted out of me this time. Money or more time?

''See, the thing is, we don't have trouble getting volunteers to come work,'' she said earnestly, brushing back a lock of sweat damp hair. Her blue chambray sundress showed darker half-circles at the armholes. ''We could begin another house tomorrow if we could afford to buy the materials.''

I mentally reached for my checkbook. ''I can't give you very much right now, but—''

Lu shook her head impatiently. ''No, no. I don't want money from you. But you could—if you *would*—clear the way for Kimmer Norris's house.''

Every word she spoke set my suspicions quivering like a blue tick on point and I waited for the gunshot that would drop the bird.

"Graham Ogburn called me this afternoon," she said, and everything went up like a covey of bobwhites. "He saw that story about us in the paper yesterday. Your picture."

"No, no, and no!" I said.

"Would you quit shaking your head and just listen? He'll give us all everything for another house just like this one. At his cost. Kimmer and her kids could be out of that broken-down trailer before Christmas."

"Don't do this to me, Lu."

"He's not asking you to drop the charges. He's not even asking for no bail. Just something he can reasonably raise. Heck, Deborah! Even murderers get a fair bail."

"Layton Ogburn was just one step away from murdering someone with a car."

"But he didn't, did he? And his father promises he'll keep him out from under a steering wheel till he comes up for trial. It's tearing his wife apart to see their only son sitting in a jail cell. Come on, Deborah. Show a little Christian compassion, okay?"

"Think of Laura Ogburn's ravaged face," whispered the preacher.

"Sooner or later, Zack Young's gonna find a superior court judge who'll give him his writ of habeas corpus," said the pragmatist. *"Might as well let Lu get something for WomenAid out of it while she can."*

"Okay," I said at last. "Tell Mr. Ogburn I'll enter an order for reduction of bond first thing in the morning."

"How much?"

"I'll drop it to fifty thousand. And I'll let him post a surety bond."

"Neat-o!" Lu beamed. Her slang's always been ten years out of date. She took a deep breath and squared her shoulders, as if she'd never had any doubt that she'd persuade me. "Well, I'd better go lay it on the line to those Norris young'uns. Don't y'all work too hard, now."

9

Soil Bearing Capacity

*"The ability of the earth to support a load...varies
considerably with different types of soil, and a
soil of given bearing capacity will bear a heavier
load on a wide foundation or footing than it
will on a narrow one."*

Despite Lu Bingham's parting injunction, Annie Sue kept
me busy fetching and carrying for another hour till she had a
lot of the preliminaries done. Paige Byrd came by looking
for her and she, too, wound up pulling stiff cables across the
ceiling joists or threading them through the drilled holes.

Each time I saw Paige these days, she seemed another
pound thinner and just a little more self-confident as she
emerged further and further out of her shell. Annie Sue
assured me that when the three girls were alone together,
Paige could get almost as intense as Cindy at times. (Not by
the littlest twitch of my lips did I let on how funny this
sounded coming from someone who could make a broken
fingernail sound like a major disaster.)

Paige's fingers were still chubby as she pulled and poked,
and her lingering plumpness gave her skin a creamy trans-
parency that did little to disguise her emotions.

When Annie Sue told her that Carver Bannerman was

married, Paige flushed with partisan indignation, and work almost came to a full stop.

"I knew it!" She rocked back on her heels and tucked behind her ears the locks of red-gold hair that kept falling over the broad planes of her face. "I just knew it! That nasty, whoremongering adulterer!"

Irrelevantly, I couldn't help noting that, if nothing else, a strict church upbringing certainly does provide a richer assortment of synonyms than the variations of "that cheatin' summanabitch" I usually hear in court.

"Does Cindy know?"

"Not unless he told her," said Annie Sue. "You think we ought to go over there after supper?"

"Too late. She said he was picking her up after work. And she just laughed when I asked where they were going."

They stared at each other grimly.

"He's older than we thought, too," said Annie Sue. "Twenty-five, didn't you say, Deborah?"

"Or twenty-six. Reid wasn't sure."

There was an appalled silence. At sixteen, older men were nineteen-year-old college freshmen. Someone ten years older?

"I *knew* he was no good," Paige said again, but there was no satisfaction in her tone.

They didn't ask my advice and there was nothing I could say that would make any difference. They might not be grown, but they weren't children either and there was no way to put raging hormones back in the box once they were loose.

•   •   •

By the time Annie Sue was ready to admit that it was getting too dark to see, mosquitoes were about to eat us alive and all the wall boxes had wires to them although nothing was actually hooked to the panel box yet.

As we loaded tools and ladders back into the truck in the gathering dusk, Herman drove up in the company's newest truck. I saw right off that he wasn't in the best of moods, but I couldn't tell whether it was because he'd had a hard day or because he was half sick.

He was determined to inspect Annie Sue's work and snapped at her impatiently when she couldn't put her hands on the big flashlight that was supposed to be in the back of the truck. Annie Sue got tight-jawed and defensive, and Paige went beet red with sympathetic impotence. It didn't help Herman's temper when I spotted the missing flashlight on the seat of his truck—right where he'd left it.

Tension crackled like heat lightning in the starless sky, but I was too hot and tired to play the thankless role of peacemaker. A mosquito whined in my ear, another was gnawing on my ankle, and my deodorant threw in the towel as perspiration trickled down between my breasts. Suddenly, all I could think of was how nice it'd feel to be floating in Aunt Zell and Uncle Ash's pool, a bourbon and Pepsi floating in an untippable tumbler beside me, far, far away from quarrelsome people.

"See you tomorrow," I said and left them to it.

*   *   *

When I called that evening to tell Ned O'Donnell that I was reducing Layton Ogburn's bail, he was suspicious. "Don't you do it on my account."

"A little ol' district court judge doing favors for a superior court judge? Never in a million years, Your Honor."

I told Zack Young the same thing when he stuck his head in during the midmorning recess next day and thanked me for my cooperation.

"Raising that much cash would've cost your client more than his profits on a WomenAid house," I said, pouring myself another glass of ice water. "Better in their pocket than in a mortgage company's."

"If it came to that," Zack agreed blandly. "I had an appointment with a superior judge over in Wake County this afternoon. You just saved me a trip to Raleigh."

*   *   *

The day continued overcast and heavy, but the rain held off, tormenting us with a promise of relief that wouldn't come. I sweated through morning court in my heavy robe, then drove home at lunch, took off all my underwear and panty hose, and drove back to court wearing only an opaque cotton sundress and sandals under that horse blanket.

On the afternoon docket, a flasher was followed by a thief who'd stolen his next-door neighbor's air conditioner right out of the window. Both pleaded the heat as a mitigating circumstance. I sent the flasher for a Mental Health evaluation and sent the thief to an air-conditioned jail cell for forty-eight hours.

When I met Annie Sue after work, I warned her that I'd have to leave early for a political meeting over in Makely. She seemed as listless and dispirited as the weather.

"Your dad give you a hard time last night?" I asked.

She shrugged. "Not really. In fact, at breakfast this morning, he told Mom I was doing good. I don't know why he couldn't just tell me though. Why does he have to be like that?"

"At the risk of sounding sexist, honey, that's just the way some men are."

Her smile was wan. "Yeah."

"Did you talk to Cindy?"

She grimaced. "For all the good it did. Guess what? He doesn't love his wife. They're going to get a divorce. 'And what about the baby?' Paige asked her."

"*Baby?*"

"That's what Cindy said. Yeah, baby. Paige did some asking around. Remember Saturday, that tall black-haired woman? She had on that funny Calvin and Hobbes T-shirt you liked?"

I nodded.

"Well, she lives in the same trailer park as them and she's friends with Rochelle Bannerman. She told Paige that Rochelle and Carver were going through a rocky time of it 'cause neither of them wanted a baby this quickly—they've only been married about a year—but Rochelle's never said anything about a divorce. *And* he's still living with her."

Annie Sue climbed up on the stepladder and started splicing wires into a ceiling box. "We told Cindy all that, but she won't listen. She's talking about dropping out of school and marrying that creep."

Her fingers worked furiously the whole time and as she finished one box and moved her ladder into the dining area to begin on another, thunder rumbled and drops of rain began to fall, tentatively at first, then gathering in volume and tempo till there was a steady drumming on the tar-papered roof over our heads.

We raced out to close the windows on the car and truck and came back damp and cooler as the wind rose and sheets of rain swept down the road in front and even blew vagrant drops onto us as we stood in the doorway and watched. The trees around the house swayed and danced, their leaves turning inside out, and lightning popped somewhere nearby.

After the first rush, the skies lightened somewhat and the winds died down, but rain continued to fall steadily as if it were fixing to set in and go all night. Annie Sue had rigged a droplight so that we had no trouble seeing what we were doing, but it made me lose track of time. Suddenly I realized I only had an hour to shower, change, and get to Makely before the meeting started.

"Want me to help you put this stuff away?" I asked.

"I'll do it. I just need to finish up a couple of more things."

Even though this was a stable, low-crime neighborhood and even though there was plenty of daylight left, I hesitated. "I don't know, honey. I don't think you ought to be here alone."

"It's okay. Besides, Paige's coming. We're going to practice some harmony on a song we're doing at her church next Sunday. She should've already been here." She smiled down at me from her perch. "Don't worry. If she doesn't come soon, I'll pack up and go before dark. Promise."

Just to be on the safe side, I stopped at the convenience store and got Patsy Reddick to lend me the phone again. Eleanor Byrd, Perry Byrd's widow answered on the third ring. I didn't identify myself, just asked for Paige.

"Paige? She left a little while ago to go help work on that WomenAid house." She didn't ask who I was, so I thanked her, hung up, and headed off for a very dull, very routine, but thankfully very short meeting.

• • •

It was only a little past eight-thirty when I got back to Dobbs. Had the skies been clear, it wouldn't even be full dark yet. All evening, one storm after another had rolled across the Triangle, misty showers followed by frog-strangling gully washers. At the moment, it was raining fairly hard, but straight down. The temperature hadn't dropped much and I had my window lowered to enjoy the cool wetness on my arm.

My route through town took me only a few blocks from the construction site, and a guilty memory had surfaced on my drive back: I had left Herman's fifty-foot tape measure and brand-new hammer up on one of the cross-braces in the living room. I was sure Annie Sue would overlook them in the twilight; I was equally sure that three little sharp-eyed Norris vandals wouldn't if they disobeyed Lu and came back in the daylight.

There was nothing for it but to go by and pick them up. The convenience store was still open as I turned up Redbud Lane and a light was on in the house diagonally across the way. I pulled into the muddy yard so I could shine my car lights in through the open door space.

To my surprise, Annie Sue's van was still parked there. So was Carver Bannerman's red Jeep. At least I assumed it was his vehicle, only now it was covered by a black vinyl snap-on top.

No one appeared in the doorway and I could see no light. I splashed through the rain and onto the covered porch where I paused to call Annie Sue's name.

No answer.

My car lights did little to illuminate the front room and I nearly tripped on something.

Herman's hammer.

When I picked it up, the handle felt as if someone with

greasy hands had been using it, but I barely noticed as I called again.

Rain drummed on the rooftop but beneath the steady pounding, I thought I heard a moan. Something moved at the far end of the house. At first glance it appeared to be a roll of tar paper propped in the corner, then I saw the pale oval of her face.

"Annie Sue?"

"Deb'rah? Dad?" Her voice sounded dazed.

My eyes had become accustomed to the dark and now I saw the overturned stepladder. Broken glass twinkled in the car lights from the smashed light bulb that had been her droplight.

"What's wrong?" I cried, stubbing my toe and banging my shins as I threaded a path through the normal building rubble.

She started to cry as I reached her. "Daddy?"

"He's not here, honey. It's just me. What's happened? Are you all right?" I dropped the hammer and reached to help her stand.

Even in the poor light, she was shocking to see. Her hair was wild, her cheek was scraped, the front of her shirt gaped open, and her shorts and panties were down around her ankles.

She felt her nakedness and groped for her clothes as a wave of nausea hit her. Aflame with a murderous anger I didn't know I could feel, I held her until her stomach was empty and only dry heaves wracked her body.

That bastard. That—

"Did he do it?" Annie Sue sobbed. "Oh sweet Jesus, please don't let me get pregnant! Please, Jesus! Oh Deborah, Mommy and Daddy are going to be so mad at me. I tried to kick him in the—you know—but he just laughed, and I fought and I tried to get away and please, Jesus, don't let me get AIDS!"

Making soothing noises, I helped her pull up her shorts, then coaxed her through the house and out to my car.

"It's okay, honey," I said, smoothing her hair as she cried in my arms. "It's going to be all right, but you have to tell me now what happened. Did Carver Bannerman do this to you?"

She gulped back another sob and nodded.

"You were here all by yourself? Where was Paige?"

"She and Cindy—Dad— They don't like him much. And when he started on me, they left."

"When who started?"

"Dad." Old resentments mingled with misery in her voice. "He was mad at Reese because he'd fouled up a job and then he got over here and I'd wired the kitchen stove outlet to the same circuit as the air conditioner instead of putting them separate and I *knew* it was wrong as soon as I showed it to him, but he could've just said. He didn't have to yell in front of my friends. So they left and then he left and I was so mad I stayed to fix it right and then *he* came in."

"Bannerman?"

"I think I want to go home now," she whimpered.

"We will," I soothed. "Just as soon as you finish telling me."

"I didn't know he was anywhere around. It was raining hard and I didn't hear him come in. I was almost finished and when I turned around, there he was. I told him if he was looking for Cindy, she'd already gone and how come he was out tomcatting around to dances anyhow when he had a pregnant wife at home?"

She shivered and pulled away from me to roll down the window and take long deep breaths of the wet night air. "Oh, God, Deb'rah! What if I *do* get pregnant?"

"What happened next?" I prodded.

"He said, 'What's the matter, dollface? You jealous?' I told him not to be a jerk, but he started bragging about how he'd made a woman of Cindy and I probably wanted him to do me, too. I thought maybe he'd been drinking or was on dope or something and I tried to change the subject. Told him if he was there to inspect the rough-in, I was all finished. I was picking up my tools and he said something nasty about inspecting *my* wiring first and he grabbed me. I tried to get away and that's when the ladder tipped over and smashed the light bulb. He started cursing me and pulled me toward the back of the house. I fought and kicked and he yanked at my shirt and threw me down on the floor and next

I must have hit my head because I don't remember anything else till you came and oh, please, Deborah. Let's go home! Please?''

"We'll go home," I promised. "But first, I want to take you to the hospital."

Streetlights along Redbud Lane were few and far between, but they threw enough light for me to see her head shaking back and forth wildly. "No! I can't—I don't—''

I put my arms around her again and tried to make her understand the necessity. "They'll have a rape kit there, honey. They're trained to collect the evidence we're going to need to put that bastard in prison."

She tried to pull away but I held her tighter. "I know you don't think you can stand it, but you have to, Annie Sue. You can't let him get away with it."

"But Mom and Dad—''

I knew I was on shaky legal ground. Annie Sue was a minor and I was not her mother. I couldn't force them to prosecute; it wasn't my decision to make. But damned if I wasn't going to try to preserve the evidence if they did want that slimeball put under state prison.

It took a few minutes, but eventually Annie Sue calmed down enough to see my reasoning. She agreed to let me take her to the hospital if I'd stop and call Nadine first. This time, despite the pouring rain, I used the pay phone in the parking lot beside the convenience store. It rang several times, then clicked into their answering machine.

Where the hell were they? I was so sure Nadine and Herman would be there, that for a moment I blanked. This wasn't a decision an aunt should make. What if I committed Annie Sue to something they might not want? Frustrated, I slammed up the phone without leaving a message and dashed back to the car. Even with an umbrella, my sandals and skirt were sopping wet as I climbed back in.

Tears streamed down Annie Sue's battered face when I told her Herman and Nadine weren't there, but she didn't argue as I turned my car toward the hospital.

• • •

I parked at the emergency entrance and the nurse who came forward as we hurried in out of the rain was Bambi Cobb. Her sister Sherry manages the law office I'd shared with Reid and John Claude and from what I'd seen of Bambi, she was every bit as sharp as Sherry. No dramatics, no superfluous lamentations, just a real efficient professional.

"We want a full rape kit workup," I said.

She nodded, then put her arm around Annie Sue and led her down the hall to an examination room.

I ducked into a nearby rest room, and one look at the mirror made me wonder that Bambi hadn't asked if I needed help, too. I washed my face and hands and did what I could with my sandy blonde hair—in wet weather, it thickens up even more and tries to curl instead of falling smoothly around my face. My soggy coral sandals had walked through so many puddles tonight that they were ruined. Paper towels helped with my muddy feet, but nothing could be done about the smudges on my coral silk blouse. As for my no-longer-white skirt, how did I get so much mud and— were those blood stains? No cuts on my hands. Annie Sue?

The skirt was full enough to let me briefly consider turning it around.

"Right," said the pragmatist who could remember every humiliation of junior high. "That's all we need—Colleton County's first female judge walking around with bloodstains on the back of her white skirt."

"Only dirty minds think dirty thoughts," the preacher said primly.

I left my skirt where it was, slashed on fresh lipstick and went on down to the waiting room.

And stopped short.

There stood Nadine with tearstained, anxious face and beside her stood Dwight Bryant. Both of them stared back at me.

"What are *you* doing here?" we asked each other.

"Herman's had a heart attack," Nadine said tremulously.

Dwight cocked a professional eye at my white skirt and frowned. "Is that blood?"

10

Dead Load

"The total dead load is the total weight of the structure, which gradually increases as the structure rises and remains constant once it is completed. The total live load is the total weight of movable objects (such as people, furniture, bridge traffic or the like) which the structure happens to be supporting at a particular instant."

I looked down at my white skirt and Dwight's question triggered a memory of how I'd wiped my hand across it before I reached for Annie Sue tonight.

"The hammer," I said.

"Hammer?" he asked, but I brushed him aside.

"Herman had a heart attack? When? How bad is it?"

"They don't know yet," said Nadine. "They found him collapsed behind the steering wheel of his truck. Just a few minutes ago." She glanced at the clock on the wall above us and shook her head in bewilderment over how much time had passed. "An hour ago."

Dwight took her by the arm and led her over to a dark purple couch. "Come sit down, Nadine."

It seemed to be a quiet night. Except for an elderly man half-dozing in an easy chair near the door and a nurse absorbed in paperwork, we were the only ones here in the waiting room as I followed Dwight across the polished vinyl tile and took an adjacent armchair. All the chairs and couches were harmonizing shades of plums and grays that simulated soft leather but were really wipe-down vinyl.

"I heard the Dobbs dispatcher and recognized the description of Herman's truck," Dwight told me. "Soon as they identified him and said they were going to bring him here, I went and got Nadine."

"Annie Sue!" Nadine exclaimed. "I didn't leave her a note or anything. She'll be worried to death. And I should call Reese and Haywood, too."

"I just did that," Dwight reminded her.

"But how's Herman?" I insisted.

"They're still trying to get him stabilized," said Dwight.

"Dr. Worley's in there with him. And another doctor. I tried to make him come. For over a week. Didn't I? I told Dr. Worley I tried to make him come. You know I did, Deb'rah!"

I patted her arm sympathetically. "You did everything you could."

"You saw him drop that hymn book in church Sunday?" I nodded.

"He said the ends of his fingers just went numb on him all of a sudden. Like they went to sleep or something. And his toes keep feeling sort of numb, too."

It didn't sound good. Numbness in the extremities—didn't that mean serious blockage in the veins? I remembered when I went to call him for dinner Sunday and found him stretched full length on the couch in front of a televised news program. His eyes were closed, his face was a putty gray, his breathing labored.

"You should have just picked him up and hauled him to a doctor right then," scolded the I-told-you-so voice of the preacher.

"You and whose army?" the pragmatist asked sarcastically.

Nadine was struggling to her feet again. "Annie Sue," she murmured.

I took a deep breath and caught her hand. "Wait, Nadine. She's not at home. She's here."

She and Dwight both looked around blankly, then Dwight's eyes searched mine and immediately dropped to the ghastly stains on my skirt.

"She's okay. At least, she's *going* to be okay." There was no gentle way to put it. "She's been raped."

Nadine lost color. Her legs buckled and she sank back onto the couch.

Before I could say more, Bambi came down the hall, followed by a tired-looking intern in a rumpled blue lab coat. They crossed the large room and paused discreetly until I motioned them over.

"This is my niece's mother," I said. "Nadine, this is Bambi Cobb. She's been taking care of Annie Sue."

"Is she all right? Where is she?" Nadine said, struggling to her feet.

"She's going to be just fine," said the doctor who was on ER duty that night.

"Did Deborah tell you?" Bambi asked.

"That someone—" Nadine couldn't make herself say the horrible words.

Impulsively, Bambi took her hand. "It's okay, Mrs. Knott. She wasn't raped."

"What?" I was dumbfounded.

"She was assaulted," the doctor said grimly. "Facial contusions, bruises to her upper extremities, but there was no penetration, no semen smears, no bruising in the vaginal area itself. And the hymen is still intact. Your daughter has a mild concussion—it would appear that she was thrown down rather violently—but I'd guess that he panicked and fled when he realized she was unconscious."

Nadine was suddenly an enraged mother tiger ready to kill. "I want to see my baby. Now!"

"Of course," the intern agreed. "I've given her a tranquilizer and I want to check her blood pressure again, but then she can go home."

As they left the waiting room, Dwight turned to me. "What happened, Deb'rah? Who did it?"

I gave him as many details as I could remember, carefully editing out Cindy McGee's involvement with that hound's leavings. No point smearing her with his slime.

"I'll try to get Nadine to swear out a warrant against Bannerman," I said, "but she may not want to if she thinks it'll hurt Annie Sue. And with Herman—how is he really, Dwight?"

He shrugged bleakly and held out an arm to me. "Don't look good, shug."

I've known Dwight since I was a little girl and he was one of the gang of neighborhood boys that used to hang out at the farm and play whatever ball my brothers were tossing around at the moment. He fusses at me, tries to watch out for me, comforts me just like one of them; and I let myself be enfolded by his big arm because sometimes you just need to lay your burdens down for a few minutes and take refuge in a loving human hug. •

I leaned against his broad chest and tucked my head under his chin as reaction set in.

"I swear to God," I told him, "if that slug had come back for his car right then, I'd have bashed his head in with Herman's hammer."

"Shh," said Dwight, his voice muffled by my hair.

But my words suddenly registered in both our heads and we pulled apart.

"Blood!" I said.

"His car?" asked Dwight.

"I'll bet he hit Annie Sue with that hammer," I said. "That's why there's blood on my skirt."

"Hold on a minute," he said. "How come Bannerman left his car there?"

Before I could speculate, the waiting room was flooded with Knotts.

Reese and his girlfriend tumbled through the door one step ahead of Haywood and Isabel and two of their kids. Andrew and April came with A.K. and Ruth. Seth, Minnie and their kids arrived moments later because Minnie had stopped to call one of Nadine's sisters. Will and Amy were right behind them and they'd brought Daddy, who came in grim-faced and resigned to hear the worst. Soon I saw Aunt Zell and Uncle Ash and some New Deliverance Church people.

Brothers who lived away had been called and were just waiting for the word to get on plane or car, but by the time Nadine appeared with her arm around a shaky Annie Sue, every Knott in that end of Colleton County knew everything we knew about what had happened to both my brother and my niece. The women rushed to comfort Nadine and Annie Sue; the men buzzed around like an overturned hornet nest. My brothers were talking horsewhips; their sons and daughters were talking hanging trees.

They all fell silent though when Dr. Worley appeared in the doorway. For a moment, he seemed taken aback by so many of Herman's kinfolks, but we moved aside automatically and he made his way to Nadine, who sat between Daddy and Annie Sue. Someone gave the doctor a chair so he could face all three of them, then we all circled around so we could hear, too.

"We've got him stabilized," he told Nadine. "But frankly, I don't know for how long. It's not his heart, although there may be some peripheral involvement. His white blood count's way down and there's definite neurological damage. It may have been a stroke, but there's some kidney blockage—it's a medical nightmare. Frankly, all we can do right now is treat the symptoms until we can do more tests. And Dobbs Memorial just isn't equipped for what he needs. I want to airlift him to Chapel Hill."

"Airlift?" Nadine looked around our circle of faces.

"Helicopter," said Daddy. "That sounds pretty serious, son."

"It is, Mr. Kezzie."

Their eyes met and Daddy nodded.

"Whatever it takes, whatever it costs—" He broke off and put his gnarled hand over Nadine's. "But it ain't mine to say. You're his wife, girl. You want them to do this?"

"Yes!" she said. "Of course, yes. Only"—her eyes sought out the preacher, who'd come as soon as her sister had called him—"could we have a prayer first?"

The only times I'd heard New Deliverance's preacher pray, he'd struck me as overly long-winded. Tonight, he was brief and to the point as we all joined hands and bowed our heads: "Lord God who hears us when we cry thy name, thy will be done on earth as it is in heaven, but we pray mercy on this family, Lord, and on thy good and faithful servant Herman. In Jesus' name we pray it. Amen."

"Amen," we echoed.

• • •

It was quickly arranged after that. Nadine would go in the helicopter with Herman. Some of the girl cousins would drive Annie Sue home to bathe and change and pack a suitcase for her mother, then they would drive her over to Chapel Hill, which was about an hour or so west of us. Reese called Charlotte and Greensboro to let Edward and Denise know what was happening. Everyone else would either go on home to wait for news or head over to Chapel Hill to sit with Nadine.

Dwight had waylaid Nadine and Annie Sue for a few quiet words and before the rest completely scattered, he had another few quiet words for my hotheaded relatives.

"I don't want anybody here doing anything stupid, you boys hear what I'm saying? I'll take care of Bannerman as soon as I can swear out a warrant. It's gonna be done legal and by the book, so I want all y'all to give me your word you'll leave it alone."

"Too late for Reese's word," said Stevie. "He and A.K.'ve already gone looking for him."

As Dwight headed out to his car to radio for someone to head Reese off at the trailer park, I snagged Stevie.

"One of Herman's trucks is over at the WomenAid house," I told him. "I'll run you over and help you pick up the tools Annie Sue was using and you can drive it home, okay?"

"Sure," he said.

• • •

By the time we got to Redbud Lane, it was after ten, the rain had dwindled to a thin drizzle, and the convenience store on the corner was locked and dimly lit. Bannerman's Jeep was still parked beside the white van and I suppose we could thank the rain that the van hadn't been stripped because neither Annie Sue nor I had thought to lock it when we left.

All my brothers and I are in the habit of leaving our keys under the front seat if we aren't locking up, and Annie Sue had evidently picked up the same habit. Stevie, too, because he went right to the floor, fumbled around and came up with them jingling in his hand.

I found a flashlight and we went inside. He folded up the overturned stepladder and carried it out to the truck while I started gathering up the scattered tools. When we'd almost finished, I remembered the hammer I'd dropped at the rear of the house where I found Annie Sue.

Okay, easy enough to say I should have realized as soon as I first touched the hammer hours earlier, but dammit, my niece was battered and bloody. I thought she'd been raped. And then Herman—

But yeah, I suppose the minute I saw that stupid red phallic symbol still parked in the yard, I should have known Carver Bannerman had never left.

We found him draped over a sawbench at the back of the house with his head smashed in.

Like Herman, he got sent to Chapel Hill that night, too.

Except that Herman went to Intensive Care and Bannerman went to the medical examiner's morgue.

11

Line Levels

"The line level is used to test whether a line or cord is level. It is particularly useful when the distance between two points to be checked for level is too long to permit the use of a board and the carpenter's level. However, the line level will show a disadvantage at a long distance because the line has a tendency to sag."

Few crime scenes are what Aunt Zell would call neat, but the WomenAid house was a real mess.

Literally.

The yard was a muddy pigmire. Although it had been crisscrossed with car tracks and footprints, hours of rain had blurred them into a sameness impossible to differentiate.

Inside, the floors were littered with scraps of two-by-fours, bent nails, pieces of tar paper and insulation, and plastic drink cups. Plastic tarps lay crumpled in the corners or draped over the wall spacers. When we were there working in the late afternoon, Annie Sue and I had mucked back and forth to the truck, through the sawdust that had drifted over the concrete floor; and every time Stevie and I went in and out with stepladder and tools, we'd tracked yet another load of wet mud.

Dwight's crime scene people brought portable floodlights and they began to photograph every inch of the place inside and out, but I couldn't see as how they'd find much to help them. The heat they generated made the humid air even steamier.

I showed Dwight exactly where I thought I'd stumbled on the hammer near the front door. As it turned out, when I carried it back to where I found Annie Sue, I wound up dropping it less than three feet from where Carver Bannerman's body still lay, slumped over a sawbench like one of the plastic tarps, his pants unzipped but still in place.

"And you didn't see him lying there?" Dwight asked skeptically.

"Oh sure, you can say that, lit up like it is now. When I came in, though, there was nothing but my car lights. Everything was dark and shadowy. I told you I sort of thought Annie Sue was a roll of tar paper till I heard her moan, remember? And after that, taking care of her was all I thought about. It certainly didn't occur to me to start fumbling around to see if any of those other dark lumps were human bodies."

"Come here a minute," he said and took me off to the far side of the small house, out of earshot of his officers. His brown eyes were troubled as he looked deeply into mine. "Now listen, Deb'rah, and don't mouth off at me, 'cause this is for real. You sure this is the way you want to tell it?"

"*What?*"

"Well, think about it. If Annie Sue was the one who bashed his head in, it seems to me it'd be a clear-cut case of self-defense. The doctor can attest to her bruises and that blow on her head. She might not even have realized what she was doing. Fighting him off and all, what if she just grabbed the hammer and flailed away?"

"And then carried the hammer out to the living room for me to trip over and came back in here to pass out close to his body?"

"People with concussions do crazy things," he said stubbornly.

"True. But then wouldn't her hand be even bloodier than mine was?" I asked.

"Did she wash or—"

I was shaking my head. "No, no, and no. That's why I took her straight to the hospital instead of home. I wanted every scrap of physical evidence to remain on her body until it was documented. You and I both know that the first thing rape victims want to do is take a long hot shower, get clean again."

He nodded.

"I didn't want her near a bathroom till a nurse with a rape kit had gone over her body with a fine tooth comb." I winced at the cliché, suddenly remembering that it wasn't a trite figure of speech: Annie Sue's pubic area would indeed have been combed for foreign hairs.

"Bambi probably took fingernail scrapings, too," I said. "Even if Annie Sue'd rinsed her hands in the rain, his blood would still be there."

"I'll check," said Dwight. "But if Annie Sue didn't do it . . ." His voice trailed off and his face got even gloomier.

I was incredulous.

"You think *I* killed him?"

"Your fingerprints will be on the hammer. That's probably his blood on your skirt," Dwight said. "Say you came back and found Bannerman in the act of raping your niece. Say you had a hammer in your hand. Wouldn't you have smacked him over the head with it?"

"Damn straight!" I agreed. "But it didn't happen that way."

"You're sure."

"Dwight!"

"Okay, okay. If you say you didn't, you didn't. One more thing though." He seemed to be picking his words carefully. "You hear where they found Herman?"

My heart started to sink. "No."

"On Troop Road."

That was less than a mile from here and not on any beeline between his office and his house. "Going which direction?"

"Toward his house," said Dwight. "Away from here. It was like he wasn't going too fast when he passed out. The truck sort of coasted to a stop on the sidewalk, but he did bang his head. His face was bloody. And the time's about right.''

Dwight thrust a big hand into his off-duty jeans and rattled his pocket change as he gazed at me speculatively. ''So if you're sure that hammer was already sticky when you picked it up, guess I'd better have my techs take samples of the bloodstains in Herman's truck.''

''I'm sure.'' I hated this scenario just as much as Dwight's first two, but if it were true . . .

''No jury in Colleton County ever convicted a man who killed his daughter's rapist.''

''Even if he ran away and left his daughter behind, half-naked?''

''*If* he did that, it's because he was sick,'' I argued. ''Not thinking clearly.''

''Well, we'll worry about that down the road,'' Dwight said. ''Right now, I want you to let Richards drive you first to Annie Sue's and then take you home.''

''I'm perfectly capable of driving myself and—''

He huffed at me in exasperation, just like one of my brothers. ''You always got to argue, don't you? I swear I don't know why you gave up being a lawyer and took up the one job where you're supposed to listen to what people say and not fly off the handle before they finish talking.''

''So finish,'' I snapped.

''I want Richards to collect the clothes Annie Sue was wearing tonight and I want that skirt and blouse you have on, too.''

Before I could bristle, he gave me a sardonic look. ''Preacher's wife, okay?''

He was right. And if I hadn't been so tired, he wouldn't have had to spell it out for me. As a judge, I not only had to appear above suspicion, I had to be able to prove it, too. Better to let them run my clothes through the system and verify that the bloodstains were wipes, not splatters, than to have awkward questions raised after the garments were cleaned.

● ● ●

Deputy Mayleen Richards and I got to Annie Sue's clothes just seconds before Seth's Jessica tossed them in the washer. The whole house seemed to swarm with energetic young women and every single one of them had grown up watching their mothers so they knew how southern women were supposed to behave in a crisis.

Some were in the kitchen to load the dishwasher and put away the food Nadine had cooked before she'd rushed off to the hospital. Others had tidied the house, including cleaning up the bathroom behind Annie Sue. In fact, Jessica was only waiting for the last damp towel before starting the washer. Had I stayed to argue with Dwight, we'd have been too late.

The girls hadn't heard about Bannerman's death until we arrived, and they were wide-eyed as Richards scooped the clothes from Jessica's hands and put them in a brown paper sack.

"Carver Bannerman got his head smashed in?"

Some of my eye-for-an-eye nieces immediately declared he got what he deserved. Andrew's Ruth looked apprehensive though. When Reese rushed out of the hospital to look for Bannerman with violence in his eyes, her brother A.K. had gone with him. I squeezed her hand and told her not to worry, that Bannerman was probably dead before I carried Annie Sue to the hospital.

Paige Byrd and Cindy McGee were also there at the house. Paige kept saying, "If only we hadn't left when we did!"

Cindy's face was splotched and her eyes were red and swollen. When she heard that Bannerman was dead, fresh tears rolled down her cheeks, but at least she didn't moan and shriek and overdramatize like some of my nieces would have.

Amazingly, they didn't seem to notice, and Annie Sue had loyally kept her mouth shut about Cindy.

Knowing what I did, Cindy's misery seemed palpable, but I honestly couldn't tell whether it was (1) because her erstwhile lover was dead, (2) because he'd tried to rape her best friend, or (3) because, like Paige, she was blaming herself for leaving Annie Sue when Herman's tongue-lashing made them too uncomfortable.

Maybe it was (4)—all of the above.

Despite all the evening's shocks and a mild concussion that would have me in bed sound asleep by now, Annie Sue seemed to be bouncing back okay. As soon as she'd realized that all her injuries were external, she'd become giddy with relief. Before she'd had time to come down from that, she'd been sucker-punched with her father's collapse, which sent her into a crying jag, terrified that Herman might die.

Now, just as abruptly, her attacker was dead.

"It's so weird," she told Jessica and me as we helped her pack Nadine's cosmetics and night clothes. "I don't know whether to laugh or cry or just throw my head back and simply *howl*. It's like that time when I was little out at the farm, remember? When I almost stepped on a copperhead and started screaming and Granddaddy came and chopped his head off?"

Jess and I nodded. More of Annie Sue's dramatics, but it had become family lore. First she'd screamed from fright and then she'd bawled for an hour because the snake, though poisonous, had been killed.

Driving to Chapel Hill with Jess and a couple of the others would help. If she didn't fall asleep driving over, by the time they got there, they would have hashed and rehashed every detail of the whole evening. "I said— Then he— So what did *you* do? And then?"

Telling and retelling ought to blunt the knife edge of trauma before it could cut her too deeply.

Annie Sue had already packed her overnight bag and now she closed Nadine's.

"Wait a minute, honey," I said as the others picked up the bags and headed down the hall with them to Jessica's car.

Mayleen Richards didn't want to let me—or rather my clothes—out of her sight, but I asked her to wait down the hall and I stood in the open doorway so that she could watch without hearing.

Annie Sue's eyes grew large, but she sat down on the white hobnail spread that covered her parents' bed. She had changed into a pink floral jumpsuit and her shining chestnut hair was caught up in pink hair clips. Except for the scrapes on her elbows and chin, there were no outward signs of the mauling she'd taken.

"Dwight Bryant'll probably talk to you sometime tomorrow," I said, "and I'm sure he'll ask you if you were aware of anyone else in the house when Carver Bannerman jumped you?"

She shook her head. "No."

"Think carefully, honey. Could someone have been waiting for him out in his car?"

"Maybe," she answered slowly. "I didn't see. He didn't *act* like anybody was there to walk in on us. Not the way he grabbed me."

"And after he threw you down?"

"Honest, Deb'rah, I can't remember. I must have been unconscious. But when I was starting to come out of it . . ."

"Yes?"

"Something . . . a noise? Something fell? And then . . . yes! A car! I heard a car start up and drive away. I guess I sort of thought it was him. Driving away in the rain. Because I remember feeling like maybe everything was going to be all right. And then I guess I must have gone under again because I don't remember anything else till I heard you calling me."

"Did you recognize the sound of the motor?" I asked cautiously. Herman's new truck was only a few months old. Maybe it had no distinctive sounds yet.

She looked at me blankly. "Nope. It was just a car. Or a truck, I suppose."

"No loud rattles, no shriek when the gears changed?"

She smiled. "Like Chitty-Chitty-Bang-Bang or something?"

I smiled back, not wanting to put ideas in her head. "Or something."

She smoothed the lace collar of her jumpsuit as she

considered. I could tell that she was replaying the sound of the engine in her head. A shadow flicked across her face and was instantly gone.

"It was just an ordinary car motor," she said and looked me straight in the eye as she said it.

12

Handscrews and C-Clamps

*"The wooden handscrew is relatively limited with
regard to both scope and pressure.... When a
metal C-clamp is used for wood, the wood must be
protected against damage from the metal jaw
and the screw swivel on the clamp."*

I probably could have borrowed a change of clothes from
Annie Sue, but I'd still have to hitch a ride back with
Deputy Richards to pick up my car; so I had her drive me
home. She came upstairs with me, a stolid young woman
who grew up in the tobacco fields near Fayetteville and who
was not inclined to be too chatty with a judge that her
immediate boss treated like a younger sister. After a few of
her yes-ma'am, no-ma'am answers, I quit trying to put her
at ease.

She took my bloodstained skirt and my soiled but
unsplattered shirt and put them in a brown paper bag
separate from Annie Sue's things.

"I'll just wait out in the car for you, ma'am."

"Be right with you," I promised. Stripped down to a
white silk teddy, I stood barefoot in front of my closet and
flipped through the hangers for fresh clothes. What's appropriate for a murder scene? I slipped a scoop-necked black

cotton knit over my head and pulled a pair of old jeans over my hips. This time I meant to be ready for mud *or* blood.

Aunt Zell came in as I finished tying the laces on my raggedyest pair of sneakers. She had the puppy in her arms and was feeding it with its nursing bottle. "Ash wants to know how come there's a sheriff's car parked in our drive."

"We're just leaving," I said lightly. "She's going to drop me off to pick up my car."

After Mother died and Daddy went back to the farm, I moved into these two rooms that once belonged to Uncle Ash's father. Daddy and I weren't getting along too well then, and Uncle Ash was on the road even more in those days, so it seemed a sensible solution all around.

No kitchen, but otherwise it's like a self-contained apartment: sitting room, bath, and a large bedroom that opens onto the upstairs back veranda. There's even a side entrance and a second staircase, so I can come and go in private if I wish.

I've lived here off and on ever since that eighteenth summer, so Aunt Zell knows me about as well as anybody. Normally she's enough like my mother to enjoy stringing me along just to see how far I'll go before I tell the whole truth. Tonight she wasn't playing, and the lines in her face were deeper than I'd seen them in a long time, as the puppy nursed with little snorts and grunts.

"How'd you hear?" I asked. "The family tom-toms been working overtime?"

She shifted the puppy to a more comfortable position so that he could drain the bottle. "Ruth called Andrew from Herman's house. That odious creature's dead?"

I nodded.

"Are A.K. and Reese involved?"

"Is that what Andrew's afraid of? He doesn't have to worry. Honest. If any of us are in trouble, it's probably me."

In twenty-five words or less, I hastily explained how Dwight was pretty sure Bannerman was already dead when I found Annie Sue, and how we expected to find my fingerprints on the hammer that killed him, and how it'd all happened at least an hour before Reese and A.K. even heard about the incident.

She pushed my pillows up on the headboard and leaned back against them. The puppy, his fat little tummy thoroughly full again, nuzzled into the sleeve of her robe and went sound to sleep. As I talked, Aunt Zell stroked the pup's silky hair and relief smoothed away some of the tension between her eyes.

"Would you please call your brother and tell him that?"

Like Mother, she always did have a tender heart for him.

•   •   •

Andrew was one of the wild ones who came along during the Depression years when things got a touch rough around here. I've never known all the details of that period. Somehow it seemed a little disloyal to Mother to ask too many questions about Daddy's first wife. She was from that swampy area where Possum Creek runs into the Neuse River, much more of a backwoods in those days than now, but the land was just as sorry—"no good for nothing 'cept keeping the world stuck together right yonder"—and the people there just as suspicious of outsiders and revenuers.

Her people were dirt poor and nearly illiterate, and they made her quit school in the sixth grade and set her running trot lines and boiling mash when she wasn't picking cotton for two cents a pound like the rest of her family. No wonder she married Daddy when she was fifteen and started kicking out baby boys every two years regular as clockwork. A man who owns his own land never has to let his family go hungry long as seeds sprout and hogs can be fattened, but fresh vegetables and cured hams couldn't always be traded for boys' shoes or a widowed mother's medicine. I expect that's why Daddy kept on running his own shine. It was his only dependable source of cash money.

Was it a good marriage?

I don't know.

They say she was certainly a good helpmeet. When the revenuers came sniffing around local stores to see who was buying up lots of sugar, they say it was her idea to visit every grocery store in Raleigh, Wilson, Goldsboro and Fayetteville three or four times a summer, never buying more than twenty-five or thirty pounds of sugar at a time. "And better let me have some of them big canning jars. Looks like hit's gonna be a good summer for blackberries/cherries/peaches/pears. These young'uns shore do love my [insert one] preserves."

And every other year, here came another son to help with the plowing when Daddy starting buying up farms that were going under. Poor Andrew didn't get his turn as knee baby because the next lying-in brought twins, Herman and Haywood, and their mother's lap wasn't big enough to hold two infants and a toddler. He was only seven when she died of child-birth fever after birthing Jack, and Daddy remarried within the year.

Mother gentled the twins and the younger boys, but the older ones never did completely tame and seems like Andrew was worst of all. I don't think they ever resented her, they just couldn't get used to a woman who made Daddy turn loose some of his money and fix up the old farmhouse with paint and wallpaper. She brought her own things, too: bright clothes, china and crystal, family heirlooms. Rural Electrification reached the farm a few years before Mother did, but there'd never even been a radio in the house. She brought along her phonograph and a stack of records taller than baby Jack.

An upright piano, too.

"I fell in love with your daddy's fiddle, before I knew he had a houseful of boys," she used to tease them. "Hadn't been for his fiddle, I'd have stayed in Dobbs and married me a man with a fine big empty house."

Then the little ones would shiver to think what they almost missed and they'd look up at the tall fiddle-playing man who'd sired them and love him all the more for playing her into their lives.

Hymns and folk tunes weren't all they played either. She banged out bebop on the piano and soon had the boys singing right along with the Andrews Sisters and a young Frank Sinatra.

"And books," Haywood always says. "She read to us every night at bedtime. *Aesop's Fables*, fairy tales, Bible stories."

Because even though Mother was a hard worker and even though she added more boys to the ones Daddy already had, she didn't try to do it all herself the way his first wife had worked herself into the ground. She hired some of his best barn help right out from under his nose and paid them good wages to help with the cooking and cleaning, the chopping and picking, the canning and freezing, so she'd have time for the children.

Even stolid old Herman can get downright lyrical when he lets himself remember. "The first time I saw *The Wizard of Oz*—you mind the first part of the movie, how it's all black and white and gray? Your mama coming was like when Dorothy opened the door and there was all that *color*. That's what she brought us. Color."

Andrew and the older boys were dazzled, too, but they were like ditch cats that had never been hand-gentled, and they kept the feral streak even after she came. Took them all past forty before they really settled down "and got right with the Lord," as they put it.

In his younger, wilder days, Andrew had more than once seen the inside of a jailhouse, so he knew firsthand what kind of trouble two young men can find when they go looking for it with anger in their hearts. Didn't matter if it was righteous anger or not. Their lives could be just as wrecked, take just as long to put back together. Hadn't all that helling around lost him his first wife and little girl? Carol ran so far and so fast it was years before I got to meet the niece who was born six months before me.

Andrew tried to pretend he wasn't worried when I called; but he snatched up the phone on the first ring, and I could feel his relief when I repeated what I'd told Aunt Zell.

"You see him or hear tell of him tonight, you tell A.K. to git his butt on home where it belongs," he told me gruffly. "If it quits raining, we got ten acres tobacco needs housing tomorrow."

"I'll tell him," I promised. "You go on to bed and don't worry."

"I ain't worried," he said again. "It's his mama that's worried. You tell him that, you hear?"

"I hear," I said gently.

• • •

Paramedics were loading Carver Bannerman into an ambulance when we got back to Redbud Lane.

Every house on the street was lit up like a Christmas tree. Tomorrow might be a workday, but no one was going to miss this. Even the convenience store on the corner had reopened and was doing a brisk business in soft drinks, junk food, and cigarettes as people wandered back and forth between the store and the house, undeterred by the light mist that continued to fall.

Deputy Jack Jamison was questioning them and taking down names; and as soon as she was free of me, Richards joined him.

Almost midnight and the temperature was finally beginning to moderate. I'd brought along an unlined windbreaker made of red water-repellant nylon, but the misty air felt so clean and cool that I slung it in the trunk of my car before ducking under the police line to see what was happening.

"Here comes trouble," said Dwight when he saw me.

The man he'd been talking to turned and gave me a considering smile. He was shorter than Dwight, so his light eyes were about on the same level as mine.

Bowman Poole. Colleton County's sheriff. He's late fifties, thin hair the color of broom straw, the compact build of a gamecock in fighting trim, and a folksy style that's carried the county every election for sixteen years.

"Your Honor," he said.

We'd nodded at each other across the crowded meeting over in Makely earlier, but we hadn't actually spoken since my reception and I cocked my head at him. "You acting like a stranger because I'm a judge or because Dwight's told you I'm a suspect?"

Bo laughed. "The hands are the hands of Esau, but the voice is Kezzie's. You won't never change, will you, girl?"

Dwight had brought him up to speed on the killing, but he asked if I'd mind going over it again. Practice makes perfect. This was about my fifth telling and I was getting pretty glib. For Dwight's benefit, I added what Annie Sue had said about hearing a car drive away just before I arrived.

"Yeah," said Dwight. "The lady across the street told Jack Jamison she saw headlights as she was pulling her shades for the night, but she didn't pay any mind to them. Neighbor next door saw it, too, and thinks a white woman was driving, but he's not sure."

We talked a few minutes longer, then Dwight sighed. "Reckon I'd better get Jack and Mayleen to go over and talk to Mrs. Bannerman. Unless you want to do it," he said to Bo.

I knew Dwight never liked to be the one to break bad news to the family.

Evidently Bo didn't like to either. "Nah, you're handling everything just fine," he said. "Looks like they're about finished in there, so I'll go on now. Talk to you tomorrow."

As soon as he turned and walked away from us, I pounced on Dwight. "Has anybody seen Reese or A.K.?"

He shook his head. "I canceled that order as soon as I heard Bannerman was dead. They still out there somewhere?"

"They must be. A.K. hasn't come home and Andrew's getting worried."

"They're probably sitting out at a tavern on the truck lane about now and—"

Our attention was snagged by Jack Jamison lifting the yellow police tape for a couple of young women. I recognized the taller by sight if not by name as the one who'd worn a funny Calvin and Hobbes T-shirt—Rochelle Bannerman's friend, according to Annie Sue and Paige.

That probably meant that the shorter, pregnant one that Deputy Jamison was escorting so solicitously was Carver Bannerman's widow. Bannerman's very pregnant widow. She wore shorts and a bright yellow T-shirt that read BABY

ON BOARD. A big black arrow ended at her bulging middle.

"They said he was here," she sobbed. "What've y'all done with my husband? Where've y'all got him?"

Her friend, Opal Grimes, patted her arm like she was trying to soothe her, but there was a self-important near smirk that said she was enjoying the drama. Certainly those pats only seemed to encourage Mrs. Bannerman's hysterics.

"O, Carver, Carver! My darling!" Despite the humidity, her blonde hair was freshly blow-dried around her pretty face. Her feet were thrust into yellow rubber flip-flops and mud squished between her toes as she clutched her belly and wailed, "What are me and your baby going to do without you?"

Dwight looked at me helplessly. He really does get spooked by women grieving for their dead.

I would have tried to help, but as soon as I stepped toward her, the Grimes woman whispered in her ear and her tears dried up as she turned on me.

"You the bitch judge Carver told me about?"

"Excuse me?"

"You heard me! Think just because you sit up there on that bench you can cut the balls off a man and he won't notice?"

"Now just a minute," Dwight said.

But she was beyond listening. "And then when your niece gets the hots for him, you send your brothers over to beat him up and now you've killed him and O Carver, baby!"

And here came the tears again.

13

Bridging

"The system of bracing the joists to each other is called bridging. The chief purpose of bridging is to hold the joists plumb and in correct alignment, but bridging also serves to distribute part of a concentrated heavy load over several joists next to those directly under the load."

Nosy as I generally am, it was no sacrifice when Dwight excluded me from his interview with Rochelle Bannerman.

Besides, he hit the high spots for me afterwards while we were splitting a Pepsi in Aunt Zell's cheerful kitchen: two glasses filled with ice, one Pepsi, and a bottle of Uncle Ash's best Jack Daniel's on the table between us.

Soon as I got home, I'd gone up and tapped on Aunt Zell and Uncle Ash's door to see if they'd heard any news of Herman.

"No change," said Aunt Zell from the darkened room. "We're going over first thing in the morning."

"I'll come, too, soon as court's adjourned."

She raised up on her arm. "If you're still going to be up in a half hour, would you feed that puppy?"

"Damn thing's more trouble than a real baby," Uncle Ash rumbled from his side of the bed.

"How 'bout I take care of him all night?" I volunteered.

"You need your sleep," Aunt Zell protested weakly.

"So do you!" Uncle Ash and I chorused.

"Well, if you're sure . . . ?"

"Sleep tight," I said.

•   •   •

Back downstairs, Dwight had already taken the little guy on his lap and I warmed the bottle and handed it to him.

News always travels fast in Dobbs and news of this death was no different, according to Dwight. One of the residents of Redbud Lane had called Opal Grimes in Magnolia Mobile Home Park, and Opal immediately hightailed it over to the Bannerman trailer where she found Rochelle Bannerman fending off questions about Bannerman's whereabouts from an enraged Reese and A.K.

I suppose I had Opal Grimes to thank for connecting me to those two peckerwoods; and if Bannerman had told his wife that I'd treated him unfairly in court, well, no wonder that young woman felt as if Knotts had it in for Bannermans. On the other hand, if she was going to keep interpreting her so-recently-late husband's attempted rape as attempted man snatching by my niece, she wasn't going to win any prizes from me for Euclidian logic. Besides, it was Cindy McGee who wanted to snatch him away, not Annie Sue.

"Let her go worry Gladys," I told Dwight.

"She probably will before it's all over," he sighed.

I suddenly remembered I hadn't mentioned Cindy before and glanced at Dwight with guilt all over my face like yolk on an egg-sucker.

"Yeah," he said reproachfully. "Sure do 'preciate you telling me about little Cindy McGee getting it on with Bannerman."

"How'd you hear? Mrs. Bannerman? Who told her?"

"He did. Not straight out in words, of course, but she and that Grimes woman followed him to the dance Saturday night. Saw him cut Cindy out of the herd, asked someone who she was, then followed them all the way to the Days Inn over near Fuquay."

Dwight shook his head. "I tell you, that Grimes woman is wasted babysitting trailer rats. She's watched so many cop shows she knows every tailing trick in the book."

Dwight finished feeding the pup, tucked it back in its box, then poured himself a hair more sour mash. "Got another Pepsi?"

I rooted around in the refrigerator and found one. "They didn't happen to follow him tonight, did they?"

"She says they didn't, but I sent Jack over to the trailer park to ask about 'em."

He sipped his drink, then added, "Sent Mayleen Richards to talk to little Cindy."

My heart sank. "Aw, Dwight, she's just a kid."

"Not after Saturday night, she's not," he said cynically.

"I was thinking about poor Gladys McGee. Losing Ralph and now to have to hear how her daughter's mixed up in this."

"Well, it's not like Mayleen's going to show up flashing a scarlet A. She'll be tactful. Gladys won't have to know a thing, if Cindy keeps her head. After all, she and the Byrd girl were both there with Annie Sue earlier, right? It's the most natural thing in the world to ask them if they saw anything. If Cindy went straight home, then she's got nothing to worry about. If not—"

He shrugged and sipped his drink and left me to finish his thought.

Teenagers can be creatures of impulse. I knew that. And I'd sat in enough courtrooms to know that children can kill if they act before they think.

"I guess I can see Cindy or Rochelle Bannerman doing it quicker than I can see Herman," I said.

"How you figure?"

"All three of them might've grabbed up the hammer and smashed Bannerman over the head if they walked in on him while he was trying to rape Annie Sue, but Herman wouldn't panic and run. No way would he have left her lying there."

Dwight looked skeptical.

"Think how you'd feel if it was Cal." Even though he didn't get to see his young son very often—Jonna had custody of Cal and they lived up in Shawsville, Virginia, now—I knew how he felt about the boy. "Would you just leave him there?"

"Maybe not," he admitted. "Okay. No, I wouldn't. Not unless I was on the verge of a heart attack or stroke maybe."

Thinking about the damage Bannerman could keep inflicting after his death made me broody. "Used to be they hanged first-degree rapists in this state."

"Used to be a lot of things they did in this state they don't do anymore." Dwight drained his glass. "And you can either thank the Lord or curse the devil."

I gestured toward the bottles, but he shook his head and stood up to go. "Now there's nothing else that may have slipped your mind to tell me, is there?"

"No."

"You sure?"

"I'm positive," I said and honestly believed I was telling him the truth.

*   *   *

Aunt Zell and Uncle Ash were leaving as I brought the puppy downstairs for its breakfast next morning.

"Herman's awake and talking a little," Aunt Zell reported, "but he's still awfully weak and they still don't know why."

"Tell Nadine I'll come this evening," I said, "but call me if there's any change. I'll cancel court if I need to. And don't worry about your hound. I'll come home and feed him at lunchtime."

"And don't forget to wash his little bottom."

Uncle Ash laughed and left to back the car out of the garage.

"I'm dithering, aren't I?" Aunt Zell asked ruefully. "Here I was planning to get my hair done and then run into Raleigh for a new nightgown to take to Paris, and now—but listen, honey. Sallie said you could bring him down to her if you think you're going to be tied up."

"We'll be just fine. Hug Herman for me, okay?" I gave her a hug, too, and pushed her out the door.

Almost three weeks old now, the puppy was as cute and appealing as any baby animal, a fat brown and white beagle with a white tail no bigger than my little finger that stood straight up when it tried to walk on its Jell-O legs; but tending to its needs at both ends of its alimentary canal left me with no appetite for the fruit and cereal Aunt Zell had set out on the counter. I decided to take Miss Sallie up on her offer to babysit in case I did get busy later in the day.

When I stopped off on my way downtown, she was out in her soggy front yard directing the rejuvenation of her ingrown bed of irises after all the rain. She employed the same lawn service as Aunt Zell, and Mr. Ou smiled and ducked his head at my greeting and continued to separate the tubers while Miss Sallie popped the puppy into the carton with its sibling, the only pup she had left after farming out the others with dog-loving friends.

"It does fret me not to know what happened to poor old Queenie," she said as she walked me out to my car. The sun was already converting rain puddles to steam. Beneath the broad straw brim of her gardening hat, her beautiful wrinkled face was pink and troubled. "Alice Castleberry's bull terrier's been missing two weeks now. Some man was coming up from Wilmington to mate his bitch with him and now he's got to find another registered champion. You don't reckon that sorry dogman's back sneaking around town?"

At one time, "dogmen" ("catmen," too, for that matter) used to roam the countryside picking up any stray they could find to sell to various laboratories as test animals. Public outcry eventually put a stop to their activities, and testing regulations have changed so drastically since then that few labs are willing to chance the penalties that illegally obtained animals can bring.

"Surely not," I said.

"I hope you're right," said Miss Sallie. "It'd purely break my heart to find out Queenie's hooked up to some horrible old machine just to see if mascara or nose drops hurt her eyes."

• • •

It was still early when I got to the courthouse, so I circled around and pulled into the parking lot next to the Coffee Pot. I only meant to have a cup of coffee, but the smells of fried sausage and hot bread suddenly made me ravenous.

Herman's Reese was seated at the counter, and as I slid into the empty stool beside him, I told Tink Dupree, "I'll have the regular if I can get it in five minutes."

"Only take three" he assured me and hollered through the kitchen pass-through, "Retha! One fast reg'lar for the judge!"

"Coming up!" she sang back.

Ava came around the corner of the counter and smiled shyly before disappearing behind the partition with a trayload of dirty dishes from the four booths along the back wall.

"You feel as rough as you look?" I asked Reese.

He stubbed his cigarette in an ashtray shaped like a blue tin coffee pot, pushed his cap to the back of his head, and gave a sheepish grin. "Yep. Makes me glad I'm only going to be crawling around a hundred-degree attic rewiring an old house today, 'stead of out in a field priming sand lugs like A.K."

Tink set a mug of coffee in front of me. It was just the way I liked it: hot as hell and black as sin. I sipped cautiously as Reese mashed another pat of butter into his grits.

"Talked to your mother today?"

"That's why I'm here and not over at the hospital. Annie Sue and me, we've got to keep the business going. Mama says Dad's some better, but they've got to finish up some more tests. She says we can do more good here than there."

He swallowed some sausage and glanced at me sideways. "You don't look bad for somebody that found a dead man last night."

As Tink brought me my breakfast plate, he caught the end of Reese's remarks. "Y'all talking about Carver Bannerman? He eats lunch here three or four times a week. Was you really the one found him, Miss Deb'rah?"

His question was polite formality. The Coffee Pot opens

at six A.M. and I was sure he'd had the details a dozen times by seven. Hearing it all over again from one of the horses' mouths would make fresh gossip for the lunch trade; but I wasn't sure if Annie Sue's involvement was generally known, and I certainly didn't want to broadcast it.

"Bastard got what he deserved," Reese growled and Tink nodded in such sympathetic agreement that I realized Reese'd already mouthed off.

"Was he really buck naked when you found him?" asked Ava. Trade was slack at the moment, since most of their customers begin work at eight, and she had wiped up spills and straightened all the sugar bowls and creamers along the long counter till she'd worked her way down to us.

Although Ava Dupree is only in her early twenties, her long thin face has little of youth's glowing elasticity. Plastic surgery smoothed away most of the burn damage there, but the skin on her neck is mottled pink and red where it disappears beneath her high, long-sleeved smock, and shiny scar tissue on her hands has pulled and tightened until they look like the hands of someone old and crippled with arthritis. Was that why Bass Langley ran out on her? Not wanting to make love to that body? Not wanting those hands to touch him anymore?

Normally, I don't look twice at her scars. Except for wearing long sleeves year-round, Ava never seems self-conscious about her looks. But this was the first time I'd been in the Coffee Pot since last Thursday when Herman reminded me about the fire, and I busied myself with egg, sausages, and grits till I could get over my own self-consciousness.

"I heard he didn't have a stitch on," Ava nudged.

She took back the grape jelly Tink'd given me and rummaged in the jam basket till she found my favorite orange marmalade.

I always appreciate people remembering things like that and suddenly she was just Ava again, another human being trying to get along in the world, a good-hearted waitress who enjoys good gossip.

"No, he had on all his clothes," I said, "but he was flopped over a sawbench like a bag of fertilizer."

Between bites of biscuit and egg, I told her so many gory details about Bannerman's body and the bloody hammer and how my skirt was ruined that I finished eating and had paid my bill and Reese's too and we were both out the door without Annie Sue's name even being mentioned.

"Court's due to start in fifteen minutes," I told Reese as he unlocked the shop next door, "so tell me quick: you and A.K. get yourselves in any trouble last night?"

He swore they hadn't.

"We went over and parked in front of Bannerman's trailer till his wife came home. And then we'd hardly started asking where he was till her girlfriend came running up saying he was killed."

"She wasn't home when you arrived?"

Reese shook his head.

"And you didn't threaten her? Or him?"

"We don't beat up on women," he said indignantly. "And Bannerman was already dead, wasn't he?"

He and A.K. had tailed the women over to Redbud Lane, gotten the main facts from Deputy Jamison (who hadn't thought to mention to Dwight that he'd seen the boys), and had then driven on over to Chapel Hill. "But Mama made us come on home 'cause she wanted me to open the office this morning. Besides, A.K. called from the hospital and Uncle Andrew told him he was going to be in big trouble if he didn't get home before midnight."

I glanced at my watch and knew I was going to be in big trouble if I wasn't sitting on the bench in eight minutes.

•   •   •

Around the courthouse, the connection between Bannerman's death and my brother, his daughter, and me was such a muddle that conversations broke off whenever I appeared and no one found the nerve to broach the subject directly. "Sorry to hear about your brother," was the closest anyone came; and I pushed it all out of my mind till court adjourned for the day.

I had been a district judge for a full week now and it

seemed to become more interesting every day, although cases involving drugs were more depressing than I'd expected. I can't get seriously upset about marijuana anymore. Not when there's so much hard stuff floating around the country. Heroin, crack, angel dust, China white—it's everywhere, in every stratum of Colleton County society from migrant camps to million-dollar houses, and I've pretty well reversed the never-in-a-million years position I had when I first passed the bar exam.

"Every day, legalization starts to make more and more sense," I tell Dwight. "You and Bo may *think* everybody in your department's straight, but there's so damn much money in trafficking and your salaries are so damn low—"

"Who you think's not straight?" growls Dwight.

"That's not what I said. I'm saying if drugs were legal, you could cut your operating costs in half."

"If we had stiffer laws—"

"You can't enforce the laws we have."

Dwight doesn't like to hear me talk that way. "You see that documentary they did on the needle parks in—where was it? Holland? Denmark? Kids overdosing. Hypodermics all over the sidewalks. I'm telling you: drugs are flat-out *bad*."

"Hey, I never said they weren't. A fried brain is disgusting. Wave your magic wand, make the stuff disappear, and you'll get no argument from me. But till you do, the only real difference between those needle parks and what's happening in the side streets and back alleys of Durham, Fayetteville, or parts of Dobbs right now is that at least those European addicts didn't mug helpless old people or break into houses to get money to buy the stuff."

"Yeah," says Bob McAdams, who heads up a local independent insurance company. "You guys don't put a cap on drug crimes pretty soon, everybody's premiums are going to be right through the roof. The industry's hemorrhaging money from drug-related thefts and bodily injuries."

"Legalization's not the only answer," Dwight argues. "What about education and rehabilitation? They'd work if the legislature would fund them right."

"Big *if*," says Lu Bingham, who daily tries to wheedle

more money from government agencies. "Instead of spending millions on something that works, Congress would rather waste billions on trying to keep drugs illegal."

"For the last three years, at least once a week I'd have a client that'd beg the judge to get her in a treatment program," I say. "You want to guess how long some of the waiting lists are?"

I spouted off like this in frustration to one of our state's older elected representatives at a fund-raiser last month. He'd nodded sagely. Oh, yes, indeed. He remembered Prohibition, when the U.S. government told its citizens they couldn't drink booze and then couldn't or wouldn't enforce it.

"From the White House to the courthouse, everybody kept a bottle in the desk drawer. Whole police forces were bribed, judges subverted. Gangs distributed the stuff. There were turf battles, innocent bystanders got mowed down in drive-by shootings. Sound familiar, young lady?"

"So how come you don't introduce a bill to decriminalize drugs?" I goaded.

"Too late," he said, patting my shoulder. "Too much vested interest in keeping it illegal on both sides of the law. Take away the crime and you take away the cash, cash that needs to get laundered through otherwise legitimate banks and businesses. Good ol' supply and demand."

He was just tipsy enough to keep patting my shoulder and nodding agreement. "But nobody's gonna give up that Niagara of cash without a bloody fight. I'm not saying both sides'll use Uzis or busted kneecaps, but you watch what happens to the first round of politicos who advocate legalization, little lady. Pay attention to who contributes to whose campaign. Hell, maybe I'll even introduce a bill like that myself when I'm ready to retire. Just to see what crawls out of the woodwork. Long as I want to keep this seat, though"—he tucked his tongue firmly in his cheek—"I'm going to vote for tougher laws and bigger prisons every time. Yes, ma'am!"

Disheartening.

Yet, even though I was beginning to feel we'd never get a

handle on drugs, I did as much as I was allowed to, and the view from the bench continued to fascinate.

Wednesday was no different.

A reformed alcoholic appeared before me to throw himself on the mercy of the court in regard to a fugitive warrant for arrest that had been outstanding since it was issued four years ago. He wanted to clear his record and he brought along an affidavit from the complainant that he'd made good all damages.

"So where've you been hiding these last four years?" I asked.

"In Florida, Your Honor. That's where I found a kinder, gentler way of life." He handed me a letter from the minister of a church down there attesting to his sterling character. "But Jesus told me to come back to Dobbs and get straight with Caesar."

"Caesar?" Puzzled, I looked over at Phyllis Raynor, who was clerking for me. "I thought the complainant's name was Jasper Something."

"No, no," said the defendant. "Caesar. Like in 'Render unto Caesar the things that are Caesar's.' Worldly stuff. The laws of man. That's what Jesus wants straight."

Laughter rippled along the attorneys' bench.

"Any other worldly charges against you scattered around the country?"

"No, ma'am, Your Honor. I had a policeman friend run me through his computers."

"Very well," I said. "Since Jesus has done a better job with you than jail ever did, I'll vacate this warrant. Go and sin no more."

He was followed by an elderly man and the man's even more elderly neighbor, two old white men who'd been feuding for thirty-five years from the testimony I heard. The first accused the second of killing his dog. No, he hadn't seen the act; no, the dog's body hadn't been found; but the accused had threatened the dog's life and now the dog was gone. And yes, ma'am, he'd agree that dog might've barked a lot, "but King was a pure-out scairdy cat and he'd never leave the yard on his own, so what else could've happened to him?"

Even though he brought along a second neighbor to witness the accused's threats, the witness hadn't seen or heard anything except threats either.

I had a feeling that the only reason the DA had calendared the case was because the complainant was his wife's uncle and he was tired of trying to explain probable cause to the stubborn old coot. Let me do his dirty work.

"Sorry," I said, "but until you get more proof, I have to rule no grounds for complaint."

· · ·

The waiting room at Chapel Hill's North Carolina Memorial Hospital looked and smelled like a family reunion without the laughter when I got there that evening.

Daddy wasn't there, but all my local brothers and their families were. Most of my sisters-in-law held public jobs these days, but the habit of comforting with food was so strong that they'd all brought along buckets of take-out chicken and bottles of soft drinks to supplement the waiting room's coffee urn.

Herman and Nadine's other two children, Edward and Denise, had come in early this morning.

"They let us see him twice," said Nadine. "But he's so groggy I don't know if he knew it was us." She looked haggard after a night on the hospital couch and Annie Sue was trying to persuade her to go lie down a few hours in one of the motel rooms various family members had rented.

"It's not going to do Dad a bit of good if you wind up in the hospital, too!" she declaimed. "I'll come get you the *minute* there's any change. And you don't have to worry about me. Paige says she'll stay over and keep me company. You've just *got* to lie down."

"We'll see," was all Nadine would say. "Settle down, child."

The bruises had come up good on Annie Sue's face and arms, but the scrape was healing properly. Except for worrying over Herman and Nadine, she seemed almost back to normal. Of course, dramatic worry *was* natural for Annie Sue, especially with someone as solicitous as Paige Byrd to hover and worry with her and hold her hand. I was surprised not to see the third member of their trio.

"Cindy's sister heard about what she was doing with Carver Bannerman," Annie Sue whispered, "and told Miss Gladys and Miss Gladys went nuclear! Thank the Lord for Paige! I couldn't stand it without her."

Paige turned bright red under her strawberry bangs, but I could see she was happy Annie Sue felt that way.

•   •   •

As the evening wore on, some of those who'd come directly from work were replaced by those who'd come from home. Seth and Minnie drove over with Andrew and April, but they'd worked in tobacco all day and were physically drained. Too, they needed to get home early to check on their bulk barns. One of Andrew's was nearing the point where he needed to run up the heat to set the leaf's golden color, so they left before eight, just as Dwight Bryant and Terry Wilson arrived.

Both lawmen had been in and out of our lives so long, they felt like family, too.

The seriousness of Herman's condition preyed on us, but human nature always bubbles up at even the most solemn wakes, and conversation went from dark to light in looping circles.

Aunt Zell asked me about the pup, which led her to tell the others about Miss Sallie's missing beagle, her strayed Goldie, and Alice Castleberry's registered bull terrier. I told her about the dog feud I'd had in court that morning, and we debated the possible reappearance in Dobbs of the dognaper.

Reese's girlfriend ignored the fact that most of the family didn't approve of her and talked about the time her cat got inside a friend's van and went home with them. That put Terry in mind of his second wife's cat.

"Big old gray fuzzball," he told us. "Every time I'd leave the car window down, the dang cat would crawl inside to sleep. Cat hairs everywhere. And of course *she* said if I'd keep the windows closed, the cat wouldn't get in. She was just scared that someday I'd drive off with the thing and lock it inside and it'd suffocate to death. Reckon you could see how me and that cat ranked in her affections.''

My brothers grinned and Will's Amy asked with great innocence, ''Well, Terry sugar, which one of you was most faithful?''

He gave her a mock scowl and continued. ''So this one day, I came out in a hurry, jumped in my car and ran down to the grocery store for a jug of milk. When I was coming back across the parking lot, I saw something under my car—that big old gray fuzzball. And yeah, I'd left my windows down again. First off, I thought I'd just drive away and leave it there and act dumb whenever she missed the stupid thing; but being an upright righteous husband—''

''Yeah, sure!'' everyone hooted.

''—I decided I'd better try to catch him. Now that cat and me, we never did get along too good, and I called 'kitty-kitty' till I was purple before he came out from under my car. Then I had to chase him all over the parking lot and when I finally grabbed him, he gave me such a scratch it dripped blood all the way home. But I'm a special agent for the SBI, right? And he was just a dumb old cat, right? So I did eventually throw him in the car and off we set. He stomped back and forth on the backseat and snarled at me the whole way home. Well, we get home and I pull into the driveway and there's the *real* old fuzzball sound asleep on the roof of my wife's car.''

Before he could tell us what he did with the feline doppelganger, a white-coated doctor appeared in the doorway. ''Mrs. Knott?'' he asked. ''Mrs. Herman Knott?''

Instinctively, we fell silent and clustered around Nadine.

''We've confirmed the cause of your husband's condition,'' he said briskly. ''It isn't his heart or a stroke.''

''Then what?'' asked Nadine.

''Chronic poisoning,'' said the doctor. ''Somehow or other, your husband's ingested a good deal of arsenic over the past week or so.''

14

Safety Rules

> *"The posted or promulgated rules for the safe operation of all power equipment must be strictly followed, unless an unavoidable suspension of a rule is authorized by proper authority. The suspension must end as soon as the necessity for it has passed."*

"Arsenic?"

The word ran around the room and bounced off the ceiling.

Nadine seemed bewildered. "Where would he get arsenic?"

The doctor flipped to Herman's admittance chart. "His occupation is listed as an electrician. Is he also engaged in farming where he might handle insecticides or other poisonous chemicals?"

Nadine shook her head. "Sometimes he has to crawl up under old houses where they've put out rat poison. Maybe—"

"No, that's warfarin, an anticoagulant."

"But he's going to be all right, isn't he?" asked Annie Sue. She pushed close to her mother, as if seeking physical comfort and her big blue eyes were frightened. "He's not going to die, is he? *Is he?*"

"Now hush that kind of talk," said Nadine, but she, too, was shaken. "Doctor?"

He shook his head. "I wish I could give you a cut-and-dried answer, Mrs. Knott, but chronic arsenic poisoning's a tricky thing. We don't yet know how much neurological damage there is. The lack of paralysis is encouraging, but the anesthesias in his legs and extremities, the liver involvement—"

We stood numbly as all that medical terminology flowed over us. What it boiled down to was that Herman would probably recover, but it was going to be long and slow—six months or longer—and he might never recover full feeling in his fingers and feet. A wheelchair could not be ruled out.

Nor was treatment itself going to be a simple thing. Some doctors advocated doing nothing. Let the body heal itself. If a more aggressive course were taken, the antidote might be as dangerous as the arsenic itself.

Yet even as we listened, we all kept circling back to the central question: how the devil was he getting arsenic? Because on that point, the doctor was quite clear: Herman had ingested the stuff more than once in the last ten days.

The doctor finished outlining the treatment they planned to use. As he rose to go, he cocked his head and looked around the circle of faces surrounding him. "You live close to one another? See each other every day? Then perhaps I should check. Is everybody healthy? Any stomach cramps or nausea that won't go away? Summer flu? Dizziness, pins and needles in your fingers or toes? Numbness?"

We all shook our heads, although I saw a considering expression cross the face of Nadine's sister. Her robustly healthy body imprisoned the soul of a hypochondriac.

"Great!" He closed Herman's chart with a snap. "Oh, one thing more, Mrs. Knott. Someone from Environmental Health will probably be in contact with Mr. Knott and you to try to trace the source of the arsenic. They'll want you to think what you two may have eaten or drunk differently, any places where he eats that you and your family don't, maybe a list of all the locations he's worked lately that might have old arsenic-based paint or wallpaper, things like that. Okay?"

The family milled around as he left, so simultaneously worried and titillated that no one else seemed to notice the looks Dwight and Terry exchanged before following the doctor from the waiting room. I slipped out, too, and hurried down the hall after them. As they rounded a corner, I heard the doctor say, "Well, yes, I suppose there always *is* that possibility, Major Bryant."

"What possibility?" I asked, halting them in their tracks.

The doctor turned and frowned, Terry immediately went into his official secrets mode, but Dwight said, "I don't believe you've met Herman's sister. This is Judge Deborah Knott, Doctor."

"Judge?"

"Judicial District Eleven-C," I said. "What possibility?"

"That your brother's poisoning was not accidental," he answered bluntly.

"That someone poisoned *Herman?* On purpose?"

The three men shuffled their feet and I could have laughed if it hadn't been so outrageous.

"I almost forgot. Yeah. Her husband was treated here, wasn't he? Well, you can push that notion right out of your heads," I said hotly. "Nadine Knott is no Blanche Taylor Moore. Come on, Dwight! Terry? You guys have known Nadine forever. Can't you see how upset and worried she is?"

"The Reverend Moore was never my patient," the doctor said carefully, "but I'm told Mrs. Moore was a loving wife right up to the minute they arrested her. And they say she was real attentive to the boyfriend who did die. Brought him potato soup when he was in Baptist Hospital, even spoon fed him. Held the straw for him to sip iced tea. The nurses thought she was a real sweetie."

"I know, I know," I said impatiently. "And later they found out that there was arsenic in the soup and arsenic in the tea." I turned to Dwight and Terry. "But this is *Nadine!*"

"Wives aren't the only ones who do things like that," Terry said soothingly. "Besides, it'll probably turn out to be a contaminated well or something at some old house that's being renovated."

"We're just touching all the bases," Dwight chimed in. "Laying the groundwork for the public health guy."

"Long as you don't forget this is Herman, for God's sake."

The doctor had his hand on a door marked STAFF ONLY, but I asked, "While we're laying groundwork, Doctor, can you give us any idea of when he first got the arsenic? Didn't I read somewhere that you could tell by the hair or fingernails?"

He looked amused. "Well, yes, but the simplest way, if the patient is still alive, is just to ask him when he first started feeling rotten. Mr. Knott said he went to a party or something about ten days ago—the second of July?—and that night he experienced stomach cramps. At the time, he thought he might've eaten too many cucumber sandwiches or drunk too much lime punch."

Cucumber sandwiches? Lime punch?

"Wasn't your swearing-in reception on the second?" asked Dwight.

* * *

We were allowed to go in and see Herman, a few of us at a time; first Nadine and her four children, then his brothers and me. He was groggy still and pasty-faced and looked so vulnerable lying there in a hospital gown that I had to go straight over and hug him.

"Now, now," he said with a ghost of his old gruffness. "I'm gonna be fine. You don't need to cry over me yet."

Technically, I was no longer Herman's attorney, but neither Dwight nor Terry said anything about my being there when they came in to question Herman about Tuesday night. Nadine had insisted that he not be told about Bannerman's attack on Annie Sue until he was stronger, and she wasn't real happy that he even had to know that Bannerman had died there that night.

She needn't have worried. Herman was too exhausted to wonder why we wound up asking him about a county inspector he'd barely known. Far as he was concerned, Dwight and Terry were just a couple of good old friends come to see how he was faring. As for Tuesday night, he could barely remember anything specific.

"I was feeling so terrible bad I guess I was ugly to you and Annie Sue," he told me in sideways apology.

I just patted his calloused, work-worn hand. "Did you stay long after I left?"

"Naw. I was right in behind you and her girlfriends. She was mad as fire at me for telling her what she did wrong, and I have to tell you, Deb'rah, my stomach hurt so bad I was almost to the point I didn't care. I figured one of the inspectors would catch anything too dangerous about it before it got covered up."

"The inspector came by that night," I said. "Did you see him?"

Herman shook his head.

"Some young guy," I pressed him gently. "Carver Bannerman. You ever meet him?"

"Bannerman?" He frowned. "No, can't say as I have. Not to know the name. He pass Annie Sue's work all right?"

Terry rescued me. "Well, old son, you sure gave everybody a good scare."

"Weird, idn it?" he said sleepily. "Arsenic. Wonder where in the world I got it?"

"The wonder's how you were able to keep moving," said Dwight.

"Daddy'd never let us give in to being sick," Herman said and fell asleep with a smile on his lips.

15

Surface Preparation

"Proper surface preparation is an essential part of any paint job; paint will not adhere well, provide the required surface protection, or present a good appearance unless the surface has been properly treated."

The investigator from Environmental Health, an environmental epidemiologist to give him his official title, was named Gordon O'Connor. Thirtyish, going bald early. Despite laid-back sneakers and jeans, there was an edginess about his wiry build that made me think he'd probably been a nerd in grade school. An intelligent nerd with something of a terrier's nervous intensity just before he picks up the rabbit's trail.

He wore rimless round glasses perched on a long thin nose. The lens were thinner than fine crystal and polished to a shining gloss that rivaled the gloss of his bald dome. Behind those glasses, his eyes gleamed like two large black coffee beans; yet, they couldn't have needed much correction because the lens didn't distort their appearance any more than ordinary window glass.

Every attorney is something of a pop psychologist and I decided that he'd probably been shy in his youth and maybe didn't realize he'd outgrown the need to hide behind glass. (Let the record show that edgy shyness can be oddly sexy at times.)

Not that there was anything shy about the way Mr. O'Connor delved into Herman's life. He interviewed Herman and Nadine separately and together, his terrier face darting back and forth between them in the hospital. When Nadine came back to work on Friday, O'Connor was right behind her, ready to start digging up every mole run in the county.

Nadine has a touching faith in modern medicine. Now that Herman was diagnosed and on the mend, she felt it was possible to leave him in the hospital's efficient hands while she came home to keep the business going.

So far, it had not occurred to her that Herman's poisoning was anything but accidental. The Raleigh *News and Observer* had covered Blanche Taylor Moore's trial in exhaustive detail from first suspicion till when she was sentenced to death for first-degree murder. Yet, even though the paper emphasized that most arsenic killers tended to be southern women, and most victims tended to be the man in their lives, Nadine was joking that at least Herman didn't have to worry that she'd poisoned *his* tea.

Along with the other two electricians Herman employed, Reese and Annie Sue could keep up with most of the routine field work, but only Nadine fully understood all the paperwork involved in running the business, and she didn't want to get too far behind. "Especially since we haven't got us a new accountant yet," she told me. "Thank goodness Ralph McGee got us through tax season before he died."

She looked abashed. "I didn't mean that the way it sounded. Poor Gladys."

It was a little past one on a blistering hot Friday. I had adjourned court for the weekend and stopped in to see how Nadine was getting along. The humidity was so high that just walking from my air-conditioned car to the air-conditioned office was like wading through tall grass, and I grabbed a drink from the water cooler as soon as I got inside.

Nadine was seated at her desk, going through the worksheets. As she called out all the places Herman had worked over the last ten days, Mr. O'Connor sat with his legal pad at a nearby table and wrote down the addresses.

He picked up on my name immediately. "I was hoping to see you today, Judge Knott. I'll need to know the name of your caterer. And did anyone else get sick that evening?"

I must have looked combative because he said, "We don't know that's where he first ingested it, but it's a place to start."

He took off his glasses, polished them carefully, hooked the wire frames back over his ears, then looked at me with such alert expectation in those shiny black eyes that I gave him Julia Lee's name and phone number.

"She arranged everything, but the food was prepared by the Martha Circle at the First Methodist Church, and afterwards, Lu Bingham, of WomenAid, took all the leftovers to her day care center. I'm sure if there was anything in the food or punch, we'd have heard about it by now."

"Probably," he agreed. "But—"

The tickler bell jingled over the street door. Dwight Bryant. He'd evidently met O'Connor earlier in the day and had come looking for him specifically.

"It's the darnedest thing, but I thought you ought to know."

"Yes?" O'Connor's eyeglasses gleamed like twin moons under the fluorescent lights overhead.

"They just called in the autopsy report on a man who was killed here in Dobbs Tuesday night. Carver Bannerman. His head was bashed in and that's what killed him, but they found a trace of arsenic in his gastrointestinal tract."

O'Connor's smooth round head came up like a young dog that's caught the scent.

"Nice," he said happily. "Very nice indeed!"

• • •

Two men with arsenic in their system were going to make it three times as easy to locate the source of the poison, Gordon O'Connor said. His coffee bean eyes gleamed brighter than those eggshell-thin glasses the whole time Dwight was telling him who Carver Bannerman was.

"This Bannerman inspect any of Mr. Knott's jobs?"

"Half the time we aren't there when inspectors come around, so there's no way of us knowing," Nadine replied. "You'd have to compare the worksheets I gave you with whatever records the county inspector keeps. And like I told you before, we take a lot of piddling jobs that don't require inspection."

"That's what I mean about two victims cutting the possibilities so drastically," said O'Connor. "For now I can forget about all the jobs this Bannerman *didn't* inspect and just poke around at places where they overlapped."

"One place you could start is right next door." I glanced at my watch. "It's one-fifty though, and they'll be closing in a few minutes."

Nadine frowned. "The Coffee Pot?"

"Sure. Herman stops in every morning and Tink Dupree— he's the owner"—I explained to O'Connor—"Tink told me Wednesday morning that Carver Bannerman ate lunch there two or three times a week."

"But I have a glass of tea in there almost every morning myself," Nadine protested.

"Both of 'em, hmm?" Gordon O'Connor gathered up his lists, aligned the edges in neat economical movements and stashed them in a crisp manila folder. "You never know. Maybe they both ordered something exotic."

Dwight grinned. "The most exotic thing you can order in the Coffee Pot is a side dish of chili peppers with your scrambled eggs."

"Or tell Retha to hold the mayo on your hamburger at lunch," I added.

O'Connor laughed as he stood up. He wasn't nearly as tall as Dwight, but he certainly did have long legs inside those stovepipe jeans. Long thin fingers, too. They say that men with long fingers—

Dwight was looking at me and I stopped that train of thought before it could roll on into the station. Judges really do have to be discreet.

Especially *lady* judges.

On the other hand . . .

"How 'bout I introduce you to Tink?" I volunteered.

"I'll do it," Dwight said firmly. "I probably ought to tag along for this anyhow."

In the end, we both tagged along. I don't know if O'Connor sensed what was going on, but when Dwight starts acting like he's been commissioned to keep me from doing something rash, it naturally makes me want to throw discretion out the back window.

•   •   •

"I'm afraid we already went and cut off the grill," Tink apologized when the three of us entered the Coffee Pot. "We still got some cold chicken salad, though. I could make y'all a sandwich and there's a fresh pitcher of tea if y'all are just thirsty."

"That's okay, Tink," I said. "We're not here as customers. This is Gordon O'Connor from Environmental Health in Raleigh."

As soon as he heard the word *health* mentioned, Tink gazed fearfully at a framed document over the coffee maker, an "A" inspection rating from the Health Department. Retha suddenly appeared from behind the kitchen partition, wiping her rawboned hands on a clean dishtowel. Without that high rating, they wouldn't have a business.

Dwight explained about Herman and Bannerman.

"And since both men frequented your place," said O'Connor, "I thought I'd begin here."

The Duprees just gazed back at him numbly.

"It doesn't mean a thing," I soothed, trying to reassure them. "Somebody's got to be first and y'all just happen to be it."

O'Connor already had his check sheet out and was clicking his ballpoint pen in and out.

"Let's just start with a few routine questions," he said. "What sort of pesticides do you use in the kitchen?"

•   •   •

Eventually the Duprees quit acting like deer caught in a jacklight and started answering his questions. They took him back to the kitchen and showed him the ant and roach traps, "but mostly we just try to keep everything clean and swept up," said Retha. "It's a whole lot easier to keep it so you don't never get pests than it is to get shet of 'em after they get started good."

"Ever use any Terro Ant Killer?" asked O'Connor.

The question sounded almost as casual as the others, but I thought I sensed that quivering intensity again. Retha screwed up her face and said she couldn't remember.

Ava came in from the back alley where she'd been putting out the garbage and sweeping up around the barrels. Again the introductions and explanations. She'd heard the last question and said, "Stuff's hardly worth bringing home anymore. No arsenic in it, if that's what you mean. Just borax."

"Really?" asked Retha. Like Tink, she'd quit school in the eighth grade and was constantly amazed by all the things that Ava, who'd finished high school, seemed to know. "You can kill ants with borax?"

"Not very good," said her daughter. "Not like with arsenic."

"My granny used to strew red pepper on the threshold," Tink said. "In her pantry, too. Don't nothing like to crawl through red pepper."

That reminded Retha of the tansy *her* granny had used. O'Connor just listened with one ear while continuing to poke around in the cupboards. He found corrosive drain cleaners and spray cans of pyrethrin-based insecticides— enough stuff to wipe out half of Dobbs if the Duprees were so minded. In short, the usual deadly concoctions found in your average American kitchen.

Nothing with arsenic, though, and neither Tink, Retha, nor Ava could think of anything Bannerman and Herman might have ordered in their cafe that no one else had.

"Are there any other employees?"

An awkward silence.

"Not right now," Tink said.

"Why sure there is." Dwight gave him a jocular grin. "You're forgetting your own son-in-law. Where *is* ol' Bass anyhow. Haven't seen him around town lately."

It was too late to kick him even if I'd been close enough to do it unobtrusively. Instead I had to stand and watch as Ava flushed a painful red and the mottled scar tissue became terribly noticeable. Retha moved toward her protectively, but Ava's chin came up.

"He ain't here no more," she said defiantly. "Gone back to Georgia. I run him off last week."

"He didn't never touch the plates anyhow," Retha chimed in. "We're filling in with a Mexican dishwasher part-time now, but just me and Tink and Ava are the only ones ever handle food here."

• • •

According to the preliminary autopsy report, Bannerman had probably ingested his trace of arsenic sometime during the previous weekend, Dwight said, so O'Connor went off to the county inspector's office to get a list of houses on the dead man's schedule.

Dwight walked me out to my car and we stood there in the hot thick sunshine talking.

When they widened the streets a few years ago, they cut down most of the huge old oaks that had shaded the old cracked sidewalks. Now stiff little Bradford pears marched up and down in wire support cages. One of these days they would flower and be pretty in the spring, but they'd never provide the shade those oaks had.

Depressing.

Dwight wasn't too happy with himself for embarrassing Ava. He wanted to blame me for not telling him that Bass had walked out on her, but that dog wouldn't fight and he knew it. Still, it did remind me.

"You're all the time saying I don't tell you things, but you were out of the county then, too; so do you remember how Ava got burned?"

Like me, he knew only that there'd been a fire. When I

told him about why Herman wanted to take part of the blame for Tink's miswiring of the old house, he looked thoughtful. "You thinking one of them—"

"No," I said firmly. "I don't. But we both know people can brood on things and finally do something weird. I still think O'Connor's going to find a perfectly accidental source, but if the Coffee Pot does turn out to be the only eating place they really crossed, you'll find a way to blame me if you don't have all the facts. Besides, didn't Bass leave last week about the time Herman started feeling bad? Are the two connected? You're the police officer, you tell me."

"But Bannerman had nothing to do with the fire."

"No, but he couldn't keep his fly zipped. If he ate at the Coffee Pot three or four times a week, you can bet money he made at least one pass at Ava. Just to be friendly if nothing else. She's not even twenty-five yet, and with men like him, every woman under fifty's an automatic hit. Did it flatter her or make her mad? And what did Bass and Tink think?"

Dwight allowed as how I had a point. So far, he'd had no luck finding out who'd used the hammer on Bannerman.

"Maybe I'll go question Rochelle Bannerman again. I have to tell her about the arsenic. Maybe she knows something."

I resisted the temptation to be catty and opened my car door. At the last minute, I remembered what Reese had told me. "Did either of your deputies tell you she wasn't home when Reese and A.K. got out to the trailer park Tuesday?"

"Yeah. She was over at a girlfriend's place."

"The whole evening?"

He shrugged. "You know what the trouble with air-conditioning is? Everybody stays inside with their doors and windows closed and watches television."

"Too bad you didn't have Mayleen Richards go through the Bannerman hamper for his wife's dirty clothes."

"Huh?"

"Think how hot it was Tuesday night. Rainy and muggy. Yet when Mrs. Bannerman arrived at the WomenAid house, her hair and clothes were clean and fresh. Opal Grimes was a mess, but Rochelle Bannerman looked like she'd just stepped out of a shower. The question is, when? Not after Reese and A.K. got there, that's for sure.''

Suddenly, just talking about a shower made me long for one myself and as Dwight drove off to question Mrs. Bannerman, I headed home with my air-conditioning pushed as high as it'd go.

16

Exterior Wall Insulation

"Insulation also serves a valuable purpose in moisture control, which prevents rot and fungus growth. …The fireproofing and vermin-proofing qualities of insulation should also be considered."

Much as I wanted to spend the weekend with K.C. Massengill at her lakefront cottage, I didn't see how I could get out from under all my obligations.

"You're gonna do what?" she asked when I called to tell her so Friday night.

"Don't make it worse," I implored. I didn't want to hear about cool swims and shady walks and handsome guys on screened porches, as steaks grilled on the cooker and moons rose romantically over the water.

Not when I was going to be laboring again at the WomenAid house. I had visions of sweat-damp work clothes and itchy pink fiberglass particles sticking to my skin.

Actually, Saturday turned out not to be all that bad. A high pressure system came through early in the morning and left behind crystal clear *dry* air. The previous Saturday had seen temperature and humidity both in the nineties. This weekend, it never got out of the low eighties and humidity was way, way down.

Nor did I have to put on a mask and coveralls or wrestle with rolls of fiberglass. Must be part of the covered-dish-dinner syndrome. Tell a bunch of women to bring a vegetable, a meat or a dessert to a community meal and you'll always—not once in a while, but *always*—get a balanced selection. Volunteering for specific jobs seems to work the same way. There were women who actually *wanted* to tack six-inch-thick insulation batts between all the exterior studs and joists, and I certainly wasn't going to get in their way. Another crew swarmed onto the roof and had all the shingles on before lunch. I myself got to help set the two exterior doors and nine windows, which was sort of fun.

In and around cries for more nails. "Head's up!" and "Nail it 'fore it grows," Carver Bannerman's death was the big topic of conversation. Of equal interest were the doses of arsenic he and Herman had ingested. Had it only been Herman, human nature being what it is, Annie Sue and I might have worked all morning surrounded by a cocoon of speculative silence. Enough Tar Heel wives have laced their husband's food that you couldn't blame even good friends for wondering if Nadine had suddenly decided to exchange wedded bliss for widowhood. Luckily for Nadine, young Carver Bannerman's quasi-victimship kept Herman's firmly in the realm of accidental.

Yes, poison was a woman's weapon of choice; yes, most women—most *convicted* women—seldom stopped with one victim; but since there seemed to be no connection between Herman and Bannerman, people felt free to exclaim and question.

"Good riddance to bad rubbish," said everyone who'd heard of Bannerman's attack on Annie Sue.

He was being buried over in Goldsboro that morning, so his wife's friend, Opal Grimes, wasn't around to crimp the lively discussion. If asked, most of the women wouldn't have recognized either Carver or Rochelle, but that didn't stop the cheerfully catty gossip as we hammered and sawed in the cool morning sunlight. Lazy but shrewd was the general assessment of Rochelle. Assuming he was a prize worth having—a man for whom every woman was a potential sexual conquest—she had skillfully played the cards she'd been dealt and had won the gold ring.

A car had been seen arriving and then leaving again in the rainy twilight just minutes before I got there. A woman down the street thought for sure the driver was a young woman, and her description of the car was enough like Rochelle Bannerman's that I figured Dwight was looking very carefully into her account of how she'd spent the evening. Not that he was sharing that information with me.

"He sure was handsome," conceded the woman who had approved a bank mortgage on his trailer, "but can you imagine going to bed with him?" She pounded a final nail into her end of the siding. "One of my clerks heard he'd lay anything with a vagina. Wouldn't you be terrified of waking up with some nasty infection? To say nothing of AIDS?"

"Well, *I* heard—"

"My brother-in-law said—"

"—and her husband was right there in the room!"

None of the volunteers acted as if they knew of Cindy McGee's involvement with the dead man because the dirt was dished too freely as she moved back and forth from one task to another. Except for Paige and Annie Sue, I seemed to be the only one who noticed her drawn face and her lack of chatter.

Attention was showered on Annie Sue. She got praise for her bravery and commiseration both for the attack and for Herman's illness. Her self-esteem had lots of bolstering that day.

Poor Cindy had nothing; and every time another comment about Bannerman's womanizing went round, Paige Byrd flushed crimson and looked equally miserable. Sympathetic mortification for her friend, no doubt. Yet she, too, had to hold her tongue.

Somehow they got through the morning and at lunchtime, one of the women from Paige's church called upon the three girls for a song. They were scheduled to sing at services the next morning, "but I've got to go to Greensboro tonight, so I won't get to hear you," she said.

"Yes, do sing for us!" others urged.

Cindy and Paige both looked like they'd just as soon go eat worms, but when Annie Sue stepped up onto the porch, they didn't have much choice.

I'd never heard the girls sing together and their close harmony was a pleasant surprise. No accompaniment, just an a cappella rendering of some old hymns. Annie Sue had always enjoyed the spotlight, and I was glad to see an easing of tension in Cindy's face. Even Paige seemed to lose herself in the melody. Their fresh young voices twined in and out, point and counterpoint, until they infected the rest of us.

A black woman beside me began to croon along. Another joined in with a more solid gospel swing. I've always adored sing-alongs—never do I feel so connected to other people around me as when my voice lifts with theirs—and soon we were all so much into it that BeeBee Powell's new front yard sounded like the Benson Singing Grove over in Johnston County.

Lu Bingham had served a Peace Corps stint, and she taught us a women's work song from West Africa. We went back to our tools more refreshed than if we'd spent the whole lunch hour resting. Throughout the afternoon, occasional bursts of song spurred us on. Everything from *Michael, Row the Boat Ashore* to *There Was an Old Woman Who Swallowed a Fly*. Lu had to cut us off after one chorus of *We Are Climbing Jacob's Ladder*, though, because our hammers went from a brisk 78 rpm to a lugubrious 33⅓.

* * *

After a quick shower that evening, I drove over to Chapel Hill while it was still light, taking back roads that wound past stands of lush green corn and fields of half-cropped tobacco. Almost every yard was lined with watermelon red crepe myrtles or yellow daylilies. *Knee-deep in summer!* Whoever wrote that knew about ditch banks tumbled with yellow sneezeweeds and wild pink roses, about powerlines and bridge abutments draped in camouflage curtains of kudzu vines, about jack oaks heavy with broad dark leaves.

Near Holly Springs, I got stuck behind a farm truck piled high with huge burlap bundles of cured tobacco, but I was in no hurry and didn't really mind. Occasionally, a beautiful yellow leaf would work its way out of a bundle and drift back past my windshield like an exotic golden butterfly.

Daddy always shakes his head when he sends tobacco off to market like that—"like bundles of dirty clothes," he says—because he was a grown man with sons working alongside him before farmers quit marketing tobacco in the old way.

First the cured leaves went from stick barns to the packhouse where they were gently stripped from the four-foot-six sticks, each leaf sorted according to grade, then hand-gathered into bundles thick as a woman's wrist and the stem ends hidden by wrapping them in a smooth "tie leaf." Next, each bundle was hung back over the stick and packed onto the truck's flatbed for the drive to market. At the warehouse, the sticks were unloaded and carefully piled in a neat stack on the market floor. "And any young'un who carelessly stepped on a bundle of prime-grade leaf was lucky not to get a switching," my brother Andrew tells me.

By the time I came along and started helping by driving tractor, Daddy and my brothers had switched over to gas-fired bulk barns that look like the box trailers of an eighteen-wheeler. No more tying the leaves onto sticks, no more hand-grading. Just dump the cured leaves out onto big burlap squares, knot the four corners and toss them onto a truck headed for Fuquay or Wilson.

· · ·

Herman was cranked up in bed when I got to the hospital and he looked more alert than I'd yet seen him. His feet and legs had sustained the most neurological damage. They had started physical therapy, but it was still too soon to know what the final outcome might be.

"I'll be clomping up and down the hall with one of them metal walkers like an old crippled person," Herman said ruefully.

"Better than a wheelchair," said Nadine.

But it might be a wheelchair.

It was his first stay ever in a hospital; and, since Nadine was probably the only woman who'd touched his body since he was married, he was finding the experience almost as embarrassing as it was interesting. Certainly it was a novelty to have a pretty young physical therapist manipulate his legs and massage his hands and feet.

The tips of his fingers were still numb, too. He was aware of pressure, but not tactile discernment. He could handle a fork well enough to do justice to his supper tray, "but I don't know as I'll ever be able to hold little screws again."

"Sure you will," said Nadine.

"And if you can't, you'll let Annie Sue do it while you ride around from job to job and supervise," I said.

He'd been told all the details of the night he collapsed and he shook his head stubbornly. "If I hadn't let her stay there working by herself, that bastard'd never touched her."

"You can't wrap her in cotton. Anyhow, the kid's pretty good at it. Rufus Dayley sent over another inspector sometime this week and he gave her an 'A-OK' on the rough-in."

"Did he now?" He tried to look nonchalant and didn't quite succeed.

It was still a wonder to him where he could have gotten arsenic. He and Nadine had wracked their brains for Mr. O'Connor and neither could think of a single place he'd eaten when others hadn't partaken of the same dishes.

"Abandoned wells?"

"I carry my own water cooler for my workers and an ice chest with drinks."

"What about pottery juice mugs? I've heard that the acid in fruit juice can leach arsenic out of ceramic cups and pitchers."

"His orange juice comes right out of the Minute Maid carton and right into the same plain glasses we've had for ten years," said Nadine.

As for Carver Bannerman, Herman knew he was a county inspector and remembered now that he'd seen him several times at the Coffee Pot. They had never exchanged more than a few words in passing, though, and certainly they'd never shared a meal anywhere else that he knew of.

"Dwight and Terry," Herman said. "When they were here the other night, they think I was the one killed Bannerman?"

"You, Annie Sue or me, one. But only because of the circumstances."

He nodded. "I reckon any of us would've."

"Would've what?" chirped Annie Sue from the doorway.

Inevitably she was trailed by Cindy and Paige, and I was touched by the sadness in Paige's brown eyes as my niece scampered over to Herman for a big bear hug.

"Think how much you'd miss your daddy," whispered the preacher.

"Perry Byrd was an intolerant bigot and racist," the pragmatist sniffed. *"He must have been hell on hinges to live with."*

"He was her father, and now he's gone forever."

"Humph! Ralph McGee's gone forever, too, but you don't see Cindy mooning over Herman and Annie Sue."

Indeed, her face was brightly animated as she chattered with Nadine.

The girls were quickly followed by more friends and relatives who still believed in visiting the sick and comforting the afflicted. By eight-thirty, the room was so full that we spilled out into the hall, a dozen different conversations going at once.

Nobody would miss me if I left, I reasoned, and maybe it was still early enough to zip over to K.C.'s cottage. Watch the moon rise above Jordan Lake. See how the steaks were holding up.

Not to mention the men.

• • •

The night air was deliciously cool as I headed toward the parking lot, but I'd only gotten as far as the ramp when I heard running footsteps behind me.

"Miss Deborah! Judge Knott?"

Paige Byrd.

"Are you going home now? Could I ride with you? Please?"

I hesitated, and she drooped like a bright-headed zinnia deprived of water. "Oh. You're going somewhere else, aren't you? I'm sorry."

"No, no," I lied. "Come along. It'll be nice to have company."

"K.C.'s party," whined the pragmatist. *"Why are you feeling guilty about this child? This is so irrational. Let her ride home with Cindy and Annie Sue."*

"You have an obligation," said the preacher. *"You don't have to take her to raise, only to remember that you're sitting in her father's seat and that gives her a claim on you."*

The pragmatist sat sulking in the corner of my brain, but I made myself smile at the girl as I unlocked my car door. "Did you tell Annie Sue you were leaving?"

She nodded. "Suddenly, it was just so smothery in there. I thought I was going to faint if I didn't get out."

We talked of claustrophobia and scary experiences with elevators and tunnels, yet even after we had cleared the lights of Chapel Hill and were out on I-40 East zooming toward Dobbs, I kept feeling waves of tension from her. Nothing I said seemed to put her at ease.

Inevitably our talk drifted toward Carver Bannerman, his opportunistic treatment of Cindy and his attack on Annie Sue, and how Annie Sue was more worried about Mr. Herman and what was going to happen to him than what had nearly happened to her.

"At first she was scared maybe he was the one who'd hit Carver with the hammer," Paige said.

"I know. But he didn't. Major Bryant's narrowed down the time to when he ran off the road and collapsed, so that proves he couldn't have."

"If he had, what would've happened to Mr. Herman?"

"He'd probably have been charged with voluntary manslaughter."

"And gone to jail?"

"Not necessarily."

She picked up on the curiosity in my voice. "Are these stupid questions? Dad never talked about his work much and the only time I was in his courtroom was when our whole history class went."

"Well, manslaughter's usually defined as the unlawful killing of a human being without malice," I explained. "There's voluntary, involuntary and vehicular. Vehicular's when a death is caused by driving recklessly. You didn't mean to kill someone, but you weren't being careful. Involuntary manslaughter is usually from criminal negligence. You might argue that death occurred because of a tragic accident; the prosecution will argue that you should have realized that the situation could result in someone's death."

"And voluntary?"

"That's when you meant to kill him, but—"

"If you meant to," she interrupted, "why isn't it murder?"

"For it to be murder, you'd have to think about killing somebody ahead of time and you'd probably try to do it so nobody would know you were the killer. In other words, intent to kill *and* premeditation. Those are the two elements of murder in the first degree. But voluntary manslaughter is when you did it in the heat of passion, without malice aforethought—no intent, no premeditation—and usually with plenty of provocation."

"Like Carver trying to rape Annie Sue."

"Exactly. No jury in the world would convict a man for trying to prevent his daughter's rape. At the most he'd get a suspended sentence. Maybe some community service. Under the circumstances, a district attorney might decline to prosecute or the judge might well dismiss the charges."

She was silent as we exited from I-40 before reaching Raleigh and angled south onto Forty-Eight.

I glanced over and by the lights of the dashboard, I saw that her cheeks were wet with tears.

"Paige?"

"It's all my fault! I shouldn't have left." Her voice was ragged with repressed sobs. "Annie Sue's the very best friend I ever had—the *first* best friend I ever had—and I went and left her both times! But when Mr. Herman—''

''Hey, wait a minute,'' I said, reaching out to pat her shoulder with my free hand. ''Carver Bannerman was slime. If it hadn't been Annie Sue, he would have jumped someone else, and sooner or later, someone was going to jump him back. You couldn't know he was going to show up that night. And as for Herman, surely by now you know that his bark's worse than his bite?''

She shook her head. ''Annie Sue always said—''

There was a service center up ahead and Paige was so distrait that I pulled in and cut the engine, and opened the windows so that the cool night air could sweep over us.

''Look, honey, I know y'all haven't known each other all that long, but don't you see how Annie Sue dramatizes everything? Her daddy growls a lot, but when it comes right down to it, have you ever known him not to let her do something she really wants to do? They're crazy about each other.''

Instead of reassuring her, I seemed to be making her more miserable. The worst thing about bucket seats is that you can't scoot over and hug somebody easily. Nevertheless, I unbuckled my seat belt and tried, but she was stiff in my arms. At this point, Annie Sue or any of my nieces would have their faces snuggled into my neck, bawling their eyes out, and already feeling better; but Paige couldn't let herself melt into the comfort of a sympathetic hug. She was choking on silent sobs and painful tremors shook her hunched shoulders.

It broke my heart to think of her going almost sixteen years without a best friend to giggle and cry with, to talk girl talk and swap secrets; and now that she did, she felt that she had somehow let her friend down, had failed Annie Sue when—

Wait a minute . . . *both times?*

''You left, took Cindy home, and then you went back to the WomenAid house, didn't you?''

Her eyes were dark pools of terror as she pulled away. She tried to deny, to shake her head, but no sound came out.

"*You* hit Carver Bannerman?"

Paige's eyes dropped and a long shudder ran through her. "I didn't mean to kill him. Honest!"

Across the broad expanse of concrete, cars pulled in and out at the gas pumps under a bright white shelter, and their headlights flashed onto Paige's pale face.

"When I got up on the porch and went through the doorway, I saw Annie Sue fighting him."

Her words began in hesitant spates, then quickened into a torrent.

"At first I didn't know if they were, you know, fighting or playing. And then, just as it hit me what was going on and I saw her trying to pull away, the light smashed and I could barely see them anymore. I couldn't hear either. Not her anyhow. Just him. Grunting like an animal. It was awful!"

"A hammer was lying there on a crosspiece and I grabbed it up—all I could think was he was hurting her and I had to make him stop. He had pulled her shorts down and was squirming all over her and she wasn't moving and when he started undoing his own pants, I yelled at him and he came up at me with a roar and I just hit him and hit him and—"

At last the sobs tore through her words and she clung to me while wave after wave of terror and anguish crashed through her body.

"I was so scared," she whispered as the first storm eased. "And my hands were all bloody. He just lay there across the sawbench and didn't move. I could feel the walls closing down on me and I had to get out. Wash my hands. Get clean. I even forgot all about Annie Sue till I was in the car and halfway down the street. It was still raining and getting dark and I drove around the block trying to think what to do. There were some paper napkins under my front seat and I wet one in a puddle by the side of the road and got the worst off my hands and off my steering wheel."

As she talked, she twisted the tissue I had given her into shreds. I fished another out of my pocket and watched it, too, come apart in her restless fingers.

"I couldn't leave Annie Sue there, maybe hurt bad, so I drove back just in time to see you getting out of your car. I knew you'd take care of her, so I went home. I was still in the shower when Cindy called and I just acted like I'd been there the whole time.''

"Your mother didn't notice how upset you were? Your clothes?"

"She wasn't there. She spends a lot of time with my Aunt Faith now that Dad's gone."

Paige swallowed past the lump in her throat and looked at me fearfully. "What'll they do to me, Miss Deborah?"

I sighed. "Who's your family attorney?"

17

Chalk Lines

*"Long straight lines between distant points on surfaces
are marked by snapping a chalk line....For an
accurate snap, never snap the chalk line over a
twenty-foot distance."*

Perry Byrd's attorney was a man who'd run against me in
the primary, Edward "Big Ed" Whitbread, from Widdington
over in the next county. They were old pat-fanny teammates
from way back, but when it came to defending her daughter,
Mrs. Byrd showed that she'd been paying attention over the
years and ignored any cronyistic instructions Perry might be
trying to send from the grave. As soon as Paige finished
telling her what she'd told me, Eleanor Byrd pulled herself
together and called Zack Young, the best criminal lawyer in
Colleton County and the man who'd tied a knot in her
husband's tail more than once over the years.

At Paige's urging, I went with them to the courthouse.
Gwen Utley was the magistrate on duty that night. She
arraigned Paige on a charge of voluntary manslaughter, then
set such a low bail that she might as well have not bothered,
just gone on and released her into Eleanor's custody.

Zack emerged from his first conference with Paige and
immediately announced his young client would not be
pleading guilty.

"This is justifiable homicide, pure and simple," he told me as we walked through the dim echoing halls afterwards. "As clear a case of self-defense as you'll find in any textbook."

He cut his eyes at me. "Conflict with anything she told you earlier?"

I set his mind at rest. "No. When she tried to pull him off Annie Sue, she said he came up toward her with a roar. She may well have thought he'd knock her out and rape her, too."

"You'd testify to that?"

"Certainly."

We came out onto the side street next to the parking lot and he slouched off toward his car. "See you in court, Judge honey."

Zack or Dwight. Bound to be one of 'em picked up on it.

•   •   •

I'd been up since six. A long physical day. Emotionally draining as well. Yet I was too wired to go home.

But I had more than one home, didn't I?

And a lopsided moon was halfway up a star-studded sky, wasn't it?

Without hardly thinking twice, I turned the car toward Cotton Grove; and once I was on Old Forty-Eight south of town, I just let it find its own way back to the farm.

Unless you're from the area and grew up knowing, there's nothing much to indicate that a house might be somewhere up the rutted lane, only a battered tin mailbox with a faded number and no name. The hogwire fence is overgrown with cow-itch vine and Virginia creeper. The posts that once held it are rotted away and the fence is now supported by jack oaks and pines that have grown up and through the rusty hog wire.

The lane curves abruptly through such a thick stand of unkempt trees that even in wintertime, you won't see house lights from the road unless you look back over your shoulder just as Old Forty-Eight crosses Possum Creek. In summer, you won't see that glimmer unless there's a party going on with the whole house lit up like a Christmas tree. Even then you'd have to look hard.

All my car windows were down, and as soon as I turned off the paved road, I killed my radio and doused my lights. Moonlight was enough to pick out the sandy lane. I drove slowly, quietly, slipping into the old game, but the air was too cool and clear for me to win.

Only Saturday night traffic back out on New Forty-Eight between Cotton Grove and Makely let me get as close as I did before the dogs let loose in their pens on the far side of the house, yipping and howling as they heard me approach.

I topped a low ridge and there was the homeplace spread out before me.

White rail fences gleamed in the moonlight. Beyond a broad expanse of grass—new-mown by the smell of it— swept across the level ground and disappeared in thick dark shadows cast by a grove of huge old oaks and fifty-year old pecans. The house itself was just a plain old two-story white wooden box, nondescript and ordinary except that it was surrounded on all sides by deep porches upstairs and down.

Despite the racket the dogs were making, there were no lights in any of the windows. Only the tin roof shone like worn silver in the moonlight.

I switched off the motor and coasted to a stop on the circular dirt drive beneath a magnolia tree my grandmother had planted in 1900 to mark the new century. Its sweet fragrance welcomed me back as gladly as the two dogs that waited silently for me to open my car door. A few more querulous yaps, then the hounds and rabbit dogs out by the barns subsided. Those penned dogs get sold or traded every few months, but the night that Blue and Ladybelle bark at me will be the night I know I've stayed away too long.

They were too well mannered to jump up on my linen skirt or rip my stockings, but they appreciated a hello scratch behind their silky ears.

Five wide wooden steps led up to the shadowy porch and I sat down on the second one to whisper baby talk to the dogs. The smell of cigarette smoke reached me just as I heard the creak of the porch swing from the deepest shadows.

"Didn't wake you, did I?" I asked quietly.

"Nah," said Daddy. "I was just setting here enjoying the night. And thinking about taking a ramble. You want to come?"

"If you'll wait for me to change."

"Take your time. I ain't in no hurry."

*   *   *

Without turning on a light, I went through the house and up the central staircase. None of the curtains were drawn, but the moon was unneeded. I could have walked blindfolded to my old room on the southeast corner.

Maidie keeps fresh linens on my bed, and I leave several changes of clothes in the closet and extra toiletries in the dresser drawers. Like a snake shedding its skin, I peeled off my town clothes in the dark and slipped into jeans and an old cotton sweatshirt. Knowing Daddy's rambles, I felt around on the closet floor for a pair of worn leather boots and tucked my pantlegs down inside their tops against ticks and chiggers.

*   *   *

The caged dogs whined in excitement as we approached, hoping this meant they were going to get to run with us through a night world sensuous with the smell of coons and darting rabbits and slow-trundling possums. They gave soft pleading yaps as we passed.

"Hush!" Daddy said sternly, and they hushed.

Blue and Ladybelle, aristocrats of the farm, strode past without turning their heads.

We walked on down past his vegetable garden, through a cut, past Maidie's little house perched on the last bit of level ground before it sloped down to the creek. No light in her windows either. She and Cletus were early to bed, early to rise and they slept soundly. The dogs never woke them unless they kept it up so long that even the soundest sleeper must come awake, knowing there were trespassers on the land.

It seldom happened.

Cletus's pickup was parked beside the porch. From atop the cab, Maidie's big black tomcat was an inky pool of watchfulness as we passed.

On the other side of the lane lay a small field of melons. Honeydews and swollen cantaloupes gleamed among dark vines, and watermelons were starting to stretch themselves.

The lane wound through another stand of trees and then we were out into a twenty-acre field of tobacco. The waning moon, almost a week past full now, sailed high in the sky, flooding the countryside with silver-blue light. A winelike aroma arose from the very earth itself, compounded of cool dirt, green tobacco, and a light breeze blowing up from the creek.

Of one accord, we stood as still and unmoving as the tall pines behind us and breathed it in. Long moments passed, then an owl swooped down into the middle of a truck row. There was a sudden frantic squeak, followed by a silence all the deeper as the owl gained altitude on noiseless wings. A small dark shape dangled limply from its talons.

The spell broken, Daddy lit a cigarette, and we walked on in the general direction the owl had taken. Another quarter mile brought us out along the edge of a deep irrigation pond. Three people had drowned in it over the years. Tonight, the still water was a sheet of shiny black glass. White moths fluttered toward the moon reflected there and were snapped up by the waiting fish.

Beyond the pond was the beginning of the farm he'd given Seth and Minnie as a wedding present years ago. On tonight's clear air, faint music mingled with distant laughter and raucous speech—Saturday night winding down at the migrant camp that straddled the line between Seth's land and Andrew's.

Thus far, we had walked the two perpendicular sides of a right triangle, now we struck across a fallow field to make a rough hypotenuse back toward the house, less than a mile away. The dogs raced out ahead of us and began casting back and forth through the weeds. Once I would have nearly had to trot to keep up with Daddy's long legs. Tonight, even though my feet had been too long on concrete, the pace was slower. Still, he didn't seem winded, and his pauses were contemplative, not for rest.

Mostly we had walked in silence, enjoying a communion that needed few words. Now as we started up the gentle rise, I remembered a warm May night back when this field was planted in corn. He and I and Mother and the little twins had been out walking in the moonlight, much like this. It had rained all night the night before, a long, much-needed soaking rain, and the sun had shone all afternoon. As we stood at the edge of the field, Daddy suddenly hushed us. "Listen," he'd said.

Crickets and cicadas stridulated all around us and a soft breeze rustled the green plants, but that wasn't what he meant. We strained our ears and there beneath the crickets came faint creaks like the opening and closing of a thousand tiny rusty hinges.

"What is it?" we whispered.

"Corn's growing," Daddy said. "Hear it? Drinking up water with its roots and stretching up its stalks. It'll be six inches taller tomorrow."

"Do you remember a night?" I asked him now.

"What night was that, shug?"

"The night we heard the corn growing?"

He smiled but kept walking. "That was a purty sound, won't it?"

Down the slope from the house, on the same side as the porch swing, lay our family graveyard; and I suddenly realized this had been his destination all along.

Under a blazing sun, the bouquet of all the old roses planted here would have met us downwind. The cool moon silvered the heavy old-fashioned blossoms. It washed away their delicate pinks and flaming yellows, and it paled their heady aroma into a ghostly fragrance.

Inside the low stone wall, we passed the black marble obelisk he'd erected to his father's memory, the act of a boy's defiant pride after revenuers shot out the tires of the older man's truck and left a young family fatherless. The inscription was in deep shadow, but I knew it by heart:

ROBERT ANDREW KNOTT
1879 - 1923
WELL DONE, THOU GOOD AND FAITHFUL SERVANT

Ten feet away was a white marble stone washed in moonlight. Its block letters were so deeply carved that they were as easy to read against the smooth surface as newsprint on a page.

ANNIE RUTH KNOTT
1915 - 1944
HER SONS WILL REMEMBER AND BLESS HER NAME

Growing up, I hadn't given those dates a second thought. Yet here I stood—now past my thirtieth birthday, but still young, still in a state of becoming—and I experienced an almost visceral shock as I realized for the very first time what it meant that she had ended while only in her twenties.

Daddy's words seemed to come from far away. "They say Herman may be in a wheelchair the rest of his life."

I slipped my hand in his. Less for his comfort than for mine.

"I been thinking on his mama all day. She named him after her daddy. You know that?"

"Yes, sir."

"She didn't have much of a life. Nothing but hard work and babies."

"And you," I said loyally.

"Won't much of a prize." He reached out with gnarled fingers and lightly touched the letters of her name. "She was such a little thing. Not much more than a baby when she come to me. Not as old as Annie Sue is right now when she lost our first son."

A newborn lamb knelt atop the miniature stone beside Annie Ruth's. After all these years, its features had weathered smooth, but as a child, I had been enchanted by the lamb and whenever I played here, I brought it flowers or ferns or colored leaves depending on the season.

Mother hadn't known Daddy's first wife; but she was the one who planted the yellow Marshall Niel rose by Annie Ruth's grave, and she was the one who sang lullabies to Annie Ruth's babies and tried to mother her boys.

The summer Mother was dying, she walked me down the slope to show me where she wanted to lie—opposite Annie Ruth with a space left between them for Daddy some day. Her stone was over there now:

SUSAN STEPHENSON KNOTT
I WILL NOT LET THEE GO, EXCEPT THOU BLESS ME

"Were you ever jealous of her?" I asked back then.

Mother's face was serene as she looked over at the white marble marker of the woman who had preceded her in all things on this farm. "Oh, Annie Ruth and I made up our differences years ago."

"Then you *were* jealous."

"Use your head, Deborah!" she answered sharply. "I had her man, I had her sons, I had her place. I was *alive*! What cause did I have for jealousy? No, it was Annie Ruth who was jealous of me at first. But we made it up."

"How?"

My mother had answered my every question that summer, even some I didn't ask. It was as if she wanted to tell me all her secrets before she died. But not this one.

"Annie Ruth knows," she said finally, "and that's enough."

• • •

"Did you love her an awful lot?" I asked Daddy now.

He didn't answer and I wasn't bold enough to ask a second time.

Suddenly a mockingbird's throat-clearing trill fell like a pebble into the pool of stillness around us. Halfway up the gradual slope between the graveyard and house stood a utility pole where generations of mockingbirds had perched to sing in the moonlight an hour or more at the time. This one seemed prepared to carry on the tradition in long liquid bursts of warbled themes. He would repeat a snatch of notes five or six times, catch his breath, and then move on to a new set of sounds. A virtuoso. In his song I heard the squeaky porch swing, a blue jay's querulous complaint, a meadowlark's clear descending whistle, the guttural cry of a cat in heat.

"Some folks faulted me for marrying your mama so quick," Daddy said at last. "Annie Ruth was a good wife for a poor man—a hard worker, careful about getting and saving, whether it was a penny or a mess of peas. She was always laying by. They had it rough back yonder in the marshes. We had it rough too; but even after they killed my daddy, there was still time for fiddling or story-telling. 'What's the good of it?' she used to ask me."

Again his fingers brushed the stone letters of her name. "No, she won't one to stand out in a field of a night and listen to corn grow. Your mama and me, we come down here the night we got married. I told her I guessed Annie Ruth must've known she wouldn't never have enough time to smell the roses, and maybe that's why she worked so hard every minute from first light to last dark. Next day, Sue carried the boys to town and let 'em each pick out a rosebush for their mama. Jack was too little to choose, so she bought this one special from him for Annie Ruth. Marshall Niel. Smells real sweet, don't it?"

"Yes," I said, wondering if he'd answered one of my questions.

18

Brick Walls

"Brick walls are poor absorbers of sound originating within the walls and reflect much of it back into the structure. Sounds caused by impact, as when a wall is struck with a hammer, will travel a great distance along the wall."

I slept in my old bed that night and next morning, I was up early to put on the coffee so I could meet Maidie at the screen door with a mugful, sugared just the way she likes it and so milky it was pale beige. I'd also begun the grits and sausage and had the bread tray and pastry cloth laid out on the counter for her. I know how to make biscuits and nobody's ever choked on them, but it's like I can play the piano good enough for a sing-along, yet wouldn't touch a key if Van Cliburn walked in the room.

Maidie makes biscuits the way Van Cliburn plays the piano.

She's only about fifteen years older than me. I remember the summer she came to my mother's kitchen as a lanky teenager, a temporary fill-in for Aunt Essie, who had gone up north to attend the birth of her daughter's first child. Aunt Essie met a widowed Philadelphia policeman, Maidie met Cletus, and both just stuck where they'd lit.

After Mother died, Maidie continued to keep house for Daddy. Once in a while she'll start nagging me: if I'm not going to get married again and set up a real house this time, how come I don't just come on back home where I belong?

Sunday mornings are relatively peaceful, though. She only gets on my case when she has plenty of time for new arguments on the old themes. On Sundays, she's usually running behind. She has to get Daddy's breakfast, clean up the kitchen, go put on a dress and hat and be sitting in the pew at Mt. Olive A.M.E. Zion church ready to open her hymnbook at ten o'clock sharp. Doesn't give her a whole lot of time to fuss at me.

Besides, today she wanted to hear all about how Paige Byrd was the one who'd killed Carver Bannerman. When I told Daddy the night before while we were sitting on the porch swing after our walk, his first response was, "You reckon her mama'll need help with Zack's fees?"

As far as he was concerned, Paige had just saved the Knotts from having to pay a defense attorney themselves. Sooner or later, one of his sons or grandsons would have found Bannerman and beat him senseless. She simply got there first, so it was only fitting to offer to pay for Zack's services.

"I never heard nothing good about Judge Byrd," said Maidie as we finished eating, "but I reckon he raised his daughter to do right."

"Probably was her mama did the raising," said Daddy, reaching for a final hot biscuit.

"Whoever." Maidie put the last piece of sausage on my plate and carried the dish over to the sink.

I was too full to eat another crumb, so I slipped the sausage inside a biscuit and wrapped them in a piece of plastic wrap. One of my nephews would probably be rummaging in this refrigerator before the sun went down. Teenage boys always seem hungry.

As I put away the blackberry jam, the phone rang and Maidie answered. Her lips curved in an easy smile. "Doing just fine, Miss Zell. How 'bout you? . . . Yes, ma'am, she's here all right . . . You, too, now."

She handed the phone to me and I heard Aunt Zell say, "Deborah? I told her I bet that's where you were."

"Her who?"

"Gladys McGee. I told her I'd track you down and get you to call her. She wants you to sign an exhumation order."

"A *what*?"

"You heard right. She wants to dig up Ralph and have him autopsied. She's convinced he was poisoned, too."

19

Checking and Cracking

*"Checking and cracking describe breaks in the paint
film which are formed as the paint becomes hard
and brittle....Both are the result of stresses in the
paint film which exceed the strength of the
coating."*

I had never been in Gladys McGee's living room before,
but I could have described it beforehand: everything beige
and rose and *pretty*. Every blonde oak tabletop polished,
every piece of glass shining. Beige wall-to-wall, a beige
couch in front of a fireplace that had never burned a single
log, a rose-flowered wing chair on either side of the couch,
a blonde oak coffee table in the middle, and a pink glass
ashtray in the middle of the table. Polished brass candle-
sticks on the sidetable. Pink candles.

A pink-faced Cindy saying, "Mom, *please* don't do
this!"

Cindy's recently married, less-recently pregnant sister
saying, "I can't believe you're going to do this to us. What
is the *point*?"

"The point is that your father may have been deliberately
poisoned."

Gladys sat in one of the floral-upholstered wing chairs

and looked with bewilderment from one daughter to the next. "Don't you girls care?"

"*Mo-ther*." Ginger sighed with exaggerated patience. "Dad had a heart attack. Two doctors said so."

"Not two American doctors," Gladys said stubbornly.

"Dr. Bhagat was born in New Jersey, for God's sake!" said Cindy.

"Cindy Elaine McGee, I will not have you use the Lord's name in that manner!"

"But, Mom—"

"But me no buts, young lady."

I was seated in the other wing chair and she turned to me with stubborn determination. "You remember, Deborah? Just week before last, at your reception—you yourself remarked what a shock it was to everybody when Ralph just dropped dead, remember? And I told you he'd had the summer flu?"

"Yes, but—"

"It was just like what happened with Herman. Nadine says that's what he thought he had at first—summer flu. And here they've found him full of arsenic! If he'd gone on and died, I bet they'd be thinking it was a heart attack, too. Am I wrong?"

"No," I admitted. Ginger gave me a disgusted look and Cindy appeared on the verge of tears.

Gladys leaned forward with a confidential air. "I never did trust that Tink Dupree. He swore it was an honest mistake, but three years in a row? He was just lucky Ralph kept him out of jail. Am I wrong?"

I didn't know what Gladys was talking about, but she was happy to explain.

Ralph had prepared the Coffee Pot's taxes ever since the Duprees bought the place. Last year, he discovered that Tink and Retha Dupree were running an unlicensed sand-wich stand at a flea market every weekend and sequestering their profits. It wasn't a regulated market, just a crossroads out in the country where people gathered on pretty Saturday mornings and sold stuff out of the back of their cars. Since it was so informal and since vendors didn't pay sales taxes on their wares, the Duprees assumed they were somehow exempt, as well. Or so they claimed.

They had been doing this for three years before a horrified Ralph realized they'd been charging expenses to the Coffee Pot, which he'd dutifully listed, which in turn lowered their apparent taxable profits, thereby making him an unwitting accomplice.

"Ralph said if ever one of those hotshot state auditors took a good look at their books, they could say that Ralph was cooking the figures and maybe pull *his* license. Ralph was really mad about it because never in a million years would he've done anything to risk that.

"He told Tink and Retha that if they didn't make voluntary restitution, he was going to turn them in. I forget how much money it took before they were straight with the state."

"Get real, Mother," said Ginger. "Even if the Duprees were mad at Dad, there's no way Tink Dupree would wait almost a year to put arsenic in Dad's iced tea."

"Well, who else would have a reason to?" Gladys asked.

"*Nobody!*" Cindy howled. "He wasn't poisoned. He had a heart attack."

Gladys leaned over and patted her younger daughter's knee. "I know it's hard for you to understand how somebody could deliberately hurt Dad, but you have to be brave, sweetie."

She turned back to me. "And another thing, Deborah. Ava Dupree *says* she ran Bass off and that he's gone back to Georgia, but how do we *know* that's what happened to him? Has anybody heard pea-turkey from him since Ava says he left?"

"I don't believe this," Ginger kept muttering. "I do *not* believe this. Tommy's parents are going to have a cow. This is the tackiest thing anybody's mother ever did."

"Dad would just hate it," Cindy moaned.

"Seems to me certain people have forgotten what else their father would have hated," Gladys said with a significant look at Ginger's bulging tummy and an equally accusing look at Cindy. "Am I wrong?"

"This is totally different," Ginger said huffily. "What Cindy and I did or did not do isn't going to be in the newspaper or on television. This will."

Gladys pursed her lips. "He'd hate it even more if Tink Dupree got away with killing him."

Nothing the girls said was going to dissuade Gladys, and, in a cockeyed way, I didn't blame her. Herman had ingested poison, so had Bannerman; and both, like Ralph, had eaten frequently at the Coffee Pot. If my husband had died as unexpectedly as Ralph had, maybe I'd be putting two and two together same as she was.

"The thing is," I told her, "I can't give you an exhumation order. You'll have to talk to one of the superior court judges."

As I left, she was dialing Ned O'Donnell's home phone. I suggested she inform Dwight or Bo Poole and I gave her Gordon O'Connor's name and number as well. As happy as he'd been to hear about Bannerman's arsenic, he'd probably do handstands if Ralph got added to the list.

Cindy followed me out to my car disconsolately. She'd been on the phone all morning with Annie Sue.

"Paige called her late last night." There was an unconscious tinge of jealousy in her voice that Annie Sue had been called and not her. "I've tried and tried to call Paige, but nobody's answering the phone. What's going to happen to her?"

I explained the elements of self-defense and how unlikely it was that Paige would be convicted under the circumstances.

"I *hate* the way everything's turning out," Cindy said petulantly. "I wish Annie Sue'd never mentioned that old WomenAid house to us."

I was getting a little tired of Cindy's attitude. "Neither Annie Sue nor that house is to blame for Carver Bannerman getting the wrong idea," I said coldly. "And if half the things we heard about that man is true, I personally would be over at the hospital asking for an HIV test."

She drew back as if I'd slapped her, glared at me, then suddenly burst into tears and fled back inside the house.

"Why don't you just go on home and pull wings off flies for a while?" sighed the preacher.

"Sounds like a good idea to me," said the pragmatist.

• • •

Aunt Zell and Uncle Ash were gone when I got there. The puppy was wide awake in his box and let me know he wouldn't mind some company. He still didn't have a name.

After a day or two of comedians (Cosby, Seinfeld, Groucho), Aunt Zell had been trying out imperial Roman names lately (Augustus, Caesar, Pompey), but so far, nothing really struck her as appropriate.

I held the squirming little butterball to my face and said, "So how's it going, Julius?"

He licked my nose.

"Visiting Herman," said a note held to the refrigerator door by a tobacco leaf magnet. "Stevie brought over your tape."

I tucked Marcus Aurelius under one arm and took the video cassette up to my room, stuck it into my VCR, pushed PLAY; then Nero and I settled into my lounge chair to watch. Piled on the low table nearby was a sheaf of rulings that the chief district judge had sent over for all district judges to read. Claudius gnawed on the manila folder while I watched my swearing-in ceremony with only half an eye; especially the part where Ellis Glover was introducing half the county.

Every time I see myself on tape, I vow to quit eating for a week. Much as I love that splashy red print dress, it certainly does emphasize every extra ounce. But I was right, it did make a nice symbolic contrast when I zipped up that black robe over it. I loved the way Stevie had zoomed in on Daddy's face at that moment. He honestly does look like an Old Testament patriarch at times.

I pressed the remote's REWIND and rolled it back a couple of minutes so I could watch his face and Aunt Zell's. She really is very dear. Mother without the wild streak.

Then FAST FORWARD to the reception in the courthouse rotunda. Stevie had gotten there before me and panned over the lace-covered serving table with the silver platters of finger foods, the cutglass punch bowl, the Martha Circle and their helpers—all in readiness before the first guest walked down the row and destroyed the pretty symmetry.

And now, there I am with Frances Tripp, talking, talking every minute. The hugs, the handshakes. Lu Bingham stuffing pecan puffs with one hand and twisting my arm with the other. I found myself smiling all over again.

And there among the dignitaries, guests, and Marthas were Annie Sue, Cindy and Paige, scurrying around to fetch fresh cups of punch and take away the empty ones. How strange to think of all that had happened to those girls in only two weeks!

And look at Herman posing with them, a glass punch cup in one big hand, a plate piled high with cucumber sandwiches in the other. I couldn't bear to think that he might never walk alone again.

Was it possible that his poisoning *had* been deliberate? The Coffee Pot? Had Bass's leaving—*"IF he's left," said the pragmatist*—made Ava or Retha flip out?

I sighed, flicked off the VCR and picked up Judge Longmire's assigned readings.

Heliogabalus fell asleep sucking on my finger.

20

Plugging the Holes

"A nail set is used to set (meaning to countersink slightly below the surface) the heads of nails in finish carpentry. The purpose of setting is to improve the appearance of the work by concealing the nail heads.... The small surface hole above the head is usually plugged with putty."

It was one of the fastest exhumations I ever heard of. I don't know if it was a combination of Dwight, Terry, and Gordon O'Connor all pushing, but by midmorning on Monday, Ralph McGee had been dug up, relevant tissue samples had been collected, and his body was back under six feet of dirt again out at Centenary Cemetery where most of the best people in Dobbs were buried.

Results of the tests would take a while. As I understand it, proving arsenic's in a body is a fairly simple reactive test; proving it *isn't* there is a bit more complicated. Still, we were hoping to hear by Wednesday at the latest.

Rumors were flying all over Dobbs, especially since Bo Poole's office had queried Bass Langley's brother in Georgia and the brother said no, he hadn't heard a thing about Bass supposed to be coming home. "He hain't showed up here. Y'all ask Ava where he mought be?"

"Something 'bout that boy makes me think Bass got all the brains in his family," said Dwight as he went off to query the Duprees again.

Wasn't like he had to fight his way through hordes of lunchtime customers, he told me later. The only ones sitting at the Coffee Pot's counter were two out-of-town salesmen, our in-town drunk, and Gordon O'Connor, who was eating the same thing Ralph McGee usually ordered: a rare hamburger all the way and a glass of sweet iced tea.

In most small places, there's always a cousin or a neighbor's elderly sister who'll tell you—for your own good, of course—what folks are whispering behind your back and Dobbs was no different. Retha was red-eyed, Tink seemed bewildered, and Ava acted belligerent when Dwight came in to ask them where else Bass might be, since he wasn't in Georgia, far as they could tell.

"What's the matter, Deputy?" said Ava. "You think we poisoned him, too? You want to look out back in the dumpster?"

"Now, Ava—"

"Mrs. Langley to you, Deputy Bryant," she snapped.

"Now, Ava," said Tink. "No need to get huffy with the customers. What'll you have, Dwight?"

Up until that minute, Dwight says he hadn't really given it much thought as to whether the Coffee Pot actually was the source of the arsenic. He hesitated and saw Gordon O'Connor watching him through those shiny glasses. The epidemiologist picked up the succulent hamburger Retha had made him and bit into it with exaggerated relish.

("Well, he could, couldn't he?" Dwight asked me defensively. "They certainly weren't going to poison somebody from the Health Department.")

"I could sure use some iced tea, thank you, Tink."

"You like it sweet, don't you?"

But that far, Dwight was not prepared to go. He has a flat belly but he patted it anyhow and said he thought he'd better start cutting back on sugar.

"Humph!" said Ava and went outside to wash the windows, the better to glare at the townspeople who hadn't stopped in for their usual morning snacks.

* * *

While everyone might've been walking around the Duprees, Paige Byrd was suffering from too much attention. She and her mother had unplugged all the phones and fled to her Aunt Faith's house the night before. Friends and relatives quickly figured it out though, and by noon on Monday, they had crowded into Faith Taylor's house to lend aid and comfort and hear all the titillating details firsthand.

The consensus seemed to be that Paige had done what she had to when she defended her honor and Annie Sue's; and while it was too bad that she'd panicked and run, well, shoot! She was only sixteen, not even over her daddy's death good, and had never said boo to a goose. Who knew if they'd've done any smarter?

Paige stood it as long as she could, then called Annie Sue, who swung by on her way to run a line of 220 wire for a customer's new air-conditioning unit. The customer was an elderly farm woman who, after her husband's early demise, had managed eight acres of tobacco, thirty acres of sweet potatoes, plus the usual corn and soybeans till her sons were old enough to take over the farm.

No big deal, right?

But she thought it was just wonderful the way young women today could do so many things. Imagine being electricians! She was so impressed. And couldn't she just fix them a plate of cookies and a Pepsi?

* * *

On Tuesday morning, I awoke to the sound of Mr. Ou's lawn mower. The deep back gardens are overlooked by screened verandas that run the width of the house upstairs and down, and I pushed open my bedroom doors and stepped outside. A lacy screen of clematis shaded my part of the veranda and I looked down onto beds of splashy summer flowers at the height of their colors and riotous beauty.

Aunt Zell has never gone in for exotic plantings. She

prefers sturdy common annuals and old-fashioned perennials: zinnias of every color and height from multicolored miniatures to four-foot red giants, clear yellow marigolds, white and pink cosmos, blue salvia, more blue in the speedwell, clumps of old-time daylilies, and stiff purple phlox.

In the middle of the yard, in a long diagonal from the house, is Uncle Ash's lap pool, forty feet long by six feet wide and only four feet deep. A narrow footbridge arches over the center to a weathered gazebo almost hidden in its tangle of purple clematis.

Along the side wall, rhododendrons had finished blooming, but hydrangeas sported deep blue blossom heads bigger than honeydew melons.

Except for a wide swath that meanders through the flowerbeds and strips each side of the lap pool, there isn't much grass here in the back; and one of Mr. Ou's adolescent sons guided the power mower along the path while he and another child weeded and a third boy used an electric edger to trim where the mower couldn't reach. A much younger child gravely lopped off dead flower heads with a pair of hand clippers.

All wore khaki shorts and shirts, brown leather sandals, and cloth hats against the July sun. Mr. Ou himself was so young that I found myself suddenly taking another look at the three older boys. They were quite close in height and build. Too close, in fact, to be brothers unless they were triplets. Perhaps cousins?

In the mad scramble to get out of the refugee camps, Mr. Ou, hardly more than a boy himself, might well have wound up claiming younger brothers or nephews as his own sons. Difficult to imagine all the hardships they must have endured before fetching up here in Colleton County—exiled to a strange land, their future entrusted to strangers.

(*By the rivers of Babylon, there we sat down, yea, we wept, when we remembered Zion.*)

I wondered what his work had been in his homeland and wished his English or my French were better so that we could speak about something other than the weather and how he was feeling.

Aunt Zell had started putting the puppy out on the grass inside a portable fence after his morning feed so he could start his training, and the youngest Ou child had discovered him. He scooped up Brinkley/Donaldson/MacNeil/Lehrer (Aunt Zell thought he'd cocked his head with interest when the news came on last night) and spoke to the others in lilting phrases that I took to be a Cambodian dialect.

There were broad grins and smiling replies as he hefted the puppy in an oddly familiar gesture I couldn't quite place. A stray breeze rippled my gown and one of the boys spotted the motion. He hissed a quick warning to the young one, who even more quickly returned Cronkite to his pen. The others paused and gave me half-bows of formal greeting.

"*Bon jour*," I called down. "*C'est un bel matin, non?*"

"Good morning," replied Mr. Ou. "Is beauty day, yes. Very hot soon."

Another round of smiles and nods and I went inside to shower and dress. I admired the courage and tenacity that had allowed Mr. Ou to survive and now, even begin to flourish in a modest way. Lu told me that she'd signed up enough home owners for his services that by next spring he would probably be able to afford a riding mower for bigger yards. Dobbs can be suspicious of strangers and foreigners and I was proud they'd let the Ou family settle in without any friction. Cultural clashes can sometimes—

"*Oh, dear Lordy!*" exclaimed the pragmatist, who often puts two and two together a step ahead of my conscious mind.

"*Now don't go jumping to conclusions,*" the preacher warned nervously.

"*Who's jumping? And why are you wringing your hands if you haven't already jumped, too?*"

I found Lu Bingham's private number in my address book and when she answered sleepily on the fourth ring, I said, "I have to be in court in exactly one hour and twenty-two minutes. If you want to keep Mr. Ou from having a cross burned on his front doorstep, you better get here in fifteen."

I skipped my shower, threw on some clothes and hurried downstairs.

"Is something wrong?" asked Aunt Zell when I came barreling through the kitchen.

"No, no. Lu Bingham's coming over to help me talk to Mr. Ou. There's a question about wages," I lied, knowing the mention of money would keep her inside.

Aunt Zell would never ask how much I was paying for her anniversary gift, but she did say, "Whatever you're giving him, dear, he's worth every penny. He and those boys do *such* a good job."

*   *   *

One thing about working in a crisis center, it does seem to give quick reflexes. Lu was still in bed when I called, yet she made it in ten minutes. I guess she was expecting, from the tone of my voice, to find an angry mob storming Aunt Zell's backyard. Instead, there was only Mr. Ou and his boys, toiling peacefully in the early morning sun.

"I ran two red lights," she began indignantly. "What's the big emergency?"

"I need you to translate, okay?"

"If you'd paid more attention in Mrs. Jefferson's French class instead of flirting with Howard Med—"

"You gonna lecture or listen?" I interrupted.

We walked across the narrow arched bridge to the vine-shaded gazebo and Lu asked Mr. Ou to join us.

He came, but he looked apprehensive; and when I gestured for him to sit, he did so gingerly.

"Tell him my aunt has been very pleased with his work," I said.

I waited till she had translated and he had warily acknowledged the compliment, then said, "Ask if he understands that I'm a judge, an officer of the court and bound by the laws of this state?"

She started to protest, took one look at my face and asked him.

Mr. Ou nodded and looked even more apprehensive, if that were possible.

"I've read that dogs are considered great delicacies in your country. Even cats."

Lu gave me an outraged glare. "Of all the stereotyped, xenophobic, racist—"

I glared right back. "Why does a recognition of basic cultural differences always get labeled racism? If I were a racist, I'd have someone from the sheriff's department over going through the bones in his compost heap. I called *you*, not a reporter from the *Ledger*, didn't I? So quit hanging insulting labels on me and ask him, okay?"

"Oh, God!" said Lu and hastily translated.

Mr. Ou listened, but said nothing. He didn't have to. Not after I'd seen that youngest boy heft Brokaw the way I've seen Aunt Zell heft a supermarket chicken or pork roast a thousand times.

"In this country, cats and dogs are pets. People here would be horrified and outraged if they knew you had cooked one." I tried not to let myself think of Aunt Zell's Goldie. Of Miss Sallie's Queenie. Or, heaven forbid, Alice Castleberry's registered bull terrier.

"There is no law in North Carolina that actually forbids the eating of these animals," I continued, "but a person who took another's pet could certainly be prosecuted for theft, perhaps even for cruelty to animals."

As Lu translated, Mr. Ou suddenly began to speak and even with my limited French, I understood a protest when I heard one.

Lu confirmed it. "He swears there was no cruelty. Death was painless and swift."

"Then he admits it."

"Not exactly. It's all couched in the conditional voice."

"Well, put this in the imperative: it must stop. No more. If I hear of another single dog or cat disappearing, he and his family will be charged. Even if there's no evidence, just the accusation will make his neighbors shun them, get his children taunted in school, certainly make people quit hiring him. Some Americans get more upset over abused cats than abused children. His very life might even be threatened if certain men were to hear of it."

"These the same men who eat squirrels and possums and shoot a Bambi for their freezer every fall?" Lu asked sardonically.

"Don't try to justify or rationalize, just tell him what I said, and put in as many cultural taboos as you can."

There was a long silence when she finished, then Mr. Ou spoke quietly for several minutes.

"He's very sorry if he's done broken our laws and offended you. It's been very difficult feeding his sons. Boys need meat to grow strong, he says, and there was not enough money to buy it. Now, thanks to his lawn service business, he no longer has to forage for meat, but can buy it at a grocery store. He promises it will not happen again. He's very grateful to you for not bringing him to court, and to show his gratitude, he'd like to do this yard for free from now on."

"That sounds suspiciously like a bribe," I said. "Tell him, thanks but no thanks. If he wants to atone, let him put in a yard at the WomenAid house."

* * *

As we walked back to the house, Aunt Zell came out to ask Lu to tell Mr. Ou how really pleased she was with his work and to express her hope that he was finding America a good place to live. She had a small box of cookies for the youngest child. "Animal crackers," she beamed.

I thought of the child's sharp little teeth biting off the head of a tiger and decided to skip breakfast and go directly to court.

21

Framing Around Openings

> *"Where a floor opening occurs (such as a stairway opening), the parts of the common joists which would extend across if there were no opening must be cut away."*

Lu Bingham and I crossed paths again sooner than I'd expected. When I walked into court after lunch Wednesday afternoon, there she was sitting in the first row behind the prosecutor's table.

Tracy Johnson was ADA that day. She's tall and willowy, with short blonde hair and gorgeous eyes, which get downplayed with oversized glasses when she's prosecuting. Tracy loves shoes as much as I do, but because of her height, she usually settles for flats and low heels. Some judges of the male persuasion don't like having to look up to a woman.

Shortly before four, Tracy called line thirty-seven. "Jerry Dexter Trogden. Assault on a female."

There was something awfully familiar about his Fu Manchu mustache, that bright green-and-purple dragon tattooed on his right forearm, and the swaggering flourish with which he signed the waiver of counsel.

"Weren't you in here a couple of weeks ago?" I asked.

"Yeah, but she took up the charges," he said.

"She" was the shame-faced teenager sitting close to Lu for moral support. Skinny white blonde. Hair pulled back by a bright pink scarf that matched her cheap summer cotton dress. I sort of remembered that she'd been as pretty as her dress, a shallow-rooted flower doomed to fade just as quickly as that poorly made garment would fade and go limp after two or three washings. She certainly wasn't pretty this afternoon. There were stitches both in her lower lip and over her eye, her face was cut and swollen, and her bruises were as purple and green as the dragon tattooed above the fist that had punched her out.

As Tracy laid out the charges, Jerry Dexter Trogden drummed his fingers on the tabletop before him and kept a sneer on his face.

"*That sneer could be a mask of apprehension,*" *the preacher reminded me.*

"*Yeah,*" *agreed the pragmatist.* "*Fear that he's finally going to get what's coming to him.*"

"*You are honor-bound to listen to both sides before you judge.*"

"*Fine with me. Give the bastard enough rope so we can hang him in good conscience.*"

The testimony of Tammy Epps was as old as the Bible she swore on, as new and unnewsworthy as the back page in tomorrow's paper. They had lived together as lovers for two years, he became violent when drinking, each time he promised he would never hit her again. Last week, she finally realized he would probably wind up killing her if she stayed. When she tried to leave, this is what he did: Exhibit A, Polaroid pictures taken before her gashes were stitched.

"Your witness," said Tracy.

Trogden had watched enough television to think he was Perry Mason.

He wasn't.

His defense? Innocent because of extenuating circumstances: she was his woman, she had no cause to leave, he had a right to keep what was his.

The longer he talked, the angrier he became. I explained

contempt of court; and when he began repeating himself, I asked if he had anything new to add.

"Nothing, 'cepting I don't think I ought to go to jail for trying to hold on to what's mine."

"How far did you get in school, Mr. Trogden?"

"I finished," he said belligerently.

"Then you've heard of the Emancipation Proclamation?"

"That the one that says women got the same rights as men?"

"No, Mr. Trogden, that's the one that says slavery is abolished. No one may own another human being."

He subsided and I pronounced him guilty of assault.

"I ain't going to jail for just 'cause she marks easy," he muttered.

"If I rule you in contempt, Mr. Trogden, I guarantee you *will* see the inside of a jail." I looked at Tracy. "What's the state asking, Ms. Johnson?"

She suggested that Trogden pay Ms. Epps's medical bills and be made to stay away from her permanently.

"Stand up, Mr. Trogden," I said. "This court orders that you be imprisoned for a term of ninety days, sentence—"

Before I could finish saying that the sentence would be suspended on condition that he pay court costs, a hundred-dollar fine, and Ms. Epps's medical bills, and that he promise not to go near her, Trogden roared to his feet and snatched up the Bible lying there in front of him.

"I ain't going to no jail!" he howled and rared back and heaved the Bible at me as hard as he could.

I ducked instinctively and it slammed into the wall behind me with so much force that one of the hard corners left a dent in the wood paneling.

Officer Mayleen Richards, a Dobbs police rookie, and an elderly bailiff wrestled him to the floor and snapped handcuffs on him.

"See?" cried Tammy Epps and promptly burst into tears in Lu's arms.

Trogden came up from the floor snarling curses for every woman that ever walked, and I changed his suspended sentence to an active one and had him removed from my courtroom.

"Court's adjourned till tomorrow morning," I said.

"Oyez, Oyez, Oyez," the bailiff intoned. "This honorable court stands adjourned until tomorrow morning at nine o'clock. God save the state and this honorable court."

"Good reflexes, Your Honor," said Phyllis Raynor.

* * *

As I left the courthouse, I ran into Julia Lee and her miniature poodle. (Ever since Miss Sallie's Queenie disappeared, Julia stopped leaving CoCo unattended.) CoCo was happy to see me, but Julia was flushed with indignation. "That Health Department man! I'm a good mind to have John Claude sue him for slander."

"O'Connor? What's he done?" I asked, shaking the dainty paw that CoCo offered me.

"Somebody told him our Martha Circle catered Ginger McGee's wedding and he's over there in First Methodist's kitchen right this minute. He's even saying that if arsenic does turn up in Ralph's body, he'll want to know the names of all the women who did both your reception and Ginger's, too. A *Martha*!" She took a deep breath to steady herself. "So what I need to know is was that Bannerman person at your reception? Gladys says he certainly wasn't invited to theirs."

"I have no idea, Julia." There had been such a crush of people and at that time I didn't know Carver Bannerman from Adam's housecat. "It was a public event though, so I suppose it's possible he could have stepped in for a cookie if he was here at the courthouse. Want me to ask Annie Sue and her friends if they noticed?"

"Please," she said crisply. "The Martha Circle does too much good with the funds they raise to have its image besmirched. Heel, CoCo."

Obediently, CoCo heeled and followed Julia on into the courthouse.

I continued down the side steps and in through the basement entrance to the sheriff's department to see if Dwight wanted to come have a quick drink before I had to drive Aunt Zell and Uncle Ash to the airport.

He was standing in the doorway of Bo Poole's office and he and Bo both grinned soon as they saw me. Might've known the bailiff wouldn't waste time telling them every detail.

"I know you're still new at the job," Dwight said, "but judges are supposed to *throw* the book, not duck it."

"You laugh, but those hardback Bibles ought to be changed to paperbacks. I could have been injured for life. Any word from the lab yet?"

"Nope," said Bo. "They've got so much on their plate it looks like Friday before we hear for sure. How's Herman?"

"We're real worried about his legs," I admitted. "They still don't know if his nerve damage is permanent. He's getting therapy, but they're also teaching him how to maneuver in a wheelchair."

"And that joker from Environmental Health still can't figure out where he got that arsenic," Bo fumed.

"Got to give him A for effort though," I said. "Julia Lee's mad because he's over at First Methodist's kitchen right this minute."

"How come? Was Bannerman at your swearing-in? Ralph sure as hell wasn't."

I explained about how the Marthas had catered his daughter's wedding, and we kicked it around a few minutes.

"Y'all locate Bass Langley yet?"

"Tell you the truth, we hadn't been looking all that hard," Dwight admitted. "His brother doesn't seem worried, and Ava says she doesn't want him back."

"Maybe you should take her up on her offer and check out that dumpster back of the Coffee Pot," I said tartly.

Dwight thought he had too much paperwork to knock off just then. All the same, when I said maybe I'd go see if Gordon O'Connor had found anything, he said he reckoned he'd come along with me.

The church was only two blocks away, but by the time we got there, O'Connor was gone. As he walked me back to my car, Dwight said, "What time you getting back from the airport?"

"I don't know. Nine or nine-thirty, probably. Why?"

"How 'bout I come over later and keep you company? You make us some popcorn and I'll bring that video you've been wanting to see."

"*The Last Wave*? Hey, great!" I'd been trying to track down a copy for months. "Where'd you find it?"

"Washington."

"*Little* Washington had *The Last Wave*?"

"Not Little Washington. Washington, D.C. I got tired hearing you whine so I asked a friend to UPS it. It'd better be as good as you say it is."

"Better!" Touched by his remembering, I impulsively added, "Listen. If I tell you something, will you promise you'll keep it to yourself?"

His eyes narrowed. "What've you done now?"

"Promise first."

"Okay, I promise, even though I can tell by that look on your face I'm going to regret it."

He listened with growing incredulity as I told him of my encounter with Mr. Ou that morning.

"Jesus H., Deborah! You know how many phone calls we've gotten about those missing dogs? Miz Castleberry's in my ear every morning; Doug Woodall's wife's uncle— you can't just take the law into your own hands like that."

"Oh, come on, Dwight. What would be gained by hauling him into court at this point? It won't bring those dogs back. All it'd do is cause hard feelings. Besides, think how you'd feel if you got plopped down in India and couldn't afford to buy meat for you and Cal. You think you wouldn't soon be inviting one of those sacred cows to come home with you some dark night?"

He shook his head at me. "Don't tell me any more secrets, okay?"

I was hurt. "I thought you'd be glad to know you don't have to worry about any more pets going missing. You always say I don't tell you things."

"And this is what you start with? Barbecued beagles?" He was already heading down the basement steps. "I didn't hear a thing you said. Remember that. See you at nine-thirty."

"Well, he's got a point," said the preacher, smoothing

the wrinkles in his favorite hairshirt. "You probably should have given Mr. Ou some meaningful community service. Maybe some hours out at the animal shelter."

"That sorry place?" snorted the pragmatist from the depths of his comfortable lounge chair. *"Ninety-eight percent of the animals taken out there get put down and their bodies burned. Would Mr. Ou see that as a civics lesson or a waste of good protein?"*

• • •

When I got home, Aunt Zell was still trying to decide between black silk slacks, which would let her forget about heels and hose, or a champagne-colored cocktail dress that would require an extra bag. She was as flustered as a teenage bride packing for her honeymoon.

Annie Sue had brought over the adapter plugs that Nadine had used with her hairdryer when she and Herman took that Holy Land tour with their church group a few years back, and Cindy and Paige were with her.

The three girls had bonded closer than ever, but there were lines of strain in all three faces as things got more weirdly complicated with each passing day. Paige had killed a rapist; because of Paige, Annie Sue had escaped rape but now faced the possibility that Herman would be permanently disabled; Cindy's father had been exhumed and, along with Herman and Carver Bannerman, might have been the victim of a successful poisoning attempt. Yet, they were each trying to act as if the most interesting thing in their lives was Aunt Zell's first trip to Paris.

"I'm going to bring back a bottle of real French perfume for each one of y'all," Aunt Zell promised as she hung the cocktail dress back in her closet and opted for a black sequinned top for the slacks. She tucked it in next to something pale pink and lacy.

"Why, Miss Zell," giggled Annie Sue, fluffing out one of the skimpiest nightgowns you'd ever hope to see.

"Oh, it's *beautiful!*" sighed Paige.

Aunt Zell laughed. "Isn't that the silliest thing?"

In went her makeup kit and she was just zipping the bag when Uncle Ash came in, handsome in navy linen blazer and gray slacks.

"All packed?" he asked.

"Ready!"

"You sure you want to make that long drive, honey?" Uncle Ash asked me for the third time. "I really can leave our car at the airport. Five days won't cost that much."

"Don't be silly," I said. Also for the third time. "I'll want to hear a full report while it's fresh."

The girls each picked up a bag and as the four of us waited in the side driveway for Aunt Zell and Uncle Ash to make a final round of the house to see if there were something they needed to tell me about besides the puppy, I remembered something myself.

"That epidemiologist that's trying to find a common denominator," I told the girls. "He asked me if Carver Bannerman was at my swearing-in reception. Did y'all see him there?"

Furrowed brows and slow headshakes as they tried to recall a man they hadn't yet met themselves two weeks ago.

I had a sudden flash of brilliance. "Stevie's video!"

"Huh?" said Annie Sue.

"Stevie," I reminded her. "He was everywhere with that camera of his. Remember? If Bannerman was at the reception, Stevie's bound to have caught him on the tape. It's sitting up there on top of my VCR and soon as I get back from the airport, I'll run through it and check it out."

As Uncle Ash and Aunt Zell came through the veranda door, I called, "Don't lock it. Dwight's coming over to watch a video with me tonight and I told him to go on in if I wasn't back yet."

Annie Sue's truck was blocking my car, so the girls wished my aunt and uncle bon voyage and drove off into the sunset as I picked up one of the bags and said, "Listen, Uncle Ash—"

22

Finish Work

*"Most of the finish work involves items of essential
practical usefulness, such as the door and
window frames, the doors and windows themselves,
the roof covering, and the stairs."*

My car was out of sight, locked inside the garage.

Uncle Ash and Aunt Zell were so caught up in the
romance of their Parisian adventure, that they didn't question my lie that I'd suddenly remembered an important
meeting I simply had to attend if I expected the fall election
to rubber-stamp my appointment. If anything, they seemed
sort of pleased to start the first leg of their trip alone.

Now I sat alone in the dark parlor of their quiet house.
Twilight shadowed the rooms, but except for dim night lights,
all the lamps were off and they'd stay off till someone came.

Dwight? Or—?

I hoped it would be Dwight. I hoped it had been my
imagination out on the drive an hour earlier, that involuntary
startled widening of the eyes, the sudden withdrawn look of
intense concentration as if she were trying to remember.

Me? Did the camera catch me?

Clever to have done it then. If she had. In such a crush of
people, who would remember which girl served whom?

Now that they could drive, the three of them were always together this year, in and out of one another's houses, one another's lives, invited to all the ceremonies, caught up in their emotions and hurts—the intense, nonsexual but *passionate* and all-consuming love that exists between adolescent best friends.

Katie Tyson. I remember the night she cried herself sick up in my bedroom, unable to tell me about the disgusting thing that blighted her life; the anger and anguish I'd felt because I knew she would be shamed even further if she told me—even me!—why she cried. I loved her so much. Would I have killed for her if I'd known for sure that a father, brother, uncle, or preacher had violated her trust?

Once, and only once, I asked my father if he'd ever killed anyone.

"No," he'd said. "Wanted to a couple of times, meant to once, but never did."

And there was Mother, who turned her back on all her chances, burned every bridge, and ran off with a fiddle-playing bootlegger.

And I'm enough their daughter that yes, I've had it in me to dance with the devil a time or two over the years.

Not that Katie gave me a chance to find out if I was ready to dance right then. She walked out of our house that dark November night and drove her mother's car straight into the headlights of an eighteen-wheeler and never touched her brakes.

Everybody else thought it was an accident.

So much ugliness, even back then. Stuff I only vaguely suspected in my safe protected world. How had I escaped? What kept things sane and normal in our household? I was the only girl child in a family of randy, roughneck boys, but never did one of them look on me with lust in his heart. Never did my own father touch me lasciviously.

Did hers?

Oh God, *which* her?

For a moment, adolescence blurred with the grown-up here and now and was overlaid with all the pathological nastiness I'd seen and heard in too many courtrooms.

Dusk deepened to darkness, and the streetlight down the block cast black shadows on the sidewalk.

Had she lost her nerve? Or were her nerves strong enough to do nothing, leave it alone, assume there was nothing incriminating on the tape, or that I'd miss it if there were because I'd be busy looking for Carver Bannerman? Surely she was too young for such self-control. Killers more mature than she were unable to leave it alone, to resist that final tidying up of loose ends.

If I ever do kill anyone, I'll just do it and walk away and never look back.

Looking back trips you up.

It was barely dark good. She'd have to get free of the other two first, then drive back alone, park her car on a nearby street, and come the last little bit on foot.

But she had to come soon or risk running into Dwi—

The back veranda door squeaked and I froze.

I'd unplugged the night light here in the front parlor but the one in the hallway was enough to light her way to the central staircase, and she hurried past without a glance in my direction.

The tape atop my VCR was clearly dated and labeled. Not the real one, of course, but I didn't think she'd take the time to watch it here.

Indeed, she was up there only a minute or two before I saw her dark shape on the stairway again. I waited till she was passing the parlor's arched doorway, then switched on the lamp beside me.

"I see you found it."

The cassette fell from her nerveless fingers, but she stooped and snatched it up again and clutched it to her chest.

"I—I thought you—"

"No," I said gently.

She looked down at the tape.

"You poisoned Herman," I said. "Why?"

Her shoulders slumped in defeat.

"He made her cry a lot," she whispered. "Like *my* father. He didn't trust her. That's what she always said. I thought she meant like Dad didn't trust me—always after me and after me, and talking about sex and what boys wanted and making it all dirty.''

"Like Carver Bannerman? You gave him poison, too, didn't you?"

"He was filth!" she said indignantly. "Married. A pregnant wife and not caring who else he made pregnant—! Dad was right. That's all any of them want. To put their hands in our pants, put their things in our—"

A great shudder of repulsion shook her.

Dwight says I never think.

He's wrong. I *do* think. It's just that I always think people will act logically.

Instead of bursting into tears and confessing that she'd administered several doses of arsenic to her father and Herman, and had slipped Carver Bannerman a first dose, too, her face filled with a dread and horror I'll see in my nightmares the rest of my life as it finally dawned on her what she was facing. In that instant, she turned and fled for the back door.

By the time I got to the veranda, she was nowhere in sight. Her car could be parked anywhere. I flicked on the yard lights and forced myself to stop and listen.

Over there! Crashing through Aunt Zell's flowers.

I raced down the grassy path and saw her balanced on the rail of the arched bridge that spanned the pool. She hesitated for only a second, then pushed off from the rail with all the force she could muster to dive straight down.

Headfirst.

Into a pool she knew was only four feet deep.

I splashed into the water after her, but when I got there and turned her face up, blood was staining the water from the top of her head, and she wasn't breathing.

"Be careful!" screamed the preacher. "Her neck could be broken."

"Her neck may be broken, but if you don't get her out of the water and begin CPR, she's going to die here and now," the pragmatist said.

It was the worst dilemma I've ever faced.

As gently as I could, I laid her over the coping of the pool with her legs still in the water and performed the Heimlich maneuver till I thought her lungs were emptied of water, then I pulled her all the way up and started CPR till finally, finally she began to breathe again.

Blood was a dark halo on the white tile around her head.

A phone, I thought. The rescue squad.

And then blessedly I heard Dwight's car door slam.

•   •   •

Another Intensive Care waiting room.

"Why? O God, why?" cried Eleanor Byrd as we waited to hear if Paige's head injuries included a broken neck.

"She thought Herman was doing to Annie Sue what Perry did to her," I said.

"*No!*" she said wildly. "Perry never touched Paige. Never!" But her eyes couldn't meet mine.

I might never know exactly what Perry Byrd did to push their daughter over the edge, but I'd bet every dime I'll ever make that she did.

Dwight came back then and took me out of there. I was still in the damp, chlorine-smelling clothes I'd worn over in the ambulance.

"I didn't get a chance to tell you before," he said as we drove the short distance home through the hot, still night. "The lab report came right after you left my office this evening. No arsenic in Ralph McGee's body."

"They dug up the wrong man. It's Perry Byrd that should be exhumed."

"You think?"

"Yes. Remember when he had that first stroke and everybody thought he was going to die? She must have realized that if he did die, she'd be free of him. Because he was getting better, remember? Then suddenly, he just keeled over again."

For the last hour, I'd been facing the fact that I got Perry Byrd's seat mainly because his daughter had poisoned him.

"I can sort of understand why she'd slip arsenic in

Bannerman's drink after he laid Cindy, but why poor old Herman? Was she starting an orphans' club or something?''

"She almost told me the night she confessed to killing Bannerman—and isn't that bizarre? Start to kill a man with slow poison and then wind up doing him in with a hammer.''

"Herman," Dwight reminded me, turning down my street.

"Herman," I said, feeling tears begin to slide down my cheek. "She did it for Annie Sue and I wish to God Annie Sue never had to know. Because if she hadn't dramatized it, if she hadn't—if—"

"Hey," said Dwight. He parked the car in the side driveway, cut the motor, handed me his handkerchief, and opened his arms.

I was grateful for both.

"Paige misunderstood the way Herman yells and how Annie Sue always overreacts. If you ever heard her, you'd think he was David Copperfield's wicked stepfather and kept her chained in the basement. Because Annie Sue was the first best friend she'd ever had—you know about teen-age girls and their best friends?"

"Tell me," he said, gently smoothing my hair.

"It's hard to find the words because it isn't sexual, even though it's almost as romantic as first love. Oh hell, who am I fooling? It *is* first love! With all that pre-Freudian intensity. Flirting with each other. Telling innermost secrets. The hurts and jealousies if you think she likes another girl better than you. You spend hours analyzing hairstyles and clothes, and then you spend even more time analyzing each other. You know her thoughts and moods as well as you know your own—*better* than your own maybe, because at that age you usually don't like your body very much and you certainly don't like the dark disturbing thoughts that are rolling around in your head. And you're protective as the devil if anything or anyone threatens her. I guess she thought Herman was abusing Annie Sue and, since she'd already stopped the abuse in her own life, why not make Herman sick and stop it in Annie Sue's?"

"Not kill him?"

I shrugged. "She could have just given him one big dose

instead of several small ones. Maybe she thought if he felt a little sick, he'd leave Annie Sue alone. At the hospital Saturday night, though. That's when she finally realized there was nothing perverted between Annie Sue and Herman, and that's the real reason she couldn't stay in that hospital room.''

 •   •   •

They found Paige's car parked in front of Miss Sallie Anderson's the next day. An empty bottle of Terro Ant Killer was in a little box under the front seat.

Her neck wasn't broken, but it was four days before she came out of the coma. There's residual paralysis on her left side and the fingers of her left hand tend to curl, but they're hoping therapy will help. She says she doesn't remember a thing about that night and that these past few months have a dreamlike quality, as if they happened to someone else. Paige doesn't deny what she's done, she just doesn't quite understand why.

Considering the severity of her head injury, her doctors say she's probably telling the truth. Zack Young's counting on their testimony when she goes to trial this fall. He thinks it'll be a mitigating factor in her sentencing.

Annie Sue and Cindy have rallied around. They say Paige isn't quite the same. Quieter. Maybe not quite as sharp as before she hurt her head. "But still real sweet."

They don't hear the pity in their own young voices.

23

Trim Work

"The part of the finish which is purely ornamental is called trim."

BeeBee Powell's house was dedicated at a ceremony the weekend before Labor Day.

Living room, large kitchen, three small bedrooms, one-and-a-half baths. The siding was painted pale creamy yellow with black shutters and porch railings, and a burnt orange door. Inside, everything was fresh and clean and sparkled almost as brightly as Kaneesha's snaggle-toothed grin.

She and Anthony Carl had colored two bright THANK YOU!! posters and hung them by the front door.

Retha Dupree and Ava donated the Coffee Pot's services and catered a picnic in the yard. (After pulling a two-week drunk in South Carolina, Bass Langley had sweet-talked his way back into Ava's good graces and was back lifting and toting and washing dishes again.)

Mr. Ou hadn't put in the grass yet, but neat borders of liriope lined the new front walk, and azaleas were mixed with Korean boxwoods around the foundation. People were trying not to step on anything.

Everyone who worked on the house was there, including a few who merely donated money or materials. Not Paige, though. She was at a rehab place over in Durham, not far from the detox center where Graham Ogburn had stashed his son to wait for his jury trial.

I could thank Zack Young for that nugget of information because there was certainly no on-the-record mention of young Layton at the dedication. This was blue sky PR all the way. Lu introduced the owner of Tri-County Building Supply, and the *Ledger*'s photographer bounced strobe flashes all over the house as Graham Ogburn announced his intention to furnish all the materials for a second house—"At cost, ladies and gentlemen! In honor of what family values can accomplish when a whole community pulls together!"

(Applause.)

Clapping loudest were Kimmer Norris and her three kids, who'd been promised that house.

The women of the community college's cabinetry class had donated their labor on the cabinet work and, in the end, they took pity on some of their male classmates who felt discriminated against, so it wasn't totally an all-woman project after all. By then, no one really cared. The point had been made.

Annie Sue and Cindy hung in till the end. They could have ducked out without blame, but Annie Sue was determined to finish what she'd begun and Cindy wouldn't admit she couldn't handle it, too.

As each person's contribution was called out and Knott Electrical was recognized, Herman didn't try to stand, just reached back for Nadine's hand on the wheelchair handle and made a joint wave. They smiled proudly when Annie Sue was named, but there was still a worried look in their eyes.

And with reason.

Annie Sue's done a lot of growing up this last month, but she knows how much blame she deserves for what happened to Herman and she's quit dramatizing anything. No more stomping off in anger, but no more flamboyance either.

Not so oddly, I think Herman sort of misses it. More than what he's lost, he's troubled by what Annie Sue has lost.

• • •

The following Saturday, I was still at the breakfast table when Dwight came by to pick me up. K.C. Massengill was having an end-of-the-summer weekend party at her lake cottage, and he'd been invited, too.

The puppy met him at the back door, yipping importantly like a real watchdog, but then spoiling it by wagging his little tail like a crazed metronome.

Dwight accepted Aunt Zell's invitation and sat down across from me with a hot corn muffin and a cold glass of milk.

"What'd you end up naming him?" he asked her.

"I just can't decide," Aunt Zell sighed. "I thought sure I'd find a name in Paris, but he's too American to be a Jacques or a Pierre, isn't he? I think I've narrowed it down, though. Copperfield, because he was orphaned, too. Or Mowgli. Which do you think, Dwight?"

"What about Q?"

"Q?"

"Short for Barbecue," he said innocently.

I about strangled on my coffee.

Aunt Zell looked at me anxiously. "You all right, Deborah?"

"Or Pork Chop's a nice na— Ow!"

Dwight suddenly reached down and rubbed his shin.

My sandals weren't designed for effective kicking, but it's like building a house: one does what one can with the tools at hand.